"Are you ready to return to Pilgrim Cove?"

Rachel transferred the receiver to her other ear and collapsed onto her chair. "Do you always start off your conversations with a punch to the gut?" she asked. "Wait, don't answer that. I seem to remember that you do."

"Because it usually works, my dear, and it can save a lot of time. But not today. I guess today requires a full conversation."

"Dr. Bennett." Rachel spoke softly. "At the risk of having you think I'm buying time, could you please repeat the question."

His laughter was the only answer for a moment. Then he said, "We're offering you the position, Rachel." He outlined the details, which she could barely concentrate on.

"But think hard, Rachel," he continued. "You'll be living under a microscope because the position is a new one. And you'll be living in the shadow of your past. Some of the people here will remember you. There will be no quarter given. I want the job done well. Which is why I'm asking, as an old friend, are you ready to come back?"

She took a deep breath. "I can handle it, Dr. Bennett. I think it's time for me to come home."

Dear Reader,

Pilgrim Cove native Rachel Goodman has come home for one good reason: to prove to the town and to her family that she's not a loser. She'd graduated from high school—barely—and gone to college on a swimming scholarship. And now the swimming jock is the new assistant principal for academic studies at Pilgrim Cove High.

Marine biologist Jack Levine has a woman in every port, and his boat, *The Wanderer*, is his most prized possession. When he winds up teaching science at Pilgrim Cove, he finds that he likes the small town very much.

Bart Quinn and the ROMEOs have a plan for this young couple: Sea View House. Living there worked for Laura and Matt (*The House on the Beach*) and for Shelley and Daniel (*No Ordinary Summer*) so why not for Rachel and Jack?

Welcome to Pilgrim Cove! Or welcome back! Everyone's invited to enjoy the goings-on in this friendly coastal town where love is as powerful as the ocean next door.

See you in Pilgrim Cove!

Linda Barrett

P.S. I'd love to hear from you. Please e-mail me at Linda@Linda-barrett.com or write to P.O. Box 1934, Houston, TX 77284-1934. Check out my Web site, www.linda-barrett.com.

Reluctant Housemates

Linda Barrett

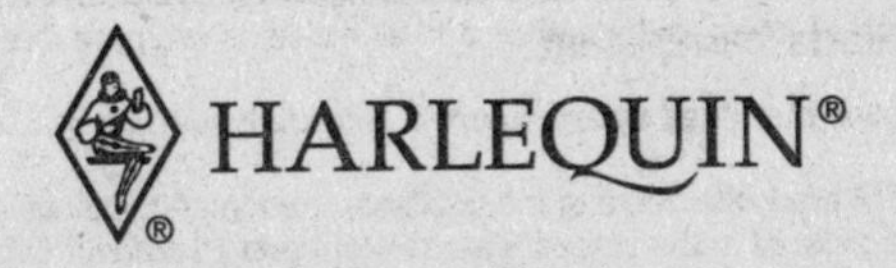

TORONTO • NEW YORK • LONDON
AMSTERDAM • PARIS • SYDNEY • HAMBURG
STOCKHOLM • ATHENS • TOKYO • MILAN • MADRID
PRAGUE • WARSAW • BUDAPEST • AUCKLAND

To Teddy and Richie Grossman, for providing the inspiration for the Pilgrim Cove series.
All it took was a house, a beach and wonderful friends.

ISBN 0-373-71256-1

RELUCTANT HOUSEMATES

This edition published by arrangement with Harlequin Books S.A.

www.eHarlequin.com

Printed in U.S.A.

CAST OF CHARACTERS

Rachel Goodman:	Assistant vice principal; leases ground floor of Sea View House
Jack Levine:	Marine biologist; leases upstairs at Sea View House
Alex and Susan Goodman:	Rachel's brother and sister-in-law Children: David and Jennifer
Dr. Bennett:	Principal of Pilgrim Cove High School
Bart Quinn:	Realtor for Sea View House
Maggie Quinn Sullivan:	Bart's daughter Partner in The Lobster Pot Married to Tom Sullivan, coach at Pilgrim Cove High School
Thea Quinn Cavelli:	Bart's daughter Partner in The Lobster Pot Married to Charlie Cavelli
Lila Sullivan:	Bart's granddaughter and partner
Dee Barnes:	Manager of Diner on the Dunes Married to Rick O'Brien

THE ROMEOS (RETIRED OLD MEN EATING OUT)

Bart Quinn:	Unofficial leader of the ROMEOs
Sam Parker:	Matt's dad; works part-time with Matt
Joe Cavelli:	Thea's father-in-law
Rick "Chief" O'Brien:	Retired police chief Married to Dee Barnes
Lou Goodman:	Retired high school librarian Rachel's father Married to Pearl
Max "Doc" Rosen:	Retired physician
Ralph Bigelow:	Retired electrician
Mike Lyons:	Retired engineer

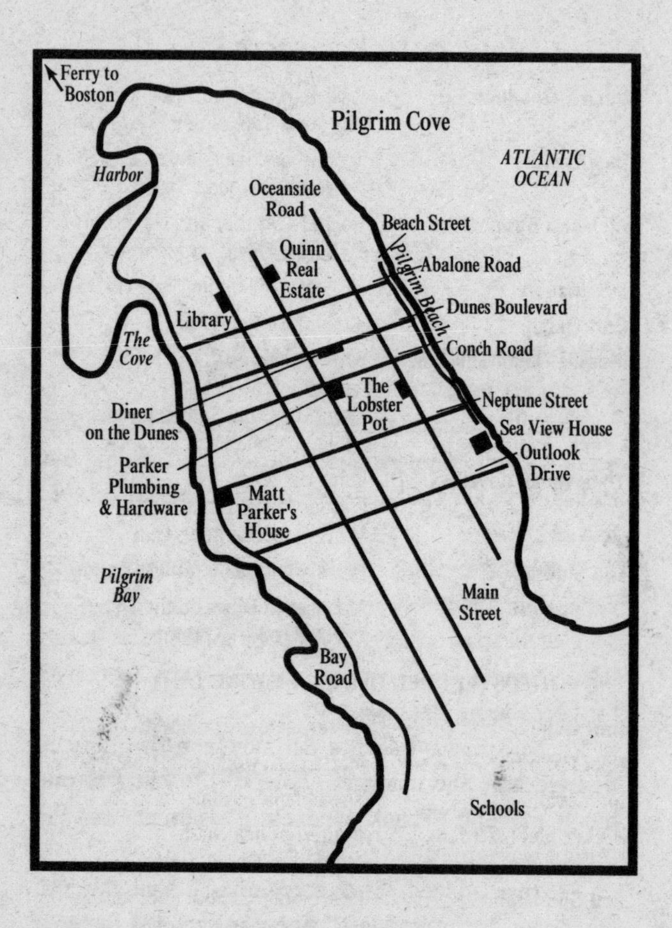
Ferry to
Boston
Pilgrim Cove
ATLANTIC
OCEAN
Harbor
Oceanside
Road
Beach Street
Quinn
Real
Estate
Pilgrim Beach
Abalone Road
Dunes Boulevard
Library
The
Cove
Conch Road
The
Lobster
Pot
Neptune Street
Diner
on the Dunes
Sea View House
Outlook
Drive
Parker
Plumbing
& Hardware
Matt
Parker's
House
Pilgrim
Bay
Main
Street
Bay
Road
Schools

CHAPTER ONE

TOTAL DEVASTATION. No roof. Barely a wall. Not a single classroom remained intact.

Rachel Goodman stared at what used to be the high school, trying to visualize the neat brick building that had stood on the spot just yesterday. Before the tornado had struck.

"It's unbelievable," she murmured to the police officer assigned to the site.

"Maybe to an easterner," the cop replied. "But Round Rock, Kansas, is in Tornado Alley. Twisters happen all the time during the season."

Rachel's hands fisted at her side as a shiver raced through her. She managed, however, to cling to one happy thought. "Thank goodness it's summer and the school was empty."

The man nodded. "But the building's done for, Ms. Goodman. Not much left." The cop scanned the area once more, his expression bleak. "Can't be used."

Rachel followed his gaze. The man was right. Her students would have to attend somewhere else when classes resumed after the summer break three weeks from now.

She waved to the officer and walked to her parked Ford Explorer. Creative planning would be needed to make sure the students' education wouldn't be compromised. As one of the high school's three assistant principals, she'd be very much involved. In fact...she glanced at her watch and realized she had barely enough time to try reaching her parents again before her three o'clock meeting with her principal and the other assistants.

Sitting in the front seat of her vehicle, she punched the auto dial on her cell phone. The landlines in town were down, and every time she'd called Pilgrim Cove, Massachusetts, on her mobile, she'd been unable to get through. Her parents were probably frantic by now.

Or maybe not. If they'd listened to the news, they'd know that no lives had been lost. Maybe she was worrying for nothing. Her dad would probably think that not contacting them was typical of Rachel. He'd expected little of her while she was growing up, and that's exactly what she'd given him—very little. C's and D's were good enough. How could she possibly compete with Alex? Ten years older than she, her brother had been the perfect one. A straight A student, president of the student council and universally popular with adults, Alex also had loads of friends and was certainly the pride of her father's heart. Rachel had recognized a no-win situation and communication between father and daughter had never been strong. After Rachel had entered college on a swimming scholarship plus some good SAT scores, she'd struck out on her own, returning home only for brief visits.

But tornadoes required some effort on her part. She listened to the normal ring at the other end of her cell and felt relieved. Finally—the promise of connection.

"Hello, hello." Her dad's voice. Tense.

"It's Rachel. It's the first..."

"Rachel! Rachel. Hold on. Don't go away."

Then she heard him call, "Pearl, pick up the extension. Rachel's on the phone. She must be fine. She's talking."

Guilt threatened to overwhelm Rachel. Of course her parents would be worried about her. She took a deep breath when he came back on. "I'm fine, Dad. The phone lines were down here, and I have a new cell phone. Just got it a couple of days ago. So, you don't have the number. I'm sorry. I've been trying every half hour.... I'm fine, Mom. Truly. Yes, totally in one piece. There were no casualties. Except for the high school—which was completely destroyed—there was remarkably little damage to the town."

"Thank God." Her dad's utterance was heartfelt.

She had more news to convey. "Listen, Mom and Dad. About my visit home next week. I may not be able to leave town. I have no idea what my principal has in mind or what the school board will decide for the next term. Whatever it is...I'm sure I'll have to stick around here."

Her parents' disappointment was audible. Rachel chatted for a little while and promised to let them know the outcome of today's meeting. Maybe she'd still be able to fly home for a quick visit. They could hardly know that she referred to her yearly treks east not as a vacation, but as her *pilgrimage* to Pilgrim Cove. Her mixed feelings about going home plagued her each time she went.

Her teenage years had been difficult. In fact, her memories of high school gave her hives. She'd been too tall, too gawky. Her breasts had forgotten to develop, and the heavy braces on her teeth hadn't helped. All she'd wanted was to fit in. Before she'd found her salvation in swimming, she'd tried joining a club but had felt out of place. She'd tried basketball because of her height, but she'd been clumsy, dropping the ball, falling. Her teammates had groaned, and the opposing side had laughed.

She hadn't cared about schoolwork or grades at all. She'd only wanted friends. Some teachers had felt sorry for her. Some had tried to reassure her father! There'd been one old biddy.... She automatically squeezed her eyes shut, intentionally dismissing the memory. Darn it! She wasn't a sensitive fifteen-year-old anymore. She was beyond that hurt now.

Her school memories weren't the only bad ones. She'd disappointed her folks throughout her childhood, and again as an adult, by choosing to live far away. And her brother still resented her. She sighed and shook her head. Family relationships were often complicated. Well, maybe she and Alex would never be close, but she was crazy about his kids! And she'd miss seeing her niece and nephew this summer if she didn't take her vacation.

Turning her key in the ignition, Rachel scanned her

surroundings. She'd been very happy in this landlocked part of the country since she'd arrived here as a college freshman. She'd been happy at her university, happy being on her own with no family history dogging her. She'd been so content with her life that she'd decided to stay in the Midwest.

The last two years as assistant principal in Round Rock had kept her busy. Most of the time, she had no regrets. But lately, sometimes…when the nights were long and she had no one to share them with, she felt lonely. At thirty-one, she'd had a couple of relationships that had gone nowhere. Always her decision, but the results were the same. She spent her nights alone.

And occasionally, when her Sundays stretched long with no family to visit…to have dinner with…to talk with…she wished Pilgrim Cove weren't so far away. In the next moment, however, her stomach would tighten and she'd laugh at herself.

She'd been on her own for thirteen years now, and an unhappy truth hit her with recurring regularity: she was alone. Her stomach often tightened at this thought, too, but somehow, she couldn't manage to laugh the idea away.

She glanced at her watch as she headed back to town for her meeting. In the end, Pilgrim Cove, Massachusetts, was her past. Round Rock, Kansas was her future. She had no intention of leaving the Midwest.

NOTEBOOK AND PEN IN HAND, Rachel sat on the end of the sofa in John Thompson's living room. For a man who was usually organized and direct, he seemed to be fumbling for words. Of course, the shock of the destroyed school could account for his loss of equilibrium, but Rachel didn't think that was the explanation. The principal was well seasoned in his job.

Rachel glanced at the other two assistant principals in the room. Both older than she, both married with families, and both looking as concerned as Rachel felt.

"You're wearing a hole in your carpet, Mr. Thompson," said Rachel with a smile. "No one was hurt, and that's the most important thing."

The principal paused in his step and sat down in a club chair opposite Rachel and her two colleagues. "You're absolutely right. And I hope you keep that in mind when I tell you what the School District has decided, in fact, why I called this meeting as soon as I learned their plans."

"Go on," said one of the assistants.

The man took a deep breath. "In a nutshell, our students will be divided and bussed to two other high schools. A few portable classrooms will be erected at each facility to handle the influx. Our teachers will be reassigned to these schools to work with the faculties there." He stopped talking for a moment.

Suddenly Rachel's stomach sank to her toes. She knew where this conversation was going. "And we administrators are out of jobs?" she asked softly.

No one moved. The silence in the room made her ears throb, wiping out the birdsong coming from the trees outside the window.

"I'm afraid so," replied Thompson with a heavy sigh. "At least for now. For this year. Or until a new school is built."

"I've got a family to support!"

"Is there unemployment insurance? John, are there any alternatives?"

The exclamations of dismay from her colleagues washed over Rachel while she faced her own situation. Completely self-supporting since college graduation, she'd saved enough money to tide her over for a little while, but she needed a job!

"I've done some preliminary research, and there might be good news for some of you," said Thompson, "if you want to return to the classroom on a teacher's salary."

"We need to work," said the woman next to Rachel. "And until our school is rebuilt, of course I'll go back to the classroom."

"Then you're in luck. There's an opening for a high school math teacher," said the principal, looking a bit more relaxed. "I can make another phone call and arrange a meeting. You should be all set."

But there wouldn't be an opening for a physical/health education teacher or coach. Rachel knew it just as surely as she knew the sun would rise the next morning. Math and science teachers were always in demand. No community had enough specialists in those subjects.

"I'm a licensed guidance counselor," said the third assistant principal. "Any openings in schools within fifty miles? Elementary, middle or high school. I don't care which." The man's voice was strained, his hands clenched on his knees, as he stared at the principal.

Thompson nodded. "I've been inquiring for all of you. There's a counselor going on maternity leave in the middle school right here in town. A last minute change."

"Thank God," said the man, shaking his head. "My own wife's pregnant with our second and…to be unemployed…." He closed his eyes and leaned against the back of the couch.

"Any rabbits in your hat for me?" asked Rachel quietly, hoping that her instincts were wrong.

John Thompson just stared at her, sorrow in his eyes, crushing even the faintest of hopes. "You'll have the strongest letter of recommendation I can write," he said. "In your two years with us, you've been a great asset. And I want you back next year if you're available."

"Count on it," said Rachel, suddenly finding it difficult to speak. She swallowed a few times, trying to absorb the implications. "I…I've enjoyed working with all of you." She looked at her colleagues. "You'll watch out for our kids…check up on them…? They'll have so many adjustments."

They reassured her. She turned toward her boss. "I'll do whatever I can to help, but right now…"

"Right now, you need some time to catch your breath. Go home! Update your résumé. I'll be in touch."

Rachel stood. "Thanks, John. Excuse me, everyone." She left the room.

When she reached her Explorer, she collapsed against it and focused on breathing. Inhale. Exhale. Two tornadoes within two days. And no warning for either.

What lousy timing! She loved her job. Loved working with high school kids. And now, just when she'd settled in and started making her mark in Round Rock, she'd have to do a job search and relocate.

She opened the car door and got in, her mind still whirling. Of course, it wouldn't be the first time she'd moved. But there was one big difference now. In the past, *she'd* been the one initiating the change. She'd wanted a school management position after earning her master's in educational administration. She'd chosen to build her career out of the classroom, and she'd loved her work at Round Rock. If the high school was rebuilt by next year, and if John Thompson called her back, great. But there were too many "ifs."

She pulled out of her spot and headed toward her apartment. Looking backward never helped—only caused pain. Now it was time to go forward, to find a new position. Time to call Pilgrim Cove, explain the situation to her folks and cancel her flight home. Finding a new job was priority now.

"DON'T GIVE UP THAT ticket, Rachel!"

Her dad's voice boomed in her ear, and Rachel jerked the receiver away from her head. What was *that* all about?

Lou Goodman rarely "boomed." Her mild-mannered father, a retired school librarian, took life in stride. She couldn't remember him ever raising his voice, not even to her when she screwed up. Between her lousy grades, arguing with teachers, picking fights with her brother and being angry at the world in general, she'd given him plenty of cause. But her dad had never said much, just always looked…sad. Or maybe disappointed.

She paced the floor of her large kitchen and cautiously placed the receiver to her ear again. "Dad? I can visit during Christmas or something. But now I have to find another job."

"Then pack your interview clothes and take that flight."

What had he said? "Interview clothes? What's going on?"

"Plenty's going on, my dear. The timing's perfect. And you'll be perfect in the position."

She sat down. Hard. "Uh…what position?"

"Isn't it quite remarkable how some things seem to work out? Yes, indeed. Truth is surely stranger than fiction."

"Dad, what are you talking about? What things are working out?" Either her father was losing it, or had had an extra glass of wine. Overindulging was not a normal Lou Goodman trait.

"I was going to tell you about it when you came home, but then again, it's not really good news. But since it's about our alma mater…"

Her dad's voice trailed off for a moment, and in her kitchen, Rachel chuckled. He wasn't losing it. He was talking about Pilgrim Cove Regional High School, a subject that always evoked emotion in him. He'd loved his career there. The school had lost an outstanding educator when he'd retired. He'd loved helping students with research and introducing them to wonderful writers. He'd fought for up-to-date technology, so the students would have up-to-date skills. Lou Goodman considered Pilgrim Cove High *his* alma mater as well as hers and her brother's.

"Want to start over, Dad?" she asked.

Now it was her father who chuckled into the phone. "I'll give it a whirl," he said. "Remember the standardized tests you used to take when you were in school?"

"Sure. We took them every spring." Oddly enough, she'd always done well on them. She handled standardized testing a lot better than regular schoolwork.

"The students' scores came in two weeks ago," her father continued, "and they were not good. In fact, it pains me to say that our students' scores have been decreasing over the last three years. Extremely disappointing."

"Oh, dear. I didn't know. I'm very sorry to hear that."

"Of course you are," said Lou, his voice more cheerful, "and that's why you're going to interview for the new position the board approved last week. They acted fast. Only took three years."

"Dad! Is that sarcasm I detect from the man who keeps his cool?"

"Cool, my petutie! In the face of this performance? But here's the important part." He paused, and despite herself, Rachel focused on what was coming next.

"We now have an opening for an assistant principal of academic studies," said Lou. "Right up your alley. The application's online. Fill it out and attach your résumé. Bring a hard copy with you when you come home."

Her dad sounded so excited, but images of her unhappy high school years flashed through Rachel's mind. Yes, she needed a job, but Pilgrim Cove High? The place she'd left with barely a backward glance? The place where her family lived? Short stays worked well for her. Despite her occasional longing, she'd be safer maintaining that pattern.

"Can people really go home again, Dad?" she asked softly.

Silence on the other end. A ringing silence filled with hurt. She could feel it vibrate through the wires and wanted to retract her words.

"Try it," said Lou. "You might be surprised."

Had her dad forgotten the distress of her teenage years? Could he not see how much happier she'd been in recent times? "Tell you what," began Rachel, "I'll stick with my vacation plans and come home, and I'll think about the job, but—I'm not making any promises. Definitely not."

"That's good enough for me," replied her dad. "We want to see our beautiful daughter."

Beautiful? That was a joke. "Then I must have a sister somewhere! This daughter of yours is built for distance swimming—tall and skinny with bony elbows and the delicate fragrance of *l'eau de chlorine* surrounding her half the time."

"Rachel...Rachel. You're slim, not skinny. Have you looked in the mirror lately?"

Rachel laughed into the phone. "Every day. And the mirror doesn't lie. But I'm not going to argue with you. Let's just agree that with the right clothes and cosmetics, I can make myself presentable."

The fact that she was ordinary-looking didn't bother her as much as it used to. Her career was what was important; her administrative and communication skills, and her ability to relate to students. These talents were the ones that counted, and she'd worked hard to develop them.

After saying goodbye to her dad, she walked to the computer in her den, pulled up her résumé and started revising. When she was satisfied with the result, she printed the document and studied it.

"What the hell?" she finally murmured. "Might as well take a look and see what he was talking about."

She accessed the job posting for Pilgrim Cove Regional High School and stared at the application form. What a joke it would be! Pure O. Henry. She could imagine the lead story in the *Pilgrim Cove Gazette*. "Swimming jock and underachiever, Rachel Goodman, returns to Pilgrim Cove High charged with improving the academic performance of the entire student body."

Laughable. Painful. Pitiful. She didn't need it.

What she did need was a swim, and the community center was open, keeping to its normal schedule. A great decision, Rachel thought. Routine countered catastrophe. She glanced at her watch as she grabbed a bathing suit and towel. She'd be at the pool earlier than usual. She wondered whether or not any of the girls would show up for the training session. While no one had been hurt by the tornado, everyone had probably been scared. Her young team, however, had to prepare for a local meet this weekend.

Rachel locked the door behind her and headed to the community center. Time to get back into the water.

IN HIS COMFORTABLE KITCHEN in Pilgrim Cove, Lou Goodman turned to his wife. "I think you're wrong, Pearl. I really think I hooked her. The job is perfect."

But Pearl shook her head. "She'll come for a week, and then she'll be gone."

"But..."

"When was the last time Rachel allowed herself to get hooked?" interrupted Pearl. "Never. She swims away like a smart fish. And not only from us. Every time a decent boy—I should say 'man'—gets serious, she runs in the other direction. So, don't get your hopes up. She's coming home because she didn't want to disappoint you. That's all."

Lou felt his smile slip as he walked to the woman with whom he'd spent forty-two years of his life. He loved her and knew her well enough to know that she was usually right about these things. He reached for her hands as she stood at the counter preparing a simple supper.

"Pearl," he whispered. "Where did we go wrong when we tried to do everything right? How did this happen?" His head drooped. "My fault. My fault."

When she looked up at him, her eyes were shiny, her mouth trembled. She didn't speak, just leaned closer and wrapped her arms around him. He embraced her as he'd done for a lifetime, loving how she nestled into his shoulder—how she felt against him. He'd hold her for many more years, God willing, as many as they were given on this earth.

But he was seventy-one years old now and still had unfinished business.

RACHEL WALKED THE LENGTH of the pool, assessing the performances of each member of her team. To her delight, all twelve girls had shown up that evening, each one eager to swim. Seemed they needed to be in the water as much as she did.

She wouldn't mention the probability of them getting a new coach. Not yet, anyway. Not until she knew for sure where she was going.

"Looking good, ladies," she called to them. "And time's up."

"Already?"

"No way!"

Rachel grinned. Her kids loved the sport.

"Think we really have a chance to place at the meet?" asked one of the girls as she got out of the pool.

Time for a pep talk. The girls were only nine and ten years old. Still learning. Still needing confidence. "Everyone, listen up," said Rachel.

They gathered around her, towels slung over their shoulders. "You have each improved tremendously this year because you worked very hard. And I promise you that your chances of placing in the events are as good as anyone else's." She eyeballed every girl. "Maybe better." She paused. "Believe me?"

Slowly, they nodded, one at a time.

"You're swimming because you love the sport. You want others to love and respect the sport. And no matter what happens at the meet, you're still going to love to swim." She paused a moment. "And who knows? You might save a life one day because you swim well. That's something more important than a meet. Isn't it?"

They nodded again, and Rachel watched their expressions change as they processed her words.

She leaned forward as if to share a secret. "In my book, you are winners right now. Every one of you."

CHAPTER TWO

RACHEL GRABBED HER SUITCASE from the carousel in Boston's Logan Airport and made her way to the water-shuttle dock. As far as she was concerned, the best part of the trip was about to start. A seven minute boat ride from the airport to Rowes Wharf in Boston Harbor followed by a half-hour ferry ride to Pilgrim Cove. How many people had the luxury of trading in bumper-to-bumper road traffic for a ferry ride as their daily commute between work and home?

Not that she was going home. Her home would be wherever she decided to live. Today she was going back to her parents' house on Atlantic Avenue, less than two blocks away from the beach. Whatever reservations she carried with her from her childhood, living by the ocean was not one of them. She bought a round-trip ticket for the shuttle, stepped on and quickly arrived at the large harbor in the heart of downtown Boston, where she bought another round-trip ticket for the Pilgrim Cove ferry.

She leaned against the rail of the boat, studying the afternoon scene before her. Busy Boston Harbor. A luxurious hotel with a grand archway and its own dock nearby, elegant restaurants and cafés, soft-rose brick buildings and a variety of office towers all stretching upward to create an impressive skyline. And in the opposite direction, sailboats glided on the water, the sun reflecting off their pristine cloth. Motorboats, too, with people who enjoyed going against the wind. People who were probably on vacation and had jobs to return to when playtime was over. Unlike Rachel.

She eyed her suitcase, which contained a navy-blue suit accented with a white collar and cuffs, a pair of low-heeled navy pumps and matching panty hose. In the end, the reality of unemployment had prompted her to e-mail her résumé to the school board. To her surprise, she'd wound up with an appointment to meet the people on the hiring committee. The fast turnaround could only mean they were in a hurry to fill the position by the time school started.

She'd come prepared, and she'd do her best. But she wasn't hungry for the job. Not deep inside. For the first time in her life, she was moving with caution. Staying at the shallow end of the pool. And it felt…weird. Better to think of this interview as practice for other opportunities she'd be seeking.

"Rachel? Sure, it's Rachel Goodman."

Rachel twirled from the railing as the familiar voice jerked her out of her musings. An energetic couple approached. The man had bristly gray hair, and his blue eyes creased in the corners as he gave her a hearty hug.

Kate Lyons spoke first. "You've just arrived, haven't you?"

Rachel nodded with a grin as the couple eyed her suitcase. "I see you're both as sharp as ever."

"And aim to stay that way!" replied Mike. "In fact, I'm doing a little consulting work with the aquarium. That's where we were today." He turned and looked back out over the bay as the ferry left the dock behind. "We have got to take better care of these waters."

Mike Lyons was a retired environmental engineer with a strong interest in the sea-coast habitat.

"You and my dad," said Rachel. "Neither of you will ever be fully retired. I think he volunteers as many hours in the town library as he put in when he worked at the high school."

"We love what we do. And that makes all the difference."

"I know what you mean," said Rachel, nodding in agreement. "I really understand."

"I can see that," said Kate. "Your smile gives you away. So, if they offer you the job, will you take it?"

Whoa! "I'd forgotten how fast news flies around town," said Rachel.

But Mike was shaking his head. "Not the whole town, my dear. Just the breakfast boys."

"The breakfast boys?" Rachel repeated slowly, trying to remember.

"You've been away too long, Rachel, or you'd never forget our *boys,*" said Kate, eyes twinkling, "and their daily breakfasts at the Diner on the Dunes."

"Breakfast at...you mean the ROMEOs!" said Rachel.

"Of course I know *those* boys. My dad's a charter member of the Retired Old Men Eating Out. And so are you, Mike."

The man pretended to pout. She and Kate looked at each other and tried to swallow their laughter. Unsuccessfully. Kate patted her husband's shoulder. "You'll always be my young stud, honey. Never an old man."

"She's right," said Rachel. "How can you be old when you're running around every day? Seems to me that the ROMEOs are misnamed! None of them acts retired."

"That's a fact," said Mike. "Sam Parker still works with Matt at the store, and Joe Cavelli puts in time at the garage. Ralph Bigelow does electric work for folks when they need him—"

"And we can't forget the one who puts in more hours than a day holds," said Kate, tightening her lips. "That Bartholomew Quinn. If his Rosemary were still alive, she'd flay him but good."

"No, no, she wouldn't," said Mike. "She had almost as much energy at Bart."

Rachel listened absentmindedly as the Lyonses brought the town alive with their descriptions and up-to-date recitation of the latest goings-on. There was only a tiny possibility that she'd remain here, so remembering any of this talk wasn't necessary.

Mike's voice penetrated when he mentioned her dad. "I had breakfast with Lou this morning. Your visit's got him walking on air. Can't remember the last time I saw him so excited."

Rachel winced.

"See what I mean?" said Mike, pointing at the Pilgrim Cove harbor.

On the big dock was Rachel's dad waving at them with the gusto of a kid. Her mom stood right next to him, hands shading her eyes as she searched the crowd on the ferry. Then a big grin crossed her face, and she waved, too.

Rachel's week at home had begun.

THE EVENING HAD GONE WELL. First, a leisurely dinner for three in her mom's comfortable kitchen, where Rachel consumed every morsel of the braised lamb roast Pearl had put on her plate. No one could outdo her mom in the kitchen. Then, she'd unpacked and had run an iron over her navy-blue interview suit. And now, Rachel was walking along the beach, wearing a bathing suit under a pair of shorts, a towel slung around her neck.

"I don't think the lifeguards are still on duty," her dad had said as she left the house. "Maybe you should postpone your swim."

"No way! It's a hot August night. I'll find someone to keep an eye out when I swim." She gave him a quick kiss. "I can take care of myself. Don't worry."

"Right. You're all grown up now." His smile was brief.

Dusk had fallen a while ago, and the beach was not very crowded. It had been a long time, however, since she'd strolled along the shore, and she was enjoying everything about it—the scent of the salt air, the sound of the waves as they ebbed and flowed in their steady rhythm. She also enjoyed stretching her legs and using her muscles against the sand. Very different from walking on hard cement sidewalks. Too bad there were no oceans in Kansas!

She'd kept a good pace for two miles, almost half the length of the entire beach, and felt warm despite the evening breeze blowing off the ocean. The moon was rising now, illuminating her way in the growing darkness. A perfect time to hit the water. Rachel scanned the area for someone who had a few minutes to spare while she swam. Her best hope was the party of teenage boys who were horsing around near the shoreline. At least she wouldn't be taking them out of their way.

She jogged toward the group, vocalizing her request as she approached.

"For Pete's sake, Aunt Rachel, you don't need a lifeguard. You could *be* a lifeguard!"

"David! Is that you? Let's see what a year's done to you, kiddo!"

Her nephew embraced her, and she had to lift her eyes to his. "Seems like the Goodman genes haven't skipped a generation. You're only fifteen, right?"

He grinned with pride and nodded before he answered. "Going on sixteen with more inches to come." His voice had reached a new low.

She turned to his friends. "Hi, guys."

They chorused a greeting. Rachel looked at the group, recognizing the boys she used to see playing with David. Bigger now. She shook her head. "This is what happens when I turn my back," she complained. "You all grow up!"

She dropped her towel and pulled off her shorts. "Can you hang out for a few minutes? I won't be long." Without waiting for a response, she ran into the water, giant-stepping through the shallows until she could strike out toward Europe.

She did freestyle strokes for a while, totally at home in the ocean, enjoying the water caressing her skin. Enjoying the exertion of energy. When she was beyond the breakers, a fair distance from shore, she flipped to her back and began swimming parallel to it. The backstroke was her second-best stroke. She could keep it up for hours if she floated at regular intervals and rested.

"Sweetheart, I know you're having fun, but it's time to get yourself back to land."

Surprise almost made her go under before she turned herself around and treaded water. A few feet away, a man faced her, quietly keeping himself upright, too. She couldn't see much in the shadowy moonlight, just a lot of hair plastered to his head. Where had he come from? And how had he managed to approach without a sound?

Rachel was completely at ease in the ocean and she took definite exception to being ordered around. Narrowing her eyes, she said, "And you are…?"

"The guy your nephew sent over to haul you in if you resist going to shore under your own steam."

She couldn't quite make out his expression, but his voice was rock-steady, and she knew he was serious. Of course, he could be a serious lunatic. Or… "What does my nephew have to do with this? Where is he?"

"The kids had their own plans. They asked me to baby-sit. So, please get your sweet tush in gear. I've got other things to do."

She turned away from him, still yearning for a long swim, her body hungry to cut through the expanse of water around her. "Don't even think about it." He purred like a tiger.

Suddenly, Rachel felt less at ease. She reversed position again and stared at him. From the light glistening off his shoulders, she could see he was at least twice her size. With his broad chest and big arms, he easily treaded water. Was probably a good swimmer, and stronger than she was. No point in arguing even if she would have liked to remain. "Shoot!" she murmured in frustration.

Was that a chuckle she heard? She glanced toward the man but couldn't make out his expression. Turning toward shore, she began a leisurely crawl.

"At this rate, we'll be here all night," said her new partner. "You can do better than that."

"Well, Aquaman, I'm not in any hurry. But don't let that stop you from surging ahead."

He said nothing, just paced himself to match her stroke, and her hypothesis was confirmed. He had good form. Her curiosity was aroused, but when she eventually touched bottom, she resisted the urge to chat. Instead, she walked toward the beach without giving him a single glance. She pushed her hair back and scanned the area for her towel.

"To the left" came the deep voice, more relaxed now.

That voice could still belong to a lunatic. She reached for her towel and started drying off. Her escort stood a few feet away, quietly watching. When she'd put her shorts back on, Rachel studied him—all of him—for the first time. She looked up. And up. Interesting.

"Good night," she said, turning to leave.

"You're welcome," he replied, his pointed tone carrying a message.

She made a half turn and counted to three under her breath. "You've been a good Boy Scout, and I'll commend you to the community. But I don't recall asking for assistance."

His silhouette blocked the moonlight, and once again she couldn't make out his features. All she knew was that his full attention was focused on her. But he didn't reply.

Instead, he shook the water from his arms and tried to dry himself off with his hands. Obviously, the man hadn't expected to take a dip this time of night. Rachel threw her towel to him.

"Thanks," he said.

She nodded.

As he used the cloth, Rachel took the opportunity to study his muscled arms and legs. Her second assessment of him in the water had been correct. The man had a swimmer's build—a definite natural for the butterfly stroke.

He returned the towel and said, "Next time don't swim alone." He turned on his heel, muttering something about women, water and trouble.

The man was leaving without getting what he'd deserved, and somehow, Rachel took no satisfaction in it. "Thank you," she called.

He pivoted back to her. "You're entirely welcome."

She couldn't see his smile, but it came through in his tone.

"Maybe I'll see you around," he added.

She shook her head. "Sorry. I'm only here for a few days visiting family."

"Well, have a nice time, and have a nice life. Stay safe." He headed for the opposite end of the beach without looking back.

She stared at his retreating figure. He seemed happy to be rid of her despite his comment about seeing her around. She shrugged. Just as well. Her own life was complicated enough right now.

She started for home. If her first night's adventure in Pilgrim Cove was any indication of what lay ahead for the rest of the week, she was in for an interesting visit. Rachel chuckled at the thought. Who would have imagined that sleepy little Pilgrim Cove could provide excitement to anyone, especially to a native like herself?

AT NOON THE NEXT DAY, Rachel stared into the full-length mirror hanging on the back of her bedroom door. The blue suit fit well—straight skirt ended mid-knee—

and had no creases anywhere. She'd pressed it lightly for the second time about an hour earlier to make sure. Her cropped dark hair was in place, longer feathered bangs brushed to one side, an easy style that suited her lifestyle. Small gold earrings, light makeup to cover freckles and a soft honey lipstick completed her professional image.

Although the interview would be held in the Town Hall offices of the school board, Rachel couldn't help feeling as if she were returning to the scene of the crime. The scene of her own high school days. Her first goal this afternoon would be to correct any impressions of herself from years ago that might be held by individuals on the hiring committee. Although the opportunity at Pilgrim Cove Regional High School was not her first choice of positions, she was going to act as though it was.

She picked up her slim briefcase, which held copies of her résumé and prior evaluations, grabbed her purse and went downstairs to the kitchen.

"Perfect!" Her mom's reaction made Rachel smile. "They'd be crazy not to hire you."

Rachel looked at her dad and winked. "All it takes is a blue suit, huh?"

"And you in it."

Four little words. They crashed against her like waves pounding the shore. Her lips trembled, her eyes filled. She grabbed the back of a chair. "Wha-what did you say?"

"My dear, Rachel…Rachel." Her dad looked stricken, his voice barely above a whisper. "I say Pilgrim Cove

High would be lucky to get you!" His step was heavy as he came closer to her. "You can handle this job or any other one you want."

Was this the same father who thought she'd never amount to anything? That she'd never measure up to her brother? Who was embarrassed by her? She stared at her dad as though seeing him for the first time, not as his teenage daughter but as one adult to another.

She shook her head slowly. "I'm not particularly clever or smart. I just like kids. And I work hard."

Her dad studied her, hardly blinking. "You're as gifted as anyone else. More than most. With your diplomas and your successful career, I thought you understood that by now." He gazed at the floor, then at her. "Why do you think you're so good at your job?"

"'Cause I hated high school," she quipped, suddenly uncomfortable.

He winced, his complexion turning pink. "That's one way of putting it," he replied in a raspy voice. "But I would say that you understand the wide range of adolescent experiences. You're the best ally a teen could have."

Shocked by his compliments, Rachel could only stammer, "Th-thank you." In fact, she was somewhat dazed. Thirty-one years old, still thirsting for her dad's approval, and getting it for the first time in her life. And yet, not understanding him at all.

"I'd love to continue this conversation, Dad," she said, "but your timing's lousy! I've got an interview shortly."

"Then, as they say in show biz, 'knock 'em dead.'"

She stepped back and shook her head in disbelief. "What a visit! Last night, it was the guy on the beach, and now this.... Life is more interesting than I anticipated. Hey, folks. I'm glad I came home."

"See!" said Pearl to her husband. "Now you can enjoy yourself, enjoy our daughter. Miracles do happen. What more do you want?"

"I want to know *what* guy on the beach?"

Rachel laughed and took her father's car keys. "Nothing to worry about. Never saw him before, and I'll never see him again. Probably a summer resident or somebody's visitor."

She let herself out the door and got into the car, determined to make a second miracle happen. Determined to become the first-ever assistant principal for academic studies at Pilgrim Cove Regional High School. What she'd formerly considered a dress rehearsal had turned into opening night.

TOWN HALL WAS LOCATED in the heart of the Pilgrim Cove business district, two blocks from the library on Sloop Street, which ran parallel to Main, just one block south. Rachel drove the two miles from her parents' house and pulled into the side parking lot of the three-story red brick building.

Rachel entered through the front door, approached the receptionist and was led into the room where she'd be interviewed. Five people sat at a round table. Paper, pens and copies of her submitted paperwork lay in front of them. In unison, they rose to their feet when she appeared. Of the five, she recognized only one. The one person who'd believed in her when she was a kid. Dr. Edward Bennett, principal of the high school, had written her recommendations for college admission, had told Lou what a terrific daughter he had within her earshot and had even attended a swim meet or two.

He greeted her warmly, then introduced her to the others. When she finally sat down, she was briefed on the hiring procedure. She quickly learned that Dr. Bennett had no vote except in case of a tie. She learned that the board wanted to fill the position as soon as possible and was canvassing hard to get a qualified pool of candidates on short notice.

"The first year of service will be provisional, not permanent," said one committee member. "No guarantees that the person in the job will be there for a second year." The woman studied Rachel. "You'd be relocating about fifteen hundred miles from your current residence, Ms. Goodman, for a position that might not work out. Does that concern you?"

Rachel took a moment before replying. "It seems to me that a provisional appointment can work both ways." A smile tugged the corner of her mouth as she met the woman's gaze. "The new hire might not like the position and might well want to leave at the end of one year. The search would have to be reopened under those conditions as well."

The questioner's eyes widened, and Rachel leaned forward. "However, that won't happen with me. Our high school was outstanding when I was a student here. I'd like to see us regain that reputation."

"I second your goal," said Dr. Bennett, "and I'd like to hear your ideas, but first, let's get everything out in the open and out of the way."

He was referring to her own student history. The poor grades, her focus on sports over academics, her genius of a brother whom she couldn't measure up to…things she wouldn't be discussing if she were interviewing anywhere else. Reputations in small towns never left a person, and the committee members were definitely aware of hers.

She purposely relaxed her hands in front of her, and nodded at her old champion. "I totally agree, Dr. Bennett." She looked around the table. "My teenage years were not happy here. Family relationships, peer relationships and schoolwork—everything was a mess. My mom says I was a 'late bloomer.' I think I was simply a confused youngster trying to find my way. In the end, I did. And that, I think, qualifies me to work with all high school students, including the misfits. I deal with each individual in a holistic way. Every child has potential. It's up to us to tap into it."

She glanced at Dr. Bennett. His eyes twinkled and he nodded. A tiny nod that warmed her. Too bad he didn't have a vote!

An hour passed. Rachel spoke about her knowledge

of state regulations, the standardized testing program, supervisory and administrative experience, and her methods of dealing with parents. As she spoke, she was also amazed at how far she'd come since she started her teaching career nine years earlier. Finally, there were no more questions.

"Would you care to make any last statements?" asked the woman who seemed to be chairing the discussion.

"Yes. Yes, I would." She looked around the table, meeting each person's glance, one at a time. "Regardless of my own issues as a youngster, I took pride in attending Pilgrim Cove Regional High School, and I want to see it on top again. I realize that the community will be watching me, judging my performance perhaps more closely than if you hired someone with no prior connection to Pilgrim Cove—the town or the school." She leaned forward in her seat. "The promise that I can make to you today is that I will do my best for the school and for each student, and that I will take full responsibility for my actions."

She took a breath and let quiet settle on the room. "I'll be in town for a week. Feel free to contact me if you have any more questions. And thank you very much."

A minute later she was back in the summer sunshine, glad to be outside, glad the meeting was over. And feeling good about it. As she tilted her head toward the sun, trying to judge the time, she stepped lightly down the short flight of stairs in front of the building, and crashed into a wall that hadn't been there when she'd come in.

"Oof!" Her arms flailed, her briefcase dropped from her hands. Sheets of paper hit the ground. Not hers. She grabbed for the banister.

"I've got you."

The voice was low, warm, sexy. And tinged with humor. Strong arms held her against a broad body. A definitely masculine body.

Her nose pressed against his chest. She wiggled her head, tilted it back and raised her glance at least six inches. A nice surprise. His green eyes twinkled down at her, then widened a bit before he released her and gathered his fallen documents.

"If you're on the interviewing committee, you're too late," said Rachel, leaning against the railing. "It's all over but the shouting. Or should I say the debating?"

"Nah," said the man. "No committee. Just complying with some bureaucratic bull….hmm." He waved the papers, then glanced at his watch. "And I've got three minutes to hand this mess in. But hey, maybe I'll see you around."

Ding! She'd heard those words recently. Last night, in fact. She studied the man's retreating back until he paused and turned toward her.

"No more swimming alone." He waved and bestowed a heartbreaker's grin, then bounded up the stairs.

So, she'd been right. He was the same guy she'd met the night before. Despite his no-nonsense demeanor about water safety, he was a dyed-in-the-wool flirt with sparkling green eyes, a square jaw and a body…yeah, he had a body.

But not for her. She didn't have a job, a home or a clear view of her future. So a relationship right now was out of the question. Besides, she wasn't good at relationships. She never allowed anyone to get too close.

She shrugged. The solution was not to get involved. Easy enough when she didn't even know his name.

CHAPTER THREE

ONCE AGAIN, HE HADN'T gotten her name! Jack Levine entered Town Hall, delivered his personnel forms and left, all the while laughing at himself. Two opportunities and he'd blown them both! Could he be losing his touch? He flinched at the thought. He'd prefer to blame the missed opportunity on the surprise of the moment. And it wouldn't be a lie at all. He'd been totally amazed at reconnecting with the same woman who'd lingered in his mind since the previous night.

Connect was the word. They couldn't have connected any more closely! He'd enjoyed holding her. He'd liked the weight of her leaning against him. Slender, but sturdy. Full of harnessed energy. He could sense her vibrations even when she stood still. And her hair! A dark, rich sable—short and sassy and temptingly thick. He'd wanted to touch it. In fact, he almost had. But touching her—even her hair—was not an option. Yet. And might never be if his technique didn't improve pretty darn quick. Of course, he hadn't used any technique last night on the beach, just old-fashioned intimidation. But…damn, she was an idiot to swim alone.

The Atlantic never gave second chances. He'd learned that the hard way—with Kevin. He clenched his jaw, then forced himself to change his thoughts as precisely as he changed a television channel.

As he walked to his car, he filled his mind with images of the mystery woman. Too bad she'd only be in town for a week. He liked tall women, women who didn't cause a crick in his neck. Seemed the tall, pretty ones were hard to find. Not that he was looking for anyone special. Not now and maybe never.

He'd never had the urge to settle down, and his social life suited him just the way it was. Short-term relationships with independent females who knew the score, and who didn't look back. Those women and lots of parties! He liked to have a good time, and all his friends knew it. Hell! His married friends depended on him to keep the single women entertained. And he never disappointed. He still had the energy of a twenty-year-old—enough for both him and Kevin.

But as much as he enjoyed his leisure time, he enjoyed his working time more. If he had a loyalty to any female on earth, it was to the mighty Atlantic. He'd grown up on her northern shores. He'd learned to read her moods and to treat her with respect.

He rubbed the back of his neck. Tension had crept in, catching him unawares. But he knew why. He slipped on his sunglasses and unlocked his truck, pausing before he climbed in. Thinking about the past always made him tense.

Jack got into his pickup and headed toward Main Street. It was time to see Bart Quinn about renting a house in town. He passed the Diner on the Dunes where he'd had a couple of good meals. In fact, he'd seen Bart and his friends arrive there two mornings ago just as he was leaving. Seemed they had a breakfast club of some kind with a funny name. What was it? His brow wrinkled in thought, but in a moment, he chuckled. The ROMEOs. He shook his head in agreement. If the old gents thought of themselves as Romeos, well, more power to them!

He pulled into a spot in front of Quinn's brick office building and found himself looking forward to chatting with the agent again. Bart Quinn was a real character.

Two long windows framed each side of the front door over which hung a sign proclaiming: Quinn Real Estate and Property Management. Jack ran up the few steps and let himself in. Mellow wood paneling, framed seascapes and pictures of Pilgrim Cove greeted his eyes. He walked farther into the entrance hall and recognized the town harbor in one print and the private marina where his own boat was anchored in another.

The reception desk was empty, but Jack heard footsteps approach from the back of the building. The agent himself appeared at the end of the hall. A leonine head of white hair, sparkling blue eyes underneath bushy eyebrows, a white short-sleeved dress shirt and belted slacks, all on a six-foot frame.

"Come on in, Jack Levine," the man said, beckoning

him. "I've been expecting you. We can chat in my office back here."

Jack followed the man and tried to follow his recitation as well.

"I took this corner because of the windows. Worth the walk to have bright sunshine everywhere, or at least the wee chance of it during the long winters here." Bart Quinn paused on the threshold of his office, turned to Jack and cocked his head. "Don't you agree, lad?"

Jack grinned and shook the man's hand. "No argument here, Mr. Quinn. I was born and bred on the Maine seacoast. I know about New England winters! Grab all the sunshine you can."

"Ah! We've got the seasons, that's true. The bitter and the better. But I wouldn't trade a one of them."

Five minutes later, sitting across the desk from Bart, Jack felt he'd known the man all his life. More than having the "gift of gab"—although the guy was no slouch with words—Quinn had a manner of listening and watching. As if he were memorizing everything—what a person said, how a person looked.

But he also shared information about himself. He was a widower. His Rosemary had passed on some years ago.

"And my girls—Maggie and Thea—they somehow talked me into giving up this beauty." Quinn held up an unlit pipe, the bowl resting in his hand. He hefted it gently, then put the stem in his mouth. "But it feels just right."

"Sometimes bad habits can feel right," said Jack,

"when you indulge in them long enough. I've spent the last ten years trying to break the habits of people and businesses polluting the North Atlantic. I wish I was as successful with them as your daughters have been with you."

The old man's blue eyes opened wide. "But you haven't given up. You're a stubborn man, and thank God for that." He banged the table with the side of his fist. "We've got to clean up the oceans no matter how long it takes, or what will our children inherit?" Bart beamed at Jack. "Very good, my boy, very good work."

Instantly, Jack felt he was in school again. A prize pupil, at the head of the class.

But now Quinn was rolling his chair closer to the desk. He reached for his calendar, pen and a thick binder. Jack stared at the black cover. Had to be the current house listings. He glanced around the room and smothered a grin. A computer sat in the corner. Dark. Unplugged. How much more information, more detail, could the man have at his fingertips if he wanted it?

Quinn glanced up just then and followed Jack's gaze.

"A sorrowful waste of good money," said Bart. "My granddaughter, Lila, made me get that. She's my business partner, and she uses one just fine. But me? I know every piece of property in this town and then some. And it's all stored in here." He pointed to his head. "In fact, I know where and when all the water mains were laid, sewer lines, too. That's what comes from seventy-five years of living in the town I love."

Jack nodded, comfortable with the old man. Comfortable in the town. The flavor of Pilgrim Cove seemed familiar. Remembrances of his boyhood in a similar coastal town wafted in and out of his mind. Sometimes, on a Saturday, he'd sit in his dad's office at the bank, looking at the big wooden desk and all the papers on it. Just like this one.

But there were differences, too. While Bart's grin was readily visible, his dad had often looked worried, taking everybody's problems to heart. When Jack was old enough to understand, he'd begun to worry as well, about the troubles that came to their friends and neighbors who depended on fishing and lobstering for their livelihoods. Worried about folks who couldn't make their payments for their homes or boats.

And sometimes the problems were worse…sometimes a boat didn't come home. Jack blinked hard and slammed that door shut fast. Before the memory took over. Damn! That was the second time today he'd had to change channels.

"Will you be needing a place for the entire school year?" asked Bart. "Or just for a couple of months while you study our waters?"

Jack refocused on Bart Quinn. "The year. My contract with the school board goes to next summer, almost the same length of time as the Pilgrim Cove pollution study. The conservation commission wants data on the water quality around the peninsula in every season." He leaned back in his chair, now totally relaxed and focused on his assignments. "I'll be measuring the amount and type of pathogens in your water and also trying to assess pollution sources regardless of the distance."

"So, you'll be working two jobs," said Bart. "Between the fresh ocean air and a bunch of high schoolers, you'll sleep well at night, boy-o!"

The agent had it almost right. Jack would be working *three* jobs, not two. But his own book project was private business, certainly not part of the federal or county budget.

"My boat's docked at the marina," said Jack, "and I'm taking a week to visit my folks in Maine. I like dropping by whenever I have the chance. So, what will you have available, if anything, when I return? Or will I have to stay at a motel until the summer renters are gone?"

But the old gent was shaking his head, a grin slowly creeping across his face. "Nope. I don't think so. We've had some big goings-on lately, and a pretty property I operate might just be available in a week. A very pretty piece for someone like you."

Jack rested against the back of his chair, content to watch The Quinn in action. "Someone like me?" he asked softly. "What exactly does that mean?"

The agent leaned over his desk closer to Jack. "Oceanfront," he said. "Right on the beach." He stabbed the air with the stem of his pipe as he spoke. "She's a sturdy old ship herself, and a real beauty. Two-and-a-half stories with a widow's walk on top. The upstairs apartment is what we call the Crow's Nest. Small but ample enough for a single man. Two bedrooms, large eat-in kitchen, a wide deck where you can view the horizon. Separate entrance on the side."

Jack knew he'd take it even if it were no more than a single room. To be right on the beach was a piece of luck he hadn't expected.

"And the price?" asked Jack.

"Aah. An interesting question." Now Bart Quinn leaned back, a faraway look in his eye.

"Interesting?" asked Jack. "The rent is the rent."

But the agent shook his head. "Not quite. Sea View House is supported by the William Adams Trust. The first William Adams founded the town, you see. It's come to be a special house for people needing it."

"Mr. Quinn," interrupted Jack, "I'm not into mysteries. I'm a self-sufficient guy, and while I'm not rich, I'm not particularly needy. Just name the price, and if I can swing it, we'll have a deal."

Quinn's eyes sharpened, and Jack suddenly felt as though he were on a slide under a microscope.

"Well, now," said Bart Quinn in a soft voice. "Seems to me that the kind of person you are remains to be seen. Many discoveries have been made around here lately—a lot of self-discovery."

Jack felt himself start to squirm, then almost glared at the man. "If you're hanging a Doctor Is In shingle next to your real estate sign outside, I'll tell you up front—I'm not interested!"

Quinn burst into laughter, picked up his pipe and

went back to stabbing the air. "You made my day, boy-o. Yes, indeed. I'm thinking that Sea View House will work out just fine." He relaxed again, his eyes twinkling. "The rent's a sliding-scale fee, and normally you'd pay full rate—what with the two jobs you're handling."

"I'm not looking for any favors," said Jack quickly. "I pay my way and no loose ends." Never any loose ends.

"No favors, Jack Levine. Just the usual off-season rate," said Bart. "Summer tenants are still there. You'll be taking over fall and winter. We've been having a lucky streak lately with that house, the kind that keeps my imagination lively. I'd like nothing better than to see that luck go on and on."

"Define 'lucky streak.' What type of luck?" *Not* that he was superstitious, but in addition to being a man of science, he was first a man of the sea and knew better than to thwart her in any way. Bart, himself, had called Sea View House "a sturdy old ship," and...uh-uh, Jack wasn't taking chances. "What kind of luck?" he repeated.

"Good luck, of course," replied Bart. "The last two sets of tenants had life-changing experiences there."

"Such as..." said Jack, still not comfortable with all the talk of luck.

"While they lived in Sea View House, they fell in love. Laura and Matt's wedding was at the beginning of the summer, and Shelley and Daniel's will take place this Christmas."

"Love? Your tenants fell in love?" repeated Jack, so

relieved he began to laugh. He laughed until his sides hurt. "Is that all? Mr. Quinn..."

"Call me Bart. Everyone does."

"Bart, then. Your imagination is going to get a rest! Bring out the lease. I'm ready to sign."

RACHEL HUMMED TO HERSELF as she finally headed back to her parents' house after the job interview. She'd detoured to the high school grounds near the neck of the peninsula, just to refresh her memory and note any external changes. There weren't any. The two-story, U-shaped brick building looked exactly the same as when she'd been a student there. The grounds were in good shape, and the football team had been practicing on the field behind the school. With land at a premium, the field was used for a variety of sports depending on the season. Rachel smiled to herself as she pulled into her parents' driveway, recalling how busy the groundskeepers became getting ready for the change of seasons and games.

She climbed the back steps to the porch and went inside through the kitchen door, inhaling the fragrant aroma of her mom's cooking. Her stomach rumbled. Loudly.

"Just in time!" Pearl beamed from her spot by the stove. "Everyone's just in time. Your brother and Susan and the kids are inside." Without waiting for a reply, she called into the adjoining rooms. "Time to eat. Rachel's home."

"What is that delicious smell?" asked Rachel as she walked toward her mother.

"Garlic, Rachel. It's always the garlic. Roast chicken,

summer-squash-and-zucchini combo, and sweet potatoes. Nothing too fancy, but healthy and filling."

"So, how was the interview?" Lou Goodman walked into the kitchen, followed by Rachel's brother, Alex, and his family.

"I'll tell you later. Now I want to see my favorite brother and sister-in-law."

"He's your *only* brother, Aunt Rachel." Patient exasperation from Alex's twelve-year-old daughter.

"Hi, Jennifer. And you're my favorite niece!"

The girl nodded. "I know. You've only got one of those, too." She walked into Rachel's open arms. "I'm glad you're here."

Unexpected tears sprang to Rachel's eyes as she hugged the child. "I'm glad to see you, too, sweetheart. I love you, Jen."

And then Susan and Alex greeted her. Susan's friendly smile was reflected in her sparkling eyes, in her tight hug. Alex studied her silently, his glance roving from her head to her toes. He bestowed a perfunctory kiss on her cheek, then said, "Still skinny and still unsettled."

"I do declare," drawled Rachel in her best Southern accent, "that you're still so-o perfect, Alex Goodman, that it's pos-i-tive-e-ly unnerving."

She turned toward her nephew who had stood apart. "Hi, dude," she greeted in her normal voice. "Enjoy yourself last night?"

"You were okay with Jack, weren't you?" he replied, a slightly wary look on his face.

So his name was Jack. "A friend of yours, kiddo?"

David shrugged. "He keeps his boat at the marina where I work. He knows a lot of stuff. About the ocean and marine life. He studies it. He's been up and down the entire coastline of North America lots of times."

The man's attitude about the ocean was starting to make sense. "He was fine, David. Don't worry about it."

Five minutes later, after satisfying her first hunger pangs, Rachel felt her dad's gaze on her.

"Are you going to relieve the suspense?" asked Lou. "How did the afternoon go?"

Rachel shrugged. "There were five people, Dad. They asked me a lot of questions, and I gave them honest answers. Whether or not they liked what I had to say, I don't know."

"It still knocks me out," began Alex, shaking his head, "that a girl who hated to study when she was in high school, and who got such lousy grades, winds up in charge of a high school's academic performance. Does that make any sense?"

Rachel took a breath, but Lou was quicker. "It makes perfect sense," he said. "Rachel's the best person for the job—she knows how teenagers feel when they have trouble in school."

"Okay, okay," said Alex, his hands up in surrender. "Don't shoot me if I just don't get it." He looked at Rachel, then at his dad. "And I really don't. If it hadn't been for swimming, she wouldn't have gotten into college at all."

Suddenly, his gaze darted toward his son, then back toward Rachel. "David's a great starting forward for the school. Are you going to tell him not to worry about grades and studying because he can always get a sports scholarship, and maybe be drafted by the NBA?"

Her original indignation at her brother's remarks began to soften. He was worried about his son—his son, who was better on a basketball court than at a desk with books. "I haven't lost a kid's trust yet, Alex," she said in a quiet voice. "Or a parent's respect. And I haven't set them against each other. Take it easy, Dad," she said to him with a wink. "We'll work it out."

Alex stared at her for a moment, then the corner of his mouth twitched. "Maybe," he said. But then he shook his head. "No offense, Rachel, but I'm not sure I want you involved with David's education."

How could she not take offense? "It's time to let go of the past and get into the present." Rachel stared at her brother, trying to will him a new attitude.

"Well, I, for one, think you'll do a wonderful job," said Susan. "Both our kids are crazy about you."

"Thank you, Sue. And I'm crazy about them." She grinned broadly at her niece and nephew. "It's so good to see you two brats."

Good-natured protest followed, just as she'd hoped. She didn't want Jennifer and David caught up in any tension among the adults.

She looked around the table at her family. "We're so lucky," she said. "In fact, I've had a lot of luck lately.

When the tornado struck Round Rock, the school year hadn't started and no kids or staff were hurt."

"Thank God for that," said Pearl.

"Did you know that the state of Massachusetts has the third-highest amount of tornadoes of all the states?" asked David.

"How'd you know that?" asked Jennifer.

"Looked it up on the Net."

"You did?" asked his father. "Are you interested in meteorology, David? That's great. There are such good colleges..."

Rachel watched the interchange. Her brother's eyes shone with enthusiasm and hope. She'd seen it all before, not only with Alex, but with other fathers who thought their kids needed a career choice by the time they hit puberty.

She watched as her nephew shrugged his shoulders. "I don't know, Dad. I like a lot of different stuff. I like working on the boats at the marina. I like playing basketball. I like fishing off the jetty. So, don't start on me, okay? School's not even in session yet."

Storm clouds on two faces. Familiar territory. Every time she visited Pilgrim Cove, a variation of the father-son discord came up.

"You and I, David, must have been on the same wavelength last week," said Rachel. "I jumped on the Internet, too, after we got over the shock of the twister. Did you see the articles about the tornado chasers?"

"Yeah," he replied. "You need special training for

that, and it's better to work in teams so one drives and one takes pictures...."

Rachel looked around the table. Everyone seemed suitably impressed as David continued to explain what he'd read. Including her brother.

Just give your boy breathing room, Alex, and he'll figure it out.

But she'd bet odds, her brother couldn't do it. Alex was so quick himself, an engineer with a fabulous memory and so much ability. But he didn't understand, couldn't understand, or didn't want to understand that David wasn't a reincarnation of himself. The truth was that David shared more characteristics with Rachel at the same age. A fact Alex wouldn't want to admit.

Rachel's heart squeezed for both these males in her family. She knew that Alex loved his son dearly. If she got the position in the local high school, maybe in time, her relationship with her brother would change.

A change Rachel would certainly welcome.

RACHEL WOKE UP EARLY the next morning, washed and dressed quickly and met her dad in the kitchen. Breakfast at the Diner on the Dunes was on the agenda.

"C'mon, Rachel. The ROMEOs all want to see you and hear about yesterday's meeting with the committee."

"I'll just bet they do," she replied. "Those guys still have their fingers in every pie around here, don't they?"

"Those guys include me!" Lou pointed at himself as he led her out the kitchen door to the driveway. "And we sure do. The library's been humming with new volunteers we've recruited—including Laura McCloud Parker, Matt Parker's new wife. And Rick O'Brien got involved when we helped out the lovely woman who's renting Sea View House right now. Her name's Shelley Anderson, and her ex-husband sent down a private investigator. We didn't like that."

"My goodness! Sounds like the ROMEOs are not slowing down at all. So the chief was put to work."

Lou nodded and headed his Plymouth sedan down Oceanside Road toward Dunes Street. "The ROMEOs still help out around the town. Sam Parker and Matt donate materials from the hardware store, and Ralph Bigelow does some electrical work for those who need a helping hand. Some older folks, some younger, down on their luck. We each do what we can. Without the red tape. That's the best part."

Rachel leaned back against the seat, glancing at the man who was her father. "You are a very good person, Dad. You and your friends. Really trying to 'repair the world.' Taking 'tikkun olam' to heart." She referred to the Hebrew phrase, one of the tenets she'd learned as a child.

She saw his face turn red at the compliment. He wasn't used to them. At least not from her.

"We can't fix the whole world, Rachel. Just one situation—one person—at a time."

But he hadn't fixed her when she'd needed him most. He hadn't even tried to help during her awful teenage years. Never told her she was pretty. His own daughter! Even now, she winced.

She thought of her students. How the best results for troubled youngsters came from one-on-one attention. "You're right, Dad. One at a time. But maybe it adds up to something."

Lou nodded, pulled into the parking lot and into a spot. Rachel got out of the car, and the aroma of rich coffee assailed her. She looked toward the entrance of the diner, glad to see the familiar place looking good. The building was a white one-story affair with port-hole-type windows aligned high on the walls. Large picture windows were beneath them.

"And your sign's still there!" Rachel pointed to the red-and-white wood carving above the entrance. "Home of the ROMEOs."

Her father laughed. "Laura, whom I just mentioned, thought Romeo was the last name of the owners."

"I bet she was surprised…."

They pushed the door open and automatically walked toward the back, where five men sat around a large table in the center of which was propped a Reserved sign. Rachel's glance went immediately to Bart Quinn, who stood up and waved her over.

"A sight for my sore eyes, you are, my dear. Welcome home, and give me a hug."

A chorus of welcomes echoed Bart's and she greeted Sam Parker, Doc Rosen, Chief Rick O'Brien and Joe Cavelli.

"You all look wonderful," said Rachel as she bestowed each with a kiss on the cheek. "I hear you're all keeping busy, just like my dad."

"Surely, we are," Bart said.

"I've no doubt about you," Rachel replied. "You're still running the 'largest and oldest' real estate and property management company in the county. Or at least as much of it as Lila allows you to."

"She *is* getting bossy, now that you mention it," Bart replied with a grin. "But I don't mind. And I get to see a lot of little Katie. A crackerjack, my great-granddaughter."

Rachel nodded in acknowledgment. Lila's seven-year-old daughter had personality to spare and made her presence felt. No doubt she was good medicine for the old man.

"And Joe, are you still working at the garage with Charlie?"

Joe Cavelli nodded. "A few hours a week, more when I'm needed, like right now. Summertime is busy. But at the end of the day, we go down to the Lobster Pot and get a pretty decent meal." He winked at her, and Rachel laughed aloud at his understatement. The Lobster Pot was a first-rate seafood house owned and operated by Joe's daughter-in-law, Thea, and her sister, Maggie. Both women were Bart's daughters. Lots of family connections among these ROMEOs.

"I'll have to treat myself to a meal there before I leave," Rachel said. Then she turned to Doc Rosen, who immediately put up his hands.

"I'll admit, I'm truly retired. Probably the only one who admits it around here!"

The other men protested vigorously. "He runs to whomever calls him," said Lou.

"Remember when Shelley Anderson's little girl almost drowned?" asked Rick. "Doc was first on the scene. Even got there before I did."

"And when my son, Matt, needed medical information to understand Laura's situation," began Sam Parker, "who did he go to? Max Rosen—that's who!" Sam banged the table for emphasis. "And now I have a brand-new daughter-in-law. My grandsons have a mother, and my son's a happy man building a new house."

Rachel reached for Sam's hand and squeezed. "I'm so glad for you all. Well-deserved happiness for the Parkers."

"One more dream left to be fulfilled," said Sam, "and I'll be content."

"Amen," said Bart, glancing at his friend.

Rachel's eyes darted from one man to the other, knowing they shared the dream of Jason Parker returning home one day soon. Sam's younger son and Bart's granddaughter, Lila, had been inseparable until the night of their senior prom when Jason's identical twin brother had been killed. Eight years was a long time for him to be on the run—not from the law—but from his own pain and from the people who loved him.

"Has anyone heard from Jason at all in recent times?" asked Rachel quietly as she finally sat down at the table, her dad next to her.

"Not directly," said Chief O'Brien. "Two months ago, we thought we had a lead. A piano man fitting his description was seen by one of my buddies in a night club in New York City. Matt rushed down to investigate, but it wasn't Jason at the keyboard." Rick fiddled with his silverware. "Our Jason is smart. Really knows how to lay low. No paper trail. No salary stubs anywhere."

Rachel pressed her lips together to bottle up her words. She'd known Jason Parker, of course. All Pilgrim Cove kids knew one another as they grew up. No one knew, however, that after she'd left town, she'd seen Jason. Only one time and by accident—on a Mississippi riverboat.

She'd been teaching in the Midwest for a short while and had joined a group of friends for a fun weekend. On the first night out, she thought she spotted a familiar profile across the boat's casino as a young man dealt cards. But it wasn't until she heard the piano in the lounge later that night and recognized the piece and the style, that a chill ran through her. She'd swiveled toward the instrument, and there sat twenty-year-old Jason Parker at the keyboard.

He'd paled when he saw her, but then looked her in the eye—and turned away—deliberately. She got the message and wasn't insulted. They'd both left Pilgrim Cove to make their own way. Each had issues to resolve and neither one was ready to return home. Jason knew that Lila was waiting for him, but it wasn't Rachel's business to urge him to go home. She knew what her own reaction would have been if anyone had tried to push her.

Now she looked around the table at the diner. What would be the purpose of revealing her unexpected encounter with Jason at this late date?

"Your mother and I almost saw him a couple of months ago when we were on vacation in California," Lou said. "When we got to Los Angeles, we found a flyer for a pianist named J.J. Parks at the hotel. And even though the picture was in shadow, I knew it was him."

"But you didn't see him?" asked Rachel.

Lou shook his head. "His engagement had ended the night before we got there. We tried to find out his itinerary, and we tried to find his manager or agent. We asked questions, but no one had answers."

Jason would have made sure of that, thought Rachel.

"So who's having what this morning?" A new voice joined in. It belonged to a petite blonde who'd raced to the table, kissed Rick quickly on the mouth, then escaped from his roving hand. Rachel noticed, however, that Rick's face had turned ruddy.

"Hello, Dee. Or should I say, Mrs. O'Brien?" Rachel smiled at the woman. "How's married life?"

"Rachel!" Dee embraced her tightly. "You look great. How was the interview? Think you'll get the job?"

Whew! The sixty-year-old spitfire hadn't lost an atom of energy.

"You know as much as I do," Rachel said. "I gave it my best shot. Now we'll have to wait and see."

Dee's foot was tapping, her expression thoughtful. "It's August already. August 7." She looked at Bart. "What do you have for her in case she's back here in two weeks with no time for house hunting."

"Good question," Rachel said. "I grew up a block from the beach. I don't suppose there's anything available before Labor Day right on the ocean, is there?"

"But what about staying with..." Lou began.

Rachel sensed her dad's unspoken words, but much as she didn't want to hurt him, she was used to living on her own. She'd definitely need her own place.

"Wait, wait," said Bart to his friend, "I have a better idea."

Rachel could have kissed the agent. She gave him her full attention, but Bart was staring at Lou. "Think a minute, Lou. Sea View House has been lucky this year with people and events. And it could happen again—the way the house has been remodeled and all." Her dad's brows lifted. A tiny smile lurked. And a significant look passed between the two men before Bart turned to Rachel.

"Sea View House would be perfect. And your folks won't be insulted. In fact, they'll be pleased."

Rachel didn't care what the mystery was all about. Let the two ROMEOs have their secrets. She was familiar with the property Bart had mentioned, and he was right. Sea View House would be absolutely perfect for her. She'd get to live right on the beach.

If she was hired.

CHAPTER FOUR

BACK IN KANSAS A WEEK later, Rachel sat in front of her computer in the early morning trying to focus on her job search. She'd been home for two days, and was finding that memories of her Pilgrim Cove vacation often invaded her thoughts. Sometimes, she smiled. More often, she pondered about the slight shift in relationships she'd detected this time, mostly coming from her dad. He'd openly supported her. Had spoken up for her. It felt damn good—wonderful, in fact. But why now? What had made him change his ways? Normally, he was a laid-back type of man allowing Pearl to take the lead with Rachel as she was growing up. Not this time.

And her mom had calmed down. She'd always been the "pusher": the one who pushed Rachel into activities. When Dr. Bennett had spoken about the USA Swimming organization, Pearl had been very enthusiastic. In the beginning, Pearl had pushed for good grades, too. But then she'd stopped. Now Rachel wondered why. Maybe someday, she'd find out.

And then there was Alex. He hadn't changed much toward her, which was too bad, but...she shrugged...

she'd deal with him if and when she had to. Fortunately, her niece and nephew didn't seem to feel the undercurrents between their dad and his sister. Susan managed to calm the waters a lot, and Rachel was grateful to her sister-in-law. The relationship Rachel had with the youngsters was strong and loving. She wanted it to remain that way.

She'd purposely spent a lot of time with Jen. They'd swum together, with Rachel coaching and encouraging the girl in the water. They'd taken long walks on the beach. She'd listened to Jennifer practice for her bat mitzvah ceremony to be held in the spring when she'd turn thirteen. The child's Hebrew reading was flawless already. Rachel wasn't surprised since Jen was an excellent student—definitely her father's daughter.

Rachel refocused on her computer screen. Every school district had its own posting, and she'd decided to start with a twenty-five-mile radius from Round Rock. She couldn't afford to pass up any opportunity, and she couldn't count on returning to Pilgrim Cove.

By three in the afternoon, her neck was stiff and her eyes were glazed. She turned her head from side to side, rolled her shoulders and stretched her arms overhead. The phone rang.

"Thank God," she said, jumping to her feet. "An excuse to move!"

She picked up the receiver.

"So, are you ready to return to Pilgrim Cove?"

Dr. Edward Bennett's voice. Immediately, goose

bumps covered Rachel's arms. She collapsed back into her chair.

"Do you always start off with a punch to the gut?" asked Rachel. "Wait, wait, don't answer that. You do. I know you do."

"Because it usually works, my dear, and it can save a lot of time in the end. But I guess not today. Today requires a full conversation."

Rachel remembered confiding in this man when she could talk to no other adult. He'd cared about her when he could have ignored her. After all, he was the principal! Instead, he'd always taken the time to listen, ignoring his ringing phone when she searched him out in his office. All those reasons would have been enough for her to respect him. But after he'd recommended the USA Swim Club to her folks, Dr. Bennett could do no wrong in Rachel's eyes. Swimming had changed her life. He'd believed in her when no one else did. Sure, her mom loved her, but in Rachel's fifteen-year-old mind, Pearl didn't count. Moms were supposed to love their kids.

"Uh…Dr. Bennett? At the risk of having you think I'm buying time…want to repeat the question?"

His laughter was his only answer for a moment. "We're offering you the position, Rachel." He outlined a competitive salary, reminded her of both the student and teacher roster numbers, the start date—which could be flexible if necessary.

"But think hard, Rachel," he continued. "You'll be living under a microscope because the position is new.

And you'll be living in the shadow of your past. Some of the people here on staff will remember you. There will be no quarter given. I want the job done well. Which is why I'm asking, as an old friend, if you're ready to come back?"

She'd been more than ready when she'd left Pilgrim Cove last week. But the reality of the offer and hearing Dr. Bennett's voice made her stomach flip-flop. He was right on two counts: the responsibility was enormous, and the whole community would be watching. Everyone had been disappointed in the school's recent academic performance.

Rachel took a deep breath. "I can handle it, Dr. Bennett. The answer is yes. Yes, thank you. I want the job."

"Excellent," replied her new boss.

"And I won't let you down."

"Never thought you would."

Tears burned her eyes as she hung up the phone. No matter what happened next, no matter how hard the job turned out to be, she'd never make him regret hiring her.

She stared at the phone. First, her folks. Then Bart Quinn. Then the important people in her life right here in Round Rock, Kansas.

She glanced around the apartment, then walked to the window and looked at the familiar park across the street. She thought about her friendly neighbors who'd welcomed her so warmly. She thought about her swim team and the girls who'd miss her as much as she'd miss them.

For the second time, her eyes filled. She was lonesome for them already! Sure, the door had been left open for her to come back, but deep inside, she knew this chapter of her life was over. Rachel Goodman was going home.

JACK LEVINE LOVED Sea View House. No question about that. He stood on his deck in the early evening as he'd done every day since moving in almost a week ago, noticing how the sun's long fingers painted shadows in the sand, listening as the ocean whispered its never-ending lullaby.

Bart Quinn had done him a good turn. Everything about his apartment was exactly the way the agent had described it. The Crow's Nest, on the second floor, had a very large kitchen with a deck running the width of the house right outside its door. The master bedroom contained an oversize desk, perfect for his computer and materials, as well as a dresser and a huge closet. The small bedroom held all his guy stuff—surfboard, football, fishing gear, boat stuff—and had a wall of bookcases that he'd almost filled. All in all, a neat setup for the coming year.

As soon as he'd returned from visiting his folks and old friends in Maine, he'd started exploring the coastline around the Pilgrim Cove peninsula. He had introduced himself to the harbormaster and staff, and had even taken a few water samples. Of course, when school began, his morning trips would be limited to weekends. His afternoons would be free, however, and he intended to meet up with lobstermen bringing their catches into port. Their observations about their catches would provide valuable clues to water quality, too.

Jack yawned and headed back inside to heat up a frozen dinner, take a shower and sack out. Maybe he'd read a little or organize some notes before closing his eyes. He really should sleep late one of these days, so he'd have the energy to hit some night spots in this town—if there were any. A long winter loomed ahead. He'd definitely need some company. If Pilgrim Cove had nothing, he could always hook up with his buddies in Boston, just thirty minutes away.

He took the dinner from the freezer and stuck it in the microwave. Everything in his kitchen was in easy reach, and he was amazed at how quickly he felt at home. Even his pickup looked as if it belonged in the driveway.

Fortunately, Bart had been right about the availability of the house. Seemed Daniel Stone, the guy who'd rented before Jack, had left early to start house-hunting in Boston. And Shelley Anderson, the attractive lady downstairs, had taken her two kids and moved out yesterday—a whole week before Labor Day—to help Daniel house hunt. Since the two of them were getting married soon, her decision made sense. But if Jack had been one of Shelley's kids, he would've raised holy hell about leaving Pilgrim Cove even a minute before summer was over.

Funny the way it had worked out for Daniel and

Shelley. They'd each come for a quiet summer at the beach. And wound up with more excitement than anyone could have imagined. Bart Quinn had told Jack the whole story when he'd been in the real estate office signing the lease. Jack had chuckled and shaken his head. "Better him than me walking down that long, long aisle."

"Your turn will come, boy-o." The agent had looked at him with an expression Jack couldn't quite read. Somewhere between compassion and humor. "And when it does, my friend, I want to be around to see it."

"You sound like my mother," Jack had replied with a grin. "I really hope the two of you live that long."

He'd gotten up to leave, but the old man called him back. "Don't forget that you'll be getting a neighbor downstairs. Not for a week or so yet. A schoolteacher. Last-minute hire."

"Just like me." He shrugged. "No problem." And at the time, he'd meant it.

Bart had nodded briefly, and Jack thought no more about it until right now. He removed his meal from the oven and walked out onto the deck to eat. Man, he'd lucked out. The well-named Sea View House was perfect for him.

AFTER TWO STRAIGHT DAYS of almost nonstop driving, Rachel pulled up to her parents' house late on the Saturday night before Labor Day. She turned the ignition key off, rested her arms on the steering wheel and lay her head down, totally exhausted.

During the past hectic week, she'd given away some of her furniture and taken other pieces to consignment shops in Kansas. She'd shipped boxes of personal belongings and some kitchen supplies to Pilgrim Cove. Then she'd packed her vehicle so full that the driver's seat was the only available space inside.

More difficult than all the physical work of a quick move, however, were the emotional goodbyes. She'd managed to recruit another coach for her team, but the girls were teary-eyed when she swam with them for the last time. And her teaching friends at school…all said they looked forward to Rachel returning the next year. But Rachel knew it was only a pretense to lessen the sadness of saying goodbye. "If you get hungry for an ocean," she'd joked, "come on over. I'll share it."

Now she had thirty-six hours before she was scheduled to meet with Dr. Bennett as well as with the director of Athletics and Clubs, the attendance coordinator and the chairman of the Guidance Department. The office support staff would also be on hand. If she didn't get some sleep, she'd make exactly the impression she was trying to avoid.

From a distance, she head a door slam and then familiar voices.

"She's here, thank God, in one piece."

Rachel sat up and opened her door. Her folks must have been standing at the window, watching for her. She got out of the Explorer and stretched, then moaned. Everything hurt.

"A meal, a hot shower and a night's sleep. You'll be as good as new." Pearl hugged her daughter and urged her into the house. "Don't worry about a thing, sweetheart. We'll all help you move into Sea View House tomorrow. The kids, too. I'll do a basic food run to get you started."

"Thanks, Mom." Rachel would have agreed to anything right then, and for once appreciated that her mother was taking charge, organizing and ordering her family around.

"We've already got the key for you. Bart brought it to the diner this morning along with the lease. You can sign it and return it sometime this week."

"I guess he knew I'd be short on time tomorrow."

"He also had Matt Parker and Ralph Bigelow do a check on the plumbing and electrical systems," said Lou. "The cleaning service came in as well." Her dad paused. "And the windows were washed."

"Wow! Windows, too?"

"Your mother took care of those. I would have paid someone, but she wanted to do it herself."

"What?" Rachel pivoted to face Pearl. "That's too much work!"

"What's the point of living by the ocean if you can't see it?"

"Come on, Mom. Were the windows *that* dirty?"

"Well…maybe not. But I wanted to do it. So you'll feel comfortable and happy there. And happy to be back home in Pilgrim Cove."

If only happiness were that simple. "I'll be happy if I do a good job at the school and improve those test scores."

"But I can't help you with that." Pearl's voice trailed off on a note of disappointment.

And then it clicked. "Mom?" Rachel walked over to hug the woman who wanted her to stay close. "Thanks. That's quite a welcome-home gift."

A tight squeeze was the response.

At eleven o'clock the next morning, Rachel stood in the middle of her kitchen at Sea View House staring at disorder everywhere. Too many cartons. Too many people. Too many voices giving directions and no one listening. Wasting time. She wished she had the luxury of standing by one of the sparkling windows to enjoy the ocean view! Better yet, she wished she had a half hour to swim. And she absolutely needed time to prepare herself for her first day on the job.

"Everybody stop!" she called. "Let's control the chaos so that in two hours we can all have lunch." Now it was Rachel who gave the orders. "Alex, if you and David could set up my office—my computer is a must. And unpack the cartons of books in the same room. The boxes are marked. And Susan, if you and Jen could work in my bedroom—the linens are in that carton under the table. The hanging clothes are in plastic over there. Dad, you and I will work the kitchen, and when Mom gets back, she'll stock the food. Everybody…ready…go!"

And they did. Without any backtalk from anyone. Not even from her brother. His participation had surprised her at first, until she realized that her parents must have insisted. Or maybe Susan had. No matter who was responsible, Rachel was happy to see him.

Five minutes later, she heard her name being called from the bedroom. "Aunt Rachel, we're booting up the computer now. Want to check it out?"

"That was fast, guys," Rachel said, walking into the study.

"That wasn't guys with an 's,'" said Alex. "David reconnected it by himself." Her brother's eyes gleamed with pride when he looked at his son.

The boy shrugged. "No biggie. Anyone can do that."

"Not true, David. Not true at all," said Rachel.

"Hey, Dad!" interrupted David. "Look what she's got as a screen saver! It's us. Me and Jen."

"Jen and I." Rachel and her brother spoke in unison, then started to laugh. They stared at each other and laughed some more. And Rachel could've sworn she heard ice breaking with a loud crack. A new beginning, she hoped.

In a little more than an hour, the Captain's Quarters was almost ready to be lived in. Rachel looked at all they'd accomplished, then walked onto the large covered deck outside the kitchen. A round table and chairs and several chaise longues provided a casual dining area. She stepped to the front of the deck and leaned against the railing. Beyond her backyard, the beach was full of bathers. Large colorful umbrellas dotted the sand. Two boys ran along the shoreline trying to fly a kite. A happy scene, and Rachel sighed with contentment before turning around and going back inside.

"As soon as we're finished, I'm going to bring the signed lease to Bart," she announced. "After tomorrow, my mind will be on other things."

"When you're finished with Bart, come to the house for an early dinner." Pearl put her hand up as Rachel was about to protest. "I know you have work to do, but you have to eat, anyway. We'll have simple hamburgers on the grill. Eat and run and I promise not to be insulted. In fact, invite Bart to come, too. I've got plenty."

"Do you think he'll give up a meal at the Lobster Pot?" asked Rachel with a grin. "If I remember correctly, he loves to play at being maître d' for his daughters. He's the best piece of public relations Thea and Maggie have."

"That's the truth," said Lou. "But ask him, anyway. We enjoy a glass of schnapps together from time to time."

Rachel wrinkled her nose. "Okay."

But Bart was on the verge of leaving the office when Rachel arrived. He filed the signed lease in the cabinet drawer marked Sea View House and sent his regrets. "I've got a new listing. Want to see the property. But tell Lou I'll stop by to raise a glass if I've got some time later."

"Will do." She turned to leave.

"By the way, lass, I *did* mention that you'd have a neighbor upstairs, didn't I?"

She spun around. "I don't think so."

"Not to worry. He's a fine man. We check out everyone who stays at Sea View House, and he passed with high scores. More important, I like him, and my gut instincts never lie."

Rachel couldn't help smiling. The statement was so Bart.

"He has two jobs and crazy hours," Bart continued, "and a separate side entrance up to the Crow's Nest. You'll be like ships passing in the night, hardly seeing each other."

"Oh. Then I guess that's all right. You just surprised me. I really don't think you mentioned it before."

"Sorry, lassie. Must be losing my touch." He met her glance, and his eyes twinkled. But he didn't crack a smile.

Losing his touch? Rachel didn't believe a word of it.

THE NEXT MORNING, RACHEL dressed in a lightweight black slack suit with a black-and-white polka-dot blouse and low-heeled shoes. Her small purse fit inside her attaché case. She felt neat and professional despite her jitters as she pulled into the school's driveway. No one was parked in front, and she continued to the back lot. Empty also. She glanced at her watch and finally chose a spot near the front entrance. It was seven-forty-five. She was definitely early, but she felt wide-awake after ten hours of undisturbed sleep.

The events and activities of the last few weeks had caught up with her the previous night. After she'd dined with her family and returned to Sea View House alone, the quiet had wrapped itself around her, and the familiar ocean tang in the air seemed to trigger a sleep response. She'd flopped onto her mattress and had heard nothing until her alarm went off at six.

She reached into her half-empty briefcase and pulled out a legal pad. Might as well put her time to good use, especially since she was walking in rather cold. In five minutes, she had composed a page of questions as well as reminders to herself as one thought followed another. Were there teacher issues? Or student issues? Family issues? Social issues? Outdated books? Curriculum? Attendance problems? Something was broken here, maybe more than one something. And it was up to her to uncover and fix it.

A car pulled into the spot beside her, then a second, and soon Rachel was being greeted by Dr. Bennett and three others. Three sets of curious eyes coupled with a mix of warm and cautious smiles.

The most enthusiastic greeting came from Judy Kramer, the chair of the Guidance Department. An attractive woman probably in her forties, she had a firm handshake and a genuine smile. "We'll take all the help we can get. Everyone's worried about performance. An objective newcomer might see more clearly than we do." No doubt Judy was sincere.

Bob Franklin, the athletic director, seemed more concerned about his players' abilities and teams' stature in the community. "Don't forget, the games raise some of the money to support the cost of the program. We've also got local sponsors. Sports are big around here. Athletics and after school clubs are crucial to developing well-rounded kids."

His statements were logical, but Rachel sensed the man had his own agenda. She stared at him and nodded. "I'm very aware of the benefits team sports have for students, Mr. Franklin. I'm an athlete myself. I'm a coach in the USA Swim Club."

Franklin's expression was comical—wide eyes, open mouth. Rachel could almost hear his sigh of relief.

"But I'm also aware of the pitfalls athletes can encounter," she added. "A swelled head and attitude, poor academics…" She smiled at the athletic director. "Let's hope the benefit side wins." She couldn't blame him for wanting her to know his position. Athletic programs were often praised to the heavens or blamed for everything that went wrong in a school. However, she planned to reserve judgment on Bob Franklin.

The man's eyes narrowed again, but he said nothing more and Rachel turned to Helen Wong, the attendance coordinator.

"Welcome, Rachel Goodman. I do spreadsheets for you—any kind you want. You want big statistics, small statistics, I can do it. By grade, by age, any demographic you want. I give you the same daily reports I give to guidance counselors. My computer sings for me. We're a team." The petite woman with salt-and-pepper hair turned to Dr. Bennett. "Is it not true?"

"Don't know what we'd do without you, Helen." Dr. Bennett tried to keep a straight face, but the corners of his mouth wobbled and his eyes glistened with suppressed laughter. Finally, he started to chuckle. "If nothing else, I can always count on you to reduce my stress."

He looked at Rachel. "She's also a whiz at monitoring budgets. And in case you couldn't tell, she has an opinion about everything. Soon she'll be running the school."

Anyone else would have blushed at his teasing, thought Rachel. Helen Wong looked Bennett square in the face and said, "I'm not ready yet, boss."

Rachel's spirit soared. The bantering was a very good sign of Dr. Bennett's management style. Obviously, people enjoyed working with him and weren't afraid. So far, so good.

Dr. Bennett led the group inside the building to the suite of administrative offices where the returning staff members disappeared. Rachel followed Dr. Bennett to his private office. "Tomorrow's faculty meeting won't be as easy. Some have sharp memories of your student days, and they're eager to see what you can do. Just remember, Rachel, the committee chose you, so let whatever remarks they make roll off your back. You'll win them over in the end."

Rachel felt herself straighten to every bit of her five-foot-nine inches. "I'll get through the first encounter with a smile. Then I'll get to know each teacher one-on-one. It'll take a little time. That's all."

He studied her. "Just make sure they know who's in charge."

"Why, Dr. Bennett, I thought that was you!"

He grinned and waved her away. "Why don't you take a stroll around the place. Refresh your memory, discover changes. Then we'll set you up in your office. Here's a master key. Explore."

"Thanks. Uh…before I do, I have one small question."

He looked at her expectantly.

"Is Cornelia Stebbins still teaching here?"

Silence rang in her ears as she waited for his response. But Dr. Bennett was shaking his head. "Retired and gone to Florida."

Yes! "I'm not sorry to hear that."

"She really got to you, didn't she?"

Got to her? The woman caused her the kind of pain that still brought tears to her eyes years later. "Let's just say, I would have had to monitor her constantly. How could I trust her not to tear out the hearts of other youngsters?"

She took the key and left, glad her old nemesis was gone, but her smile faded and her spirit plummeted, anyway. She'd put up a good front, but she'd sensed there was a whole lot of attitude about her from the staff that Dr. Bennett was keeping to himself. Which meant that tomorrow's faculty meeting would be a real challenge.

SUNLIGHT STREAMED IN through large sash windows in the double classroom. Although not all seats were taken, it seemed to Rachel that the space was filled to the bursting point. Still wearing casual summer clothes and sandals, the teachers seemed not only comfortable but excited as they chatted with their colleagues. Rachel caught snatches about summer events, family news and the upcoming school year. While Dr. Bennett mingled with his staff, Rachel stood near the desk at the front of the room, glad she'd chosen to wear a tailored skirt and blouse. First impressions counted, and she aimed to present a professional image.

At least two of the old-timers had already recognized her and stopped to ask about her dad. Then Tom Sullivan, the boys' phys ed teacher and coach, came over to welcome her home. Rachel took his warm words as a positive sign and felt herself begin to relax. Of course, Tom, who was Bart Quinn's son-in-law, might just have a soft spot because of her swimming achievements, and because he never had to contend with her in class! Regardless, his greeting lessened her concern about Bob Franklin's attitude yesterday.

"It's one-ten, and although not everyone's here yet, we're going to start," said Dr. Bennett as he walked toward Rachel. The principal motioned her to sit next to him behind the desk. The room quieted down and all eyes focused on Rachel's new boss.

"It's good to see everyone looking healthy, rested and excited about the year ahead. New beginnings are what teaching is about each fall. New beginnings for students as well as staff, and this year, a new beginning for the school as a whole. In that vein, we'll start with introductions since seven new staff members have joined us. We have six new teachers…hmm, I count only five in the room right now…as well as a new assistant principal whom you'll meet shortly. I know she has some words of welcome and her own short agenda today."

As the teachers introduced themselves and the subjects they taught, Rachel tried to memorize as many of the names as possible, tried to smile or nod to each person. She jotted a note asking Helen for a faculty list by department, length of service and class performance the prior year.

The introductions took almost half an hour, and just as the last person finished speaking and sat down, the classroom door flew open.

"Sorry I'm late. *The Wanderer* had engine problems, so I've come directly from the marina."

CHAPTER FIVE

RACHEL RECOGNIZED HIM instantly. The same set of broad shoulders, the same playboy grin, this time surrounded by a scruffy beard. With his red T-shirt, denim shorts, boat shoes, and the scent of salt and seaweed, the man loomed like a modern day pirate of the Caribbean. He overflowed with testosterone, a restless heat that couldn't be missed.

This was the same guy she'd bumped into outside Town Hall after her interview. The guy who'd ordered her out of the ocean one night during her vacation a few weeks ago. A single glance at him made her own heart stop for a moment before resuming its natural rhythm. She could hear the flutter among the staff. Hopefully, her own mouth wasn't hanging open like some of the other women's.

"Just in time to introduce yourself," said Dr. Bennett, motioning the newcomer to the front row of seats.

The man strode with confidence, his slightly rolling gait revealing a sea-going life. "Sure," he said. "Name's Jack Levine, new to town. I'm a last-minute hire for the Science Department. Life just worked out that way." He glanced at Rachel, his hazel eyes twinkling. "Nice seeing you again," he said before sitting down and stretching out his long legs in front of him.

Rachel nodded in acknowledgment and tried to stop the heat she felt rising to her face.

"Dr. Levine's being modest," said the principal. "He's a marine biologist, and we'll be taking advantage of him this year. He'll be teaching a seniors-only seminar in his specialty as well as handling regular earth science and biology courses. Science teachers are hard to find. We're lucky he was available to take over for Mrs. Zack on such short notice."

"Darn lucky." The whispered words came from an attractive blonde sitting in the second row. Rachel stifled a groan. Faculty romances could get sticky. As she studied the room, Rachel saw that the blonde had competition. Even married ladies were feasting their eyes.

Rachel refocused on Jack Levine's credentials. A Ph.D. in marine biology was impressive. More impressive was that he'd chosen teaching over more lucrative careers in science. She thought about her nephew David's admiration of the man and felt reassured. The guy must really like working with youngsters, and that was exactly the type of person she wanted on the high school staff.

Dr. Bennett finished his welcoming remarks, his announcements, and then spoke about why the school had searched for its first-ever assistant principal for academic studies.

"I'm delighted to announce that one of our own has returned to Pilgrim Cove to take on that position. She's had a remarkable teaching and supervisory career in a Kansas public school system and comes highly qualified to fill this important role for us. I know you'll make her feel welcome." He turned to Rachel and motioned her to stand up. "Some of you need no introduction, but for those who don't know her, this is Rachel Goodman. I know she has some welcoming words for you."

Dr. Bennett reseated himself, and Rachel looked at the full assembly. "Good afternoon," she began.

"Rachel Goodman!" a female voice boomed. "My memory is still razor sharp, and you owe me a term paper!"

Rachel flinched, and a couple of chuckles filled the air. Mrs. Drummond had been a martinet of an English teacher in her younger days, and her style obviously hadn't changed. She did, however, seem to command the respect of the faculty here.

"Mrs. Drummond," Rachel said, forcing herself to relax and smile. "I probably owe you more than one paper if the truth be told. But as it turns out, I got straight A's in college English including grad school, so something you did in class must have stuck."

Drummond's wide-eyed expression was followed by a reluctant grin, and Rachel hoped she'd succeeded in disarming the woman. The real problem, of course, was that Mrs. Drummond hadn't looked beyond the young Rachel's attitude and hadn't recognized the girl's ability. In all probability, she still wasn't reaching out to her students. She wasn't in the same hurtful league as Cornelia Stebbins, but she needed to pay closer attention to the kids in her classroom.

Rachel's glance fell on Jack Levine who, with a wink, nodded his approval. Could he possibly understand the historic undercurrents behind her exchange with Mrs. Drummond?

"I look forward to working with all of you, and to meeting our goals," Rachel continued. Quiet descended over the group at a rapid rate. She felt the almost-physical force of her audience's attention on her and was gratified.

"Make no mistake. We're on a mission this year. A mission to regain 'exemplary' status for this school in the state system." She paused and tried to look at each teacher individually. "As you all know, status is determined by test performance at the end of the year, so I expect every instructor to cover the mandated curriculum using whatever creative method works. We need to reach every single student."

Now people shifted in their seats, a few exchanging glances. "And yes, I know that some youngsters have learning difficulties and attention-deficit problems. We'll be working with those students, too. I will be with you every step of the way. In fact, during the next two weeks, I plan to chat with each of you. We'll discuss your classes, your concerns and your successes."

"School starts next Tuesday, the day after Labor Day. Lesson plans are due every Friday starting this week.

That means the first one is due in three days. Normally they'll be returned to you on Monday, but because of the holiday coming up, they'll be in your mailboxes early next Tuesday morning." She stopped speaking and took note of her audience. A couple of frowns. A couple of people scribbling. "Are there any questions?"

"What about books? Do we have enough?"

"There are unopened cartons piled in the general office," she replied. "Publisher names are on the label. We'll need to do an inventory."

"I have a question," said a man Rachel recognized as a teacher from the Social Studies Department.

Rachel looked at him. "Yes, Mr. Maggio?"

"Can I ask Lou how his daughter went from giving him migraines to making him proud?"

The trouble with small towns was that everyone—including those with good intentions—thought they had proprietorial rights. "I think my dad's still trying to figure it out himself, Mr. Maggio, but I'll tell him you inquired. Thanks."

"Let's hope Lou's headaches don't return now that his daughter's back." Mrs. Drummond seemed determined to have the last word and wore a satisfied grin as she met the glances of some of her friends.

Rachel felt the burn in her cheeks this time. Couldn't control it now. Had she made a mistake in returning home? Wasn't this where she'd left off years ago with Lou's colleagues commiserating with him, shaking their heads at how different his two children were?

"I think my dad is safe," she finally replied to the English teacher. "So the only headaches you need to worry about are your own." She had their attention again. "I believe every student can learn. It's up to you to tap their potential so we'll have a win-win situation all the way around. Dr. Bennett and I are expecting performance here—from teachers and students." If she hammered her message any louder, they'd all get headaches. "Any other questions?"

No one responded and Rachel was glad. "I'll be here every day for the rest of the week," she said. "Stop in and see me when you can."

The meeting broke up. Dr. Bennett was chatting to a group of people, and Rachel gathered her notes, wanting to return to her office to think. To figure out how to handle the old-timers who were at this very moment probably telling all the newer teachers about Rachel's student days and her barely passing grades.

She stood up, but before she could take a step, her path was blocked by Jack Levine. He stared at her for a moment, his eyes shining, a smile lurking. "My, my. What a handful you must have been. Appearances sure can be deceiving. You look so serious and professional today."

She tilted her chin up and looked him in the eye. "That's because I *am* serious about getting this school back on track. Make no mistake, Dr. Levine, we *will* get results. I suggest you forget everything you hear about my misspent, unscholarly youth. That part of my life is over, and I am not the same person."

Slowly shaking his head in mock sorrow, he said, "Then how do you explain challenging the ocean in the middle of the night?" He raised his eyes and deliberately scanned the room. "And why have you come back to these shark-infested waters?" He looked her in the eye. "You're here to prove something—to the town, to yourself—I don't know. But I wish you good luck. Lots of it."

She'd need it. The words reverberated silently in the air. He didn't have to say them. Well, she wasn't one to turn down any good luck that came her way, but she wasn't going to wait around for it, either. Hard work and perseverance would get her through.

RACHEL WATCHED JACK LEVINE work the crowd. He shook hands with the men, laughed with the women and made more than one of them blush. His easygoing charm seemed to come naturally to him. By the end of the day, he'd probably know every name in the room. She shrugged her shoulders and continued to gather her belongings. She couldn't and wouldn't fault him for personality. It was only when she saw him and Bob Franklin deep in conversation that doubt started to rise. Franklin was gesturing toward the back of the building, his face animated. Behind the school were the football and baseball fields. She could easily guess the topic under discussion.

She rested her hip against the desk and took a moment to observe. The athletic director continued to smile, talk and shake Jack's hand before making his way to another teacher where his actions were repeated. Jack Levine wasn't the only one working the crowd, thought Rachel. The difference was that Jack's agenda was strictly social—he was a natural flirt. Bob Franklin, on the other hand, acted as his own political action committee, reminding everyone about how important sports teams were to the school. Rachel sighed. The man felt threatened by the need for a stricter academic performance.

Hadn't he ever heard of a "no pass, no play" policy? Suddenly, Rachel wondered if Pilgrim Cove Regional had such a policy. She scribbled another note to herself. Maybe she'd have a quiet talk with Tom Sullivan.

Rachel stayed at school for the rest of the day, reviewing reports and familiarizing herself with the computer system. Her office was located in the administrative suite, near Dr. Bennett's, behind the large general office on the first floor. By four o'clock, a couple of teachers had visited her. One had a question about class size; the other was new to the school and had wanted to locate Rachel's office. She'd welcomed them both warmly. Then Mr. Maggio stopped by with the advice to ignore Edith Drummond.

"I'll ignore personal remarks, Mr. Maggio, but I won't ignore her teaching performance or her manner with the students."

He look startled, and Rachel put up her hand. "Don't worry. Everyone's starting out fresh, with a clean slate, in this new year. Even Edith Drummond. Believe me, I want her to succeed with her students. I want us all to succeed."

"Of course you do," replied the teacher, his expression warm once again. "I want the same."

A vote of confidence! Mr. Maggio had been popular with the kids when Rachel had been a student. Known as a good teacher, passionate about his subject and able to engender excitement for it among his students. Unfortunately, she'd never been in any of his classes.

"Thanks for stopping by. I appreciate it," said Rachel.

"Anytime." He waved and went on his way. Rachel stared at the empty doorway for a while. Why was it that the good teachers always took challenges to heart, while the mediocre ones ignored them? Why did they never think critique applied to them? Almost a hundred people on her staff, and Rachel had to discern each teacher's philosophy.

She stretched her arms overhead, rolled her shoulders and returned to the computer and last year's reports. She wanted to analyze the reasons Pilgrim Cove Regional High School had fallen down recently.

The next time she looked up, the room was in shadow and she was hungry. She rose from her chair just as Dr. Bennett appeared in her doorway.

"Tomorrow's another day, Rachel. For both of us."

"I agree." She reached for her purse and walked to her car with him.

"We'll have a 'reserved' sign painted for you—assistant principal—next to my spot, as soon as the maintenance crew is on full-time again, probably by the end of next week."

"Is that really necessary?" she asked in a quiet voice.

"It's about being practical and safe, Rachel, not elitist," he said with a chuckle. "You need to be close to the door. I have a feeling tonight isn't the only time you'll be here after dark."

"Point taken."

"In addition," he continued, "it won't hurt to remind the staff that you aren't part of the regular faculty. The reserved spot is a subtle announcement that you are on my supervisory team."

She stopped walking mid-stride. "You've got a devious mind, Dr. Bennett."

"Sometimes, my dear, actions do speak louder than words."

"I'll remember that," Rachel replied, "if my words don't get results."

She stopped off at the diner for a burger, too hungry to cook for herself. No ROMEOs greeted her inside. Not even Dee and Chief O'Brien were there that night. But the tasty flame-broiled burger restored Rachel's flagging energy, and she drove to Sea View House feeling content.

The pickup truck in the driveway startled her. She glanced up at the second floor. Not a light on. Completely dark. Parking at the curb in front of the house, Rachel tried to remember what Bart Quinn had said about her upstairs neighbor. She thought hard but couldn't remember much. Something about working crazy hours, maybe working two jobs for a while.

She entered her apartment and closed the door quietly. No sounds came from above. She glanced at her watch. Barely nine-thirty, but obviously the man was sleeping. He probably had to wake up very early. Until she met him and understood his schedule, she'd try to be a good neighbor and make as little noise as possible.

She prepared a cup of decaf, intending to read for a while, then found herself yawning, her own eyes closing. Maybe her neighbor had the right idea. She fell asleep a minute after lying down.

Somewhere in her dreams, she heard a door creak, then close with a slight bump. When she heard a motor come to life, she opened her eyes. The bedside clock read 4:00 a.m. Ugh! She rolled over and slept again. When she left for school at eight, the pickup was gone.

The pattern continued over the next few days. Rachel worked late; the truck was parked in the driveway at night and gone the next morning when she awoke. The arrangement suited her just fine. The more privacy, the better.

She allowed herself to sleep in on Saturday, and at ten o'clock was brewing coffee. The four-cupper made two mugs, exactly the amount of caffeine Rachel needed to start the day.

The sun shone brightly through the kitchen window where Cape Cod curtains were no deterrent to the light. Her wheeled tote, filled with lesson-plan books, stood next to the large table. Rachel was eager to get started, but the morning was glorious, too glorious for her to remain indoors. She couldn't resist drinking her coffee on the porch and enjoying a neighbor who never slept—the Atlantic Ocean.

A chilly breeze raised goose bumps on Rachel's skin, but she didn't care. This weekend marked the traditional last hurrah of summer, and she wanted to be part of it. She'd invited her family for a cookout the next day, and she'd have to go shopping later, but now, she needed to get moving!

She quickly dressed in a bathing suit and shirt, put on running shoes and set out along the beach. Smiling and waving to other beachgoers, Rachel covered a five-mile circuit with almost no effort and returned to Sea View House. Perspiration dotted her forehead, the air was warmer, and the ocean looked inviting.

She ran to the water's edge, toed off her sneakers, tossed her shirt aside and waded in. Unexpectedly, the image of a sexy swimmer came to mind, a man with a scruffy beard who'd popped in and out of her thoughts since the faculty meeting.

Cautiously, Rachel looked over her shoulder. No one appeared, and she chuckled to herself. Had she expected him to by spying on her? Or was it a guilty conscience? She shaded her eyes and scanned the beach. Lifeguards had already come on duty. "Sheesh." She was annoyed at her own hesitation. Since when did she allow someone else to regulate her swimming?

Twenty minute's later, she made her way back home,

totally refreshed, ready for a shower, ready to attack the pile of lesson plans.

By late afternoon, she wasn't laughing. Of all the plan books to lose, why did it have to be Jack Levine's? She'd checked off every other teacher's submission against her master list. Only his was missing. She searched everywhere—the hallway, kitchen floor and her car. Nothing. She grabbed her purse and drove the three miles to the school. The parking lot was empty. She parked in her usual place and searched the ground. Again, nothing. Her key to the side door worked, and she let herself into the building, deactivating the alarm system.

Maybe she'd left his book on her desk. But, no, it wasn't there. Nor was it on the floor of her office, or in Dr. Bennett's or the general office. She checked the halls leading to the front door. Nothing.

Darn it! So much for earning the confidence of the staff! How professional would the hunky scientist possibly think she was now?

"WELCOME, WELCOME," Rachel said to her parents the next afternoon, taking Pearl's offering of homemade coleslaw and placing it in the refrigerator next to her own three-bean salad, which was really six-bean plus a few other veggies. "Look around now that I'm actually settled in."

"The place looks great," said Pearl. "Those gray planked floors are wonderful. Looks like twelve-inch oak."

"They are," said Lou. "Throughout the house. Believe me, I know all the specs. With Bart giving orders, Ralph Bigelow keeps the electricals up to snuff, Matt Parker takes care of the plumbing and incidental carpentry fixes, and I help out when they need a helper." He peered at his family. "They let me hold the nails."

"Oh, Dad!" said Rachel, giving Lou a kiss on the cheek. "They couldn't accomplish anything without you."

"Actually, I help Sam and Matt in their store sometimes. Max Rosen and I both help out. Matt can be gone for hours on outside calls. Sam's arthritis frustrates him, and the Golden girls only work part-time."

"The Golden girls?" Rachel repeated slowly trying to place them.

"Blanche and Ethel Gold," chimed in Pearl. "You remember them, Rachel—the two sisters who married two brothers and wound up sharing a last name throughout their whole lives. They were the fishermen in the family, going out almost every day. They started working in the hardware store after they lost their boat and almost drowned. Did you know about that?"

Rachel shook her head. "Sorry, Mom. I just didn't keep up with everything."

"The sisters were undaunted, but their husbands said, 'No more boats. If you want fresh fish, go to the Lobster Pot.' So they did. And do. And on Wednesday nights, we all play mah-jongg."

Rachel grinned at that revelation. She had no trouble conjuring the sights and sounds of five women sitting around her mom's kitchen table playing the Americanized version of the ancient Chinese game. "Still gambling big, Mom?"

"Yup. Three dollars for a night's fun." Pearl leaned closer. "And that's only if I lose. I could win major bucks!"

"Sure. Twelve dollars, tops. If you win every game. I remember how that works."

"Hi, Aunt Rachel! We're here." Jennifer, ready for a swim, came through the kitchen door and gave Rachel a hug. "Except David's working at the marina, so Dad'll get him later."

"I hope there's room in the fridge for a whipped cream cake," said Susan. "We brought some dessert."

"You bet," replied Rachel quickly, opening the refrigerator door. Whipped cream was her favorite topping on any dessert.

Then Alex approached. "I pulled into the driveway behind Dad," he said. "How come you're not parked there?"

"The neighbor uses it, but I'm sure it won't matter. The weather's perfect," Rachel added. "How about going for a swim before we eat? A lot safer than afterward."

In five minutes, everyone was sunscreened and in the water. The beach was crowded, all of Pilgrim Cove wanting one more swim before the season ended. The summer folks would be gone in two or three days.

Susan and Jennifer jumped the waves. Pearl and Lou stroked and floated, their forms actually very good.

Alex kept Rachel company beyond the break line as she swam out to sea.

"On a day like today," he said after a while, "I can see why you wouldn't want to be anywhere but out here. Swimming is actually relaxing me."

His words sounded almost like a confession, and Rachel tried to frame her response carefully. "Exercise is known for reducing stress, Alex. Any kind of exercise."

"I'm aware of the theory." His voice sounded sad.

"Then just enjoy the day, Alex. Enjoy the day."

He grunted, then started to swim to shore. The rest of the family was already making for the house. Rachel swam for another few minutes before following. She picked up her towel, rubbed her hair semidry and started finger-combing as she walked up the beach.

From a short distance away, she realized more people had joined their group. Her nephew, David, for one. Briefly, she wondered how he'd gotten there. And—holy Toledo! Jack Levine. The one person she didn't want to see at the moment. Ah, well. She'd have to tell him about his lost lesson-plan book sooner or later.

Everyone was gathered on the big porch and turned toward her as she arrived.

"Hi, David. Hello, Dr. Levine."

"Call me Jack."

Darn, if the man didn't look as good as she remembered. Sun-bronzed and wearing dark glasses. Exuding sexuality as easily as a flower exuded fragrance. "I gather you brought David home and saved my brother a ride. Thanks."

"No problem at all."

A curious quiet descended. Rachel couldn't quite understand it. "Uh, would you like to stay and join us for a drink?" She glanced at her mom, but Pearl was smiling at Jack. Rachel focused on him again, too.

The man removed his glasses, revealing eyes that shone with suppressed laughter. "A drink would be nice, but I'm not going anywhere, Rachel." His voice trailed off, confusing her further. She waited. "I live here," he said softly.

A heartbeat passed while his words registered. "What!" She couldn't believe it. "You...you..." She pointed toward the second-floor apartment, the Crow's Nest, then turned back to him.

"Afraid so."

She looked at her family. Her parents were smiling with delight. They must have known! But it was her brother who laughed long and loud.

"This is *so-o* Rachel," said Alex. "So typical. Where's your brain? You're here a whole week, so how could you not know who lives upstairs? Why didn't you ask Bart before you moved in? Or after?"

Rachel glared at him, but he didn't seem to notice.

"Not a damn thing has changed," her brother continued. "She still needs a baby-sitter, but this time, it won't be me! You're the same—just older and...really not so skinny."

She suddenly felt all eyes on her. And her one-piece racing suit hid very little. Where was her robe when she needed one? Even better, where were some boxing gloves to use on Alex? Baby-sitter!

"Guess she's not an exclamation point anymore," said Lou, coming over and giving her a hug. "That's what I used to call you when you were a munchkin. A thin, straight line. But you did grow up."

It was Jack's eyes, however, that gleamed in appreciation. "Grew up very nicely, too," he said.

She felt herself start to blush. Quickly she went inside to change her suit for faded jeans and a T-shirt. Nothing glamorous. Not even lipstick.

When she returned, she saw that her dad had already lit the grill, and Jennifer was setting the outside table. Jack stood near Lou with a soft drink in his hand.

"Is everything under control, Dad?" asked Rachel. "I need to speak to Jack for a moment."

She looked at Jack and jerked her head toward the steps. With a quizzical expression on his face, he followed her from the porch to the end of the backyard.

Once at the low cement wall, she turned to face him. She'd forgotten that she had to tilt her head to meet him at eye level. Most men didn't have more than an inch or so on her if they were taller at all. This man was different.

"It's confession time," she began. "I hate starting off the year like this, but I seem to have misplaced your plan book. I've looked everywhere. Even went back to the school yesterday and searched, but I can't find it. I'm really sorry." She smiled. "As a peace offering, how about joining us for dinner." She rattled off the home-made goodies.

"That's nice of you," he said, his tone as relaxed as the rest of his body. "But you're not the guilty party. You didn't lose my plan book."

Surprise held her silent for a moment. "No?"

"I never handed it in, so you're off the hook, boss. It seems that I should buy you a dinner for all your lost time. And I'd be glad to."

"Never mind about that." Remembering how much time she'd wasted, she glared at him. "You mind telling me why you haven't turned in your plan book?"

"That's easy. I haven't met the kids yet. How can I make plans when I don't know who I'm dealing with?"

His answer was reasonable, and she felt her anger dissipate. "We'll talk later. Stay for dinner."

"Aye-aye, Captain." He saluted her. "Can't think of any place I'd rather be."

"And please stop flirting!"

"Excuse me?"

"At least with me. Save your moves for—" she waved her hand in the direction of the high school "—those women who were batting their eyelashes at you. They're more than ready to welcome you to Pilgrim Cove."

"You've got a very friendly town." His teasing tone was at odds with his sharpened gaze as he studied Rachel carefully. "In fact, Pilgrim Cove is becoming more interesting every minute. More interesting than I would have expected."

Confused, she turned away and led him to the porch, where they rejoined the party. Jack was an easy guest. He ate heartily and complimented everyone on the food. He joined in the conversation as though he'd known her family for years. And he seemed happy to talk about his own work.

"Basically, I'm checking for polluted waters around Pilgrim Cove. I also monitor the health of our lobster industry. I come from the coast of Maine—smack dab in the middle of lobster country."

"How are you going to manage all of this while you're teaching?" asked Rachel. "There are only twenty-four hours in a day."

"I'm flexible," he replied with a grin. "So far, I've been going out most mornings to meet the lobster boats. Talk to the men about their catches. See if they've noticed any changes." He took a deep breath. "I'll go out evenings from now on, and all day on the weekends. It'll work out fine."

"So," said Rachel, studying him, "you're a hands-on kind of person."

He paused before replying, eyes darkening as he considered her statement. "I suppose you could say that. Sometimes hands-on is the best way to learn, to discover."

Rachel nodded, then sat bolt upright. "I hope you're not thinking of taking your senior class out in your boat."

He stilled, a big smile crossing his face, and Rachel's

stomach flip-flopped. "You absolutely may not take the kids out on the water. Don't even think about it!"

When he shook his head and started to laugh, she knew she'd been set up. "Very funny," she snapped.

"You're an easy mark, Rachel. I couldn't resist. Of course I won't take the students out on the boat. But you really have to loosen up or you'll wind up with an ulcer. No job's worth it."

Her open palm slapped the table. "Just follow the printed curriculum, turn in a plan book and make sure your students know their stuff and can pass the state exams at the end of the year. Do that, and I won't get an ulcer!"

"Well, well." Alex glanced from Rachel to Jack and back again. "Game, set and match. Very interesting."

"I couldn't agree with you more," said Pearl.

Rachel reached for the dirty plates in front of her. "I don't know what you're all talking about. Let's clean up and play some volleyball."

She took the dishes and ran inside the house.

CHAPTER SIX

BEACH VOLLEYBALL HAD been part of Jack's childhood, and he looked forward to participating in the game with Rachel's family. Alex had brought the net and ball, and Jack had helped him set up the court.

Now Jack's eyes zoomed in on Rachel as she jogged to the net. What a pair of legs! And Jack definitely appreciated a good pair of legs. If Rachel thought faded jeans could hide her cute behind and shapely limbs, she wasn't as smart as she'd seemed. Besides, Jack had seen her in a bathing suit and knew the truth.

"Everybody's playing!" Rachel called from the net. "Four on a side, and no excuses."

"Then Mom and I have to split up," announced Jennifer, trudging across the sand. "We're the worst in the family. I'm even worse than Grandma and she's ol…got lots of gray hair."

The kid's final words came out in a rush, and Jack admired her last-second effort to save herself from insulting her grandmother. It didn't work.

"Old?" said Pearl. "The child thinks I'm old! I'll show

you old." And Rachel's mother started chasing Jennifer, zigzagging to cut off the girl's chance to escape.

A minute later grandmother and granddaughter had their arms around each other and were laughing. Laughing hard. It made a nice picture.

Jack glanced at Rachel, who was also watching the scene. Her expression startled him with its poignant mix of longing and resignation. She blinked and stared at the volleyball in her hand.

Jack jogged to her side. "What's the matter? Your mom's not sick or anything and just putting on an act?"

A vigorous shake of her head was the response.

"So, is it Jennifer? She looks as healthy as a horse."

"She is, thank God." Rachel turned toward the ocean, away from him. "And she's so lovely and easy to love." Her voice blended with the whisper of the waves.

He'd thought most little girls were sweet and lovable. As Jack studied Rachel's wistful expression, he recalled some of the information about her he'd picked up from the teachers who'd known her as a youngster. "She broke Lou's heart with her grades and attitude." And "She was so ungainly…her knees were black and blue from tripping on the stairs!"

"If everyone were easy to love," he said aloud, "the world would be boring. Plain old vanilla."

"I like vanilla." With that, she sped away, volleyball in hand, and started assigning sides for their game.

As if she were a general commanding her troops, she divvied them up. Alex and Jack on opposite teams. She took Jennifer and her dad and joined Alex. Jack had David, Pearl and Susan.

"I'm apologizing in advance," said Susan, smiling up at Jack. "You'll lose because of me, and I don't have gray hair…yet."

Rachel turned to her sister-in-law and him. "This is for fun, Susie Q," she said. "Every player is important. There's no winning or losing."

And who was she kidding? thought Jack five minutes later. After a few gentle volleys to warm up, his new boss was straining at an invisible leash. Her eyes gleamed, her feet pivoted, her legs had springs as she spiked the ball over the net. And yet, she kept encouraging her niece while protecting her, calling her name for volleys she thought the girl could handle while signaling the rest of her team to leave the ball alone. Concern for Jennifer seemed to be the only thing holding Rachel back at all.

Jack knew her self-control wouldn't last. And it didn't. Gradually the intensity of the play escalated. Twenty minutes after they'd started, Susan and Jennifer had had enough and left the court, content to watch from the sidelines. Five minutes later, Lou and Pearl followed suit.

He and David were strong players, but they were well matched by Rachel and Alex. None of the men, however, could match Rachel's skill. Blocks, spikes, bumps, even digs—Rachel used every technique of the game, compensating for her slighter build with good form and strategy. She played with brains, not just muscle. Jack worked hard to contain her.

"Isn't she great?" asked David, turning to Jack at one point. The pride in the youngster's voice was unmistakable.

Jack nodded, but a spark of admiration ignited inside him. What made this woman tick?

When dusk began to settle, Pearl called them for dessert. Jack walked to the net to shake hands with his opponents. Sweat poured from everyone's forehead, but all the players were smiling.

"So that's what you call a friendly little game, huh?" Jack asked, wiping his face with a towel.

"That's what my sister calls it," said Alex, glancing at Rachel with a grin.

"You boys could have backed out at any time," replied Rachel, eyes sparkling.

"Hah!" Jack replied. "And have you call me a wuss? No way."

Her laughter rang out freely, her whole face alight with the joy of her mood. She looked absolutely beautiful. And invincible.

Jack stared and forgot to breathe. He shook his head to clear it. He was hallucinating. He blinked and looked again. Her eyes still shone with pleasure, her delighted smile was still in place. And Jack felt as if he'd taken a punch to the stomach. A new layer of sweat dotted his skin, this time induced by fear. He needed to back off. For both their sakes.

"Do you always play to win?" His question sounded like an accusation even to his own ears.

She held his glance. "Yes." One word. No embroidery. No hesitation.

He shouldn't have been surprised. He'd seen her giving pep talks at the school, building confidence in the staff. She knew that victory in battle required very clear goals, and she seemed good at setting them.

"Yes," she repeated. "I play to win in sports as well as in life." She turned her head slightly to gaze over his shoulder. "I don't always succeed," she admitted before looking at him again. "But make no mistake, Jack. We are going to win at the high school this year. None of us can afford to lose that contest."

She was committed with her heart as well as with her mind. Although she might also have something to prove to herself, he'd seen and heard her devotion to the students.

He'd been that optimistic once, too, about a hundred years ago when anything had seemed possible. When he and Kevin had been invincible. Then he'd learned how easily the future could change. "Sometimes ambition comes at too high a price," he said.

"Let me worry about that." She patted his arm in a soothing gesture and walked toward the porch with a light, steady step. He watched her go, his mouth tightening as a shiver ran through him. She'd wanted to reassure him, but her confidence had the opposite effect. He exhaled and looked over the ocean. Not his problem. He wasn't getting involved.

RACHEL LOOKED AROUND the dining room table feeling very content with the day. Her first bit of entertaining at Sea View House had gone off without a hitch. No surprises—except for Jack Levine. To think the guy was her upstairs neighbor! He and her entire family looked completely relaxed, sipping coffee and enjoying her mom's whipped cream cake.

"The orchards will be open in another two weeks or so," said Pearl. "Maybe we can make a day of it on a Saturday or Sunday."

"I'll go only if Aunt Rachel goes," said Jennifer. "Gram and Mom do make great apple pies, though," she added thoughtfully.

"Can't wait to climb those trees," said Pearl with a straight face. "I'm very limber on those limbs."

"Grandma!" groaned Jennifer, shaking her head. "That was bad."

"I'll have to let you know, sweetie," said Rachel, breaking into the conversation. "Can't make promises until I see how free my weekends are after school starts." She smiled at Jennifer. "But it does sound like fun."

"Well, I won't take excuses for tomorrow," said Pearl, "from either of you." Her gaze settled first on Rachel, then Jack.

"What are you talking about?" asked Rachel.

"It's the Labor Day 5K Race for the Cure," said Pearl. "This year Laura Parker—Matt's new wife—helped Doc and Marsha Rosen organize it to benefit breast cancer research. It starts early—at seven-thirty. And I've already signed the whole family up." She looked at Jack. "You can register in the morning. It's not too late."

"Yes, ma'am."

Rachel covered her grin with her hand. "Mom doesn't have a bossy bone in her body," she deadpanned.

"I noticed." Jack smiled at her. "It's good to know you come by the trait honestly."

Rachel purposely batted her lashes and pointed at herself. *"Moi?"* she asked innocently.

He shifted back in his chair and nodded. She watched a smile slowly emerge on his very handsome face. Somehow the grunginess of the sand and exercise, plus the stubble of his beard, only made him more attractive. She studied him, trying to figure it out, until she felt someone staring at her. She turned her head.

Pearl's glance slowly traveled from Rachel to Jack and back again, a curious expression on her face. Dear God! Her mother was putting two and two together and getting five.

"This house has had an interesting history recently," Pearl said slowly, looking toward Lou.

"Sure has," he confirmed. "And the ROMEOs were in on all of it right from the beginning."

Pearl rolled her eyes. "The ROMEOs want to take credit for *everything* that happens in this town!"

"Not everything, dear. *Almost* everything. And definitely the Laura McCloud and Matt Parker story." He turned to Jack. "We knew her parents when she was young, and when her mom died recently, Laura returned here. She needed to heal. We didn't know until later that she was dealing with breast cancer, too."

"She rented Sea View House," continued Pearl, "this very apartment, and Matt Parker fell in love with her. And the rest, as they say, is history."

She beamed at everyone around the table, looking as proud and happy as if she'd arranged the entire affair. "They got married right here on the beach behind Sea View House."

Rachel had a sinking feeling that her mom had no intention of stopping her tale. She was right.

"And when Laura moved out," Pearl said, "Shelley Anderson and her two little children moved right into the Captain's Quarters."

Jack nodded. "I met them."

"And the professor—Daniel Stone—moved in upstairs with Jesse!" Jennifer chimed in and looked at Jack, who seemed genuinely interested in the story. "Jesse's his beautiful dog," explained Jennifer. "A golden retriever."

"And Shelley and Dan had a time of it, with her ex-husband showing up and making her miserable." Pearl continued as though she hadn't been interrupted. "But now, their wedding's set for Christmastime, and they'll be spending their summers in Pilgrim Cove." She clapped her hands, her delight obvious. "Two Sea View House weddings in six months. I'm telling you, people," she said, looking from Rachel to Jack, "this house is hot!"

A steam shovel couldn't have dug a hole big enough

for Rachel to fall through. "Not as hot as my face," she mumbled, jumping up from her chair, looking anywhere but at Jack. "Dad," she beseeched as she passed her father on her way to the kitchen, "take your wife home."

Rachel leaned over the sink, shaking her head. How was she ever going to look her neighbor in the eye?

She heard plates knocking against one another, footsteps coming toward her. "Mom! How could you?" she said before turning around.

"Uh, not your mom here." Jack's voice.

Rachel groaned and pointed to the sink. "Just put them right in the hot water. And I'll jump in after them."

"Aren't mothers wonderful?" he asked, eyes twinkling. "Hard to train them, though. It took me years before mine stopped setting me up with dates. Every time I went home, it seemed that someone's niece was visiting. Or daughter. Or cousin's cousin. You get the picture."

"And I don't believe a word. But, thanks."

"I'll knock on your door at seven."

"You don't have to, Jack. My mother may not have given you much choice, but she's not really your boss."

"I know," he said, a grin appearing. "That position is reserved for her daughter!" He started walking toward the door, then turned around. "I'll be here on time." He stared at her, his eyes roving from her head to her toes, then suddenly, he was gone.

So he liked her body. She couldn't find too much fault with that considering she found him attractive, too. But how inappropriate. She was his boss, for goodness' sake! And anyway, they didn't know each other at all. She shrugged her shoulders. She had lots of other things to think about besides her upstairs neighbor.

Her family poured into the kitchen to say goodbye and remind her about the race. One by one they left the house until only Susan remained. "I'll be right there, Alex," she called after her husband.

Rachel waited for what her sister-in-law had to say.

"I'll talk to your mother, tell her to lay off," said Susan. "Frankly, I don't quite know what happened in there. She's usually so level-headed."

"Great. I come home and she has a personality change."

"No-o-o. She's got a beautiful single daughter. And Jack's a real hunk. Pearl's got a few years on her, but she's not dead!"

"So, she's having fantasies about being with a young stud?"

Susan's laughter bubbled up. "No, no. Her fantasies are for you, and they just got out of hand!"

"I'm not..."

Susan kissed Rachel on the cheek and raced out the door.

"...beautiful."

But a shiver ran through Rachel as she created her own fantasy about the man upstairs. Those twinkling green eyes...those broad shoulders...the laughter that came so easily...oh, he had some fine qualities. Very fine qualities.

She looked into the sink. The dishwater had almost

filled the basin, and her arms were submerged to her elbows. She shut the spigots off quickly and opened the drain. If she daydreamed any more, she'd flood the house.

Unexpectedly, her thoughts drifted back to Round Rock, Kansas. Had her sojourn there been a fantasy, too? Or merely a lifetime ago? Pilgrim Cove was absorbing her so completely, that her time spent in the Midwest seemed almost to have happened to someone else.

THE NEXT MORNING, RACHEL dressed in a plain white tank top, white shorts and a white terry-cloth sweatband around her head. She was lacing up her running shoes in the kitchen when a knock sounded at the door. She glanced at the clock. The man was right on time.

"I'm ready," she said as she opened the door. But she wasn't ready for a black muscle shirt outlining his broad shoulders and powerfully built chest. She wasn't ready for a man big enough to block the sunshine in her doorway. She wasn't ready for his whistle of admiration.

"Cool it, bud," she said, trying to keep cool herself. "The day's just started." She grabbed a blank check for her entry fee and put it into the inside pocket of her shorts. "Let's go." She stepped to the door.

He didn't move. "Hold on a sec. Like you said, the day's just started. Save your energy for the race."

"But we'll be late."

"So what? It's not the Olympics! It's for charity and having fun."

"Which is exactly what I intend to do without being

late." She brushed past him and pulled the door closed. "Coming?"

"Wouldn't miss it."

She led the way through the backyard and onto the beach, joining the many other participants who were making their way to the starting line. Men, women, children, even babies attached to their parents in carry-all holders made the morning come alive with noise and excitement.

By the time they'd walked the half mile south of Sea View House, the registration area was swarming with people.

"Would you look at Bart Quinn and Sam Parker holding up those signs, and Chief O'Brien in the middle of them trying to direct the crowd," said Rachel. "The chief actually looks like a cop today. Even has a whistle in his mouth."

Just then the whistle sounded. The crowd slowed and looked at the retired officer, listening as he directed late registrants to one side and preregistered runners to the other.

"I've got to register," said Jack. "See you at the starting line."

Rachel nodded and went to get her number.

"Rachel Goodman? Is that you? My dad said you were home."

Rachel looked into the familiar face of Matt Parker. "It is. How's the married man?" she teased.

"He'd better give the right answer," said the pretty blonde next to him.

Rachel smiled. "You must be Laura. I've heard all about you. Congratulations." She held out her hand and Laura took it.

"And we've heard about you living in Sea View House and your new job," said Laura. "We're hoping the good luck holds for you, too."

Rachel murmured noncommittally. "Right now, I'm looking forward to a good run and raising some money. In fact, how about if I double the 5K and double my entrance fee?"

"I don't know..." began Laura.

"If you're up to it," interrupted Matt. "We don't turn down donations."

"It's still less than six-and-a-half miles," Rachel replied. "I bet others will do it, too."

"Maybe, but so far no one's mentioned it."

"Then I'll start a trend." She gave her check to Laura. "I promise not to ask for a refund if I change my mind," she joked. She took her number and pinned it on her shirt. "See you later."

"Good luck. And thanks."

She waved and jogged toward the starting line, nodded and said hello to a number of people she recognized. But there were many she didn't know. The tide was out, the beach wide, but still the starting line stretched almost the entire width of the sand—from the sea wall to the water. This event had certainly grown over the years. Participants must have come in from the neighboring towns.

Rachel scanned the crowd for Jack but didn't see him immediately. She found some space and started stretching. A minute later, however, she heard Jack's laughter. Heard other voices. Female voices laughing with him.

Rachel jogged slowly in place, continuing her warm-up. When she finally looked around, she spotted her neighbor nearby chatting with a group of teachers. Her staff. They looked as if they were having fun.

But the happy group reminded her that Jack liked being surrounded by women. He'd enjoyed their attention at the staff meeting, and they knew it. Now they were gravitating to him again, and he did nothing to discourage them. And why should he? He was single, unattached, and obviously wanted to meet new people in his new town. She couldn't really fault him. Could she?

She could. The only time she'd ever seen him have a serious discussion was when he'd joined in with her family around the dinner table. He'd probably been on his best behavior then. She pictured him at school, making his grand entrance at the meeting, mixing comfortably with every person in the room afterward. A regular social butterfly—if men could be categorized as such.

She sighed with disappointment and hoped he had a brain in his head. College degrees didn't guarantee good teaching skills or common sense. The kids at Pilgrim Cove Regional needed instructors who had both.

And she needed to use her own brains. She'd never been a groupie and she wasn't going to start now. No more fantasies about Jack Levine!

"Rachel. Over here." Jack's voice.

She looked at where he stood, and reluctantly jogged over with a pasted smile on her face.

"Of course you know Julie, Karen and Mallory," said Jack, with an ease that Rachel could only envy. Not that she was awkward with people anymore, but Jack was in a class by himself.

"Hi, ladies. Good morning."

The teachers' smiles became as polite as hers, their greetings stilted. "It's nice that you've come out for such a good cause," said Rachel, trying to reduce the awkwardness. She knew, however, that the best thing she could do was leave. Of course the women felt inhibited. Rachel was their boss. Their new boss. And today was a holiday.

"Well, I'm off to find my family. Have a good run." Rachel waved and left, ignoring Jack's "Hang on a minute...."

Men were so dense sometimes.

"Hey, Aunt Rachel!"

"Hi, David. Want to keep me company?"

"I'm with a couple of buddies, but Mom and Dad are here. They're going to walk it."

"Well, I'm looking to burn muscle today, kiddo. So, they'll have to walk without me. Have fun with your friends."

"Where's Jack?" her nephew asked. "I thought you were coming here together."

She waved toward the crowd. "He's in there somewhere. We did walk over together, but we're not *together.* If you know what I mean. We're strictly neighbors."

"Oh. Too bad. I like him."

He's easy to like.

"Uh…Aunt Rachel, one more thing…"

"What, hon?" She wasn't happy about the anxious expression that suddenly appeared on his face.

"No offense, but when school starts tomorrow, could you…ah…just ignore me in the halls? Guys don't like their families hanging around when they're with their buddies."

"Is that all? No problemo, David. I know exactly how you feel. Grandpa was the librarian when I was in school. Remember?"

His expression cleared up instantly. "Yo!" He gave her a high five and ran off. Rachel followed his progress as he made his way through large groups of people. If only every problem could be solved as easily.

The crowd started to quiet down, an air of expectation permeating the throng. The event was about to start. Rachel listened to the announcements and acknowledgments, and waited for the signal to "Go." When it came, the throng moved in waves, a messy pack of humans. Within a very few minutes, however, the runners pulled to the front and left the socializing walkers behind.

The nip in the morning air, the pale fingers of sunlight and the blue Atlantic provided perfect conditions as well as a beautiful setting for the run. Rachel inhaled deeply, exhaled and started to jog forward. She needed a half mile to establish her rhythm, another half mile to establish her place among the more serious runners. And there were a number of them who were now starting to increase the pace from slow jog to slow run. She allowed them to overtake her.

"I can't believe you're holding back. We're almost at the halfway point."

She turned slightly to see Jack pulling up next to her. Then she looked ahead and saw a water station and volunteers at the edge of the sand. The halfway point.

"Not for a 10K."

"I might have known," he said with a sigh. "Do you always have to prove something? Can't you just take it easy and enjoy the day?"

"I *was* enjoying it! Until now. So, go away and have your own fun."

"Not a chance."

She ignored him, focused on the pacing, only stopping for a small paper cup of water before continuing the race. When she picked up speed, Jack shadowed her. It was hard to ignore his steady presence over her right shoulder.

"Don't let me hold you back," she said, waving her hand ahead of them. After all, he was taller, larger and probably in as good a physical shape as she was. He could set a faster pace for himself.

"I'm happy right where I am, sweetheart."

The endearment stung her as sharply as the bite of a jellyfish. "Save your breath. I'm not interested." She raced ahead, but the finish line was only a football field length away. The five kilometers had served as a good warm-up for her.

Groups of people were milling about in the area. She swerved toward the officials' table. Max and Marsha Rosen were checking off runners as they returned. Doc waved her in.

"I'm going out again," she said between breaths, motioning her intention with her arms.

Someone handed her a cup of water. She gulped it down.

"Pace it, Rachel," said Doc Rosen. "You know better. Don't be the first one to faint on me today. Or throw up."

Of course she knew better and was annoyed at herself for getting distracted. Legs were the tools. Her mind did the planning.

"I'm putting an extra ten bucks per kilometer on you for the second round," Doc added, standing up. He cupped his hands around his mouth. "Anyone else want to back Rachel Goodman for another 5K? Let's raise some extra dollars and get rid of this disease once and for all."

"I'm putting ten dollars on the new science teacher," said Marsha with a laugh, her eyes focusing over Rachel's shoulder. "More my type."

Science teacher? Rachel jerked her head around. Jack

Levine was right behind her, his frown turning to a smile when he looked at Marsha Rosen. "I won't let you down, Mrs. Rosen."

Then he turned to Rachel and his frown returned. "We need to talk, Ms. Goodman."

Rachel smiled to herself. He'd gotten her message.

CHAPTER SEVEN

SHE WAS EITHER MAD AT HIM or she couldn't breathe. Jack had no idea what was going on in Rachel's head. All he knew was that she hadn't spoken a word to him for the first third of the course out again. Which might not mean a thing. After all, who could talk after running almost five kilometers? He was having a hard time himself. He was used to buoyancy, used to the support of an ocean or lake. He could swim forever without breathing hard, but here on land, his effort was beginning to tax him.

He wouldn't complain, however, as long as he could watch Rachel. Watching her was the best part of the race. Her legs never stopped, and her cute bottom shimmied with just enough bounce to make his palm itch. The way it itched right now. And if he continued to run behind her, he'd continue to be aroused. Maybe that was the cause of his running troubles!

He'd been happy to get a warm reception from his three co-workers earlier that morning. All attractive, bright and attentive. Interested. He knew how to pick up signals in the mating game—he'd been playing it long enough. Ordinarily, he would have schmoozed with the women and gotten to know who the party girls were.

Today, however, he'd been distracted. His attention span seemed nonexistent. None of the friendly women intrigued him the way Rachel did.

He couldn't understand it, and he wasn't happy about it. Sure, he found Rachel pretty enough, but she was certainly not a raving beauty like some of his previous girlfriends had been. She wasn't soft and cuddly, didn't have sexy long hair for a man to play with. In fact, her hair was almost as short as his. But somehow, he still wanted to play…

Obviously, Rachel didn't.

The water station was coming up again. Hallelujah! He needed that water more than he'd ever needed a cocktail in his entire life. They both paused for a cup. Rachel sipped. He gulped the liquid down. Then poured another cup over his head. He reached for a third cup and raised it to his mouth.

"Don't," Rachel said, a frown forming. "Too much, too soon, can make you nauseous when you start running again."

He paused with the cup halfway to his mouth.

"Unless," she added, "you're planning to walk back at an easy pace."

The hopeful note in her voice made him wince. "Are you walking?"

She shook her head. "I'm finishing what I started the way I planned it."

He dumped a second cup of water on his head. "Then, let's go."

She shrugged, turned her back to him and started jogging, quickly picking up her pace. And ignoring him again. He didn't like it, but he wasn't stupid enough to call her on it while still participating in the event. She took her sports seriously. Hell, she took *everything* seriously. That alone could drive him batty. At least, *he* tried to store serious stuff in a separate place from fun stuff. He divided his life into neat compartments. Every part in a different box. Work. Women. Writing. Family. Kevin.

So, why did he want to get to know Rachel better? Because she was his closest neighbor? Because she was his boss? Two perfectly good reasons. But they didn't answer his question completely.

He became aware of more people, groups along both sides of the beach, cheering on the final runners as they approached the finish line. In the end, Rachel and he were not the only ones to do the ten kilometers, but the number was small, and most participants were walking in. The race was a community activity, Jack reminded himself, not a professional marathon.

"Look, Rachel." Jack pointed to a group of boys trudging toward the finish. "Your nephew's coming in now, too, with a gang around him."

She studied the teens for a minute. "They're all as tall and lanky as David. Maybe it's the school basketball team."

"David's got a lot of friends," said Jack, turning to her again.

The delight in her expression, the love in her eyes and in her smile when she looked at her nephew stole the breath from his lungs. When she loved, she loved hard. Who knew that his simple comment would produce such a deep reaction?

"It's wonderful that he has so many friends," said Rachel. "He'll have good memories."

"High school memories are always good from the perspective of distance," replied Jack. *At least for most people.*

She didn't respond.

"What's the matter, sweetheart? Don't you agree?"

She spun around and pointed a finger at him, all traces of tenderness gone. "Please stop calling me sweetheart. Stop the flirting. With me, anyway. Save your charm for the Mallorys of the world." She plunged into the crowd and disappeared.

Taken totally by surprise, he could only stare at her retreating back. He didn't like it, but he'd gotten his answers. Now he knew why she'd given him the silent treatment for the last part of the run. Now he understood why he was intrigued enough to want to know her better.

She was different from other women. Unique. He'd picked up on that the very first time he'd met her. He'd never forget that night swim. A real live mermaid with a bite! A month had passed since then and he hadn't changed his mind about her. She really could bite hard.

And now she'd judged him, found him lacking, and she didn't bother to hide her feelings.

He was not often in the position of a rejectee! But it figured that the one time he was becoming serious, the one woman he'd started to admire didn't want any part of him. He laughed at the irony, welcoming the pang of disappointment he felt as a well-timed reminder not to get involved with her at all.

BY THE END OF THE FIRST week of school, Rachel would have sworn she'd met thousands of people. Either in person or on the phone, she spoke with students, parents, faculty, publishers' reps, school board members, more students, more parents. Maybe tens of thousands!

"I'm loving it," she said to Dr. Bennett on Friday afternoon. "Busier than in Kansas. More students at this school, but for the most part, my responsibilities are falling into place."

She wouldn't complain about the teachers who still teased her. "Rachel, I'm waiting. If your homework's not in tomorrow, you'll get a zero." Then they smiled and continued down the corridor. They thought it was harmless fun—they'd known her since she was born. What they didn't realize was how much their comments hurt. She hoped they'd get tired of their game soon. If not, she'd take steps. Maybe if Mrs. Drummond asked for her term paper one more time, Rachel might actually call the woman into the office. She swallowed a grin as she pictured the scene.

She walked back into her own office and collapsed on her chair. A pile of lesson-plan books waited for her attention. She glanced at the top one. Jack Levine's. She almost dreaded picking it up again. His first week's plans had read: "Discuss— 'What is biology?' 'What is marine biology?' 'What is earth science?'" A good starting point, but no reference to textbooks, readings, homework assignments, projects or anything resembling work for the students.

She slowly picked up his book and peeked inside. Then slammed it on the table. "Continue discussions," was all this week's plan said.

"Not acceptable," she murmured, jumping out of her chair and heading for the second-floor science wing. But his classroom was empty. Rachel checked her watch and sighed. No reason for him to still be there at four o'clock. But she was disappointed. She'd seen him only from a distance all week and would have liked to catch up with him. Instead, she'd heard about him. She'd heard a lot about the new "sexy science teacher." Unfortunately, his presence had not gone unnoticed by the female students. She wondered if he realized he was the subject of speculation.

She packed the plan books in her wheeled tote and gathered her purse. Time to go home.

To her surprise, Jack's truck was in the driveway at Sea View House. The first time all week that he'd been home after school. He probably needed to sleep if he'd been going out every day on his research job. She parked in front of the house and quietly made her way inside.

The phone rang almost immediately.

"It's Jack," he replied in response to her greeting. "How'd you like to celebrate surviving your first week by going out to dinner with me? I hear the Lobster Pot is very good."

"The restaurant is excellent, Jack, but going out together is not a good idea. Thanks for the invitation, anyway."

"I didn't think you were the type to hold a grudge," he said.

She knew he was referring to the race—to her indignation at his flirtatious behavior. "I'm not the type to hold a grudge, and your…your…let's say your kidding around is not why I'm turning you down. Have you ever heard the advice about not mixing business with pleasure?"

"Sure, I've heard of it. Never had to apply it, though."

"Oh?" Right.

"No, most of the women I've met in my field were married—usually to other scientists. So I *couldn't* mix business with pleasure. Bottom line is that I found my social life elsewhere."

"I see," replied Rachel. "So you actually have lived by the rule whether you intended to or not. Surely you can understand that you and me mixing is not a good idea, so my answer's still no. But again, thanks." She gently hung up the phone. At least, he didn't pursue married women!

She headed for the bedroom when a sharp knocking

at the back door startled her. Jack was on the other side of the glass panes.

"I'm not changing my mind," she said immediately upon opening the door.

"I recognize stubborn. Let's change the agenda. How about a swim?"

She stepped outside. The late-afternoon sun still spread its light on the ground. The temperature hovered around seventy-five and the air was dry. Too cool for most people, but…

"There aren't many days left to enjoy this," said Jack, offering words of temptation.

"You're right. Give me two minutes. And no ogling!" She closed the door in his face and heard his laughter resonate as he stepped away. She grabbed a chair back for support as his warm tones stirred a chord deep inside her. Musical, happy and so attractive. She envied him. He had a way of enjoying life that was very appealing.

HE HADN'T LIED TO HER, he thought, as they swam parallel to the shore. But how could he tell her he'd stayed away from every eligible woman who'd looked at him with hope in her eyes? He went out only with those who had no expectations. Much easier on the emotions that way. Rachel wasn't a game player, but she was pretty safe, too. She put up great barriers. Laid down lots of rules. Obviously, she had no desire for a real relationship any more than he did.

But he was finding it damn hard to play by her rules. The "no ogling" one had gone out with the tide as far as he was concerned. How could he not look at and enjoy the woman who was on his mind twenty-four/seven despite his effort to block her out? He'd just try to be circumspect about it. Not too hard as long as they were both in the water.

She always wore a one piece suit, and today was no exception. A practical style, straps crossed in the back. A suit made for swimming. Maybe someday he'd buy her a frivolous bikini. Hot pink, with flowers. He grinned as he imagined her reaction.

He dunked his head underwater. How could a man sweat while he was in the Atlantic? A new phenomenon.

He reemerged and shook the water from his face. Then watched Rachel. She cut the water cleanly, her strokes perfect. Better than his.

"So, how far did you get?" he asked.

"In what?"

"Your swimming career."

"I competed, but it was never my career. Just a way out of Pilgrim Cove."

"No Olympic aspirations? Didn't you want to show this town something?" He'd heard the scuttlebutt about Rachel's schooldays. People seemed surprised at how far she'd come. They'd thought she was a loser. It was difficult to believe they were talking about the same woman who was with him now.

"Not then," she answered. "I just wanted to get away.

Away from my brother's reputation. Away from the comparisons."

"Away from being second best?" he asked quietly.

Her eyes narrowed and she rolled onto her back. "Something like that."

"I went to the public library today," he said, floating alongside her. "Saw your dad."

"He volunteers there a lot."

"He told me. And I hired him."

She went under. "What?" she spluttered a second later, coming up for air. "Did you say you hired him?"

"Come on home," he replied, reversing direction. "I'll tell you about it." He grinned as she followed him. For once, she wasn't arguing.

Five minutes later, they waded out of the water and picked up their towels. As Jack rose to his feet, he heard a rapid clicking noise. He looked at Rachel. His boss was shivering from head to foot, her teeth actually chattering as she tried to wrap the towel around herself.

Without hesitating, Jack stepped closer, adjusted her towel and wrapped his arms around her. "I'm not ogling," he whispered in her ear, holding her snugly. "I'm just warming you up."

She said nothing but didn't pull away. He held her close, rubbed her arms and soon felt her body relax against him. This was more like it!

"Hang on, I'm going to dry your legs." He used his own towel for that and noticed her legs were just as beautiful, firm and shapely up close as in the distance.

"I guess I'm more accustomed to heated indoor pools

these days." Her voice was low and tentative. Not like the Rachel he was used to.

Jack stood. "Come on," he said, reaching for her hand. "Take a hot shower when we get back and you'll feel fine."

She nodded as she kept pace with him.

"Maybe afterward we can continue our conversation over a grilled steak?"

She stopped in her tracks and pulled away from him.

He held up his hand. "Not at a restaurant. I'll grill it on our porch. We can dine al fresco or inside. Your choice."

She looked up and down the beach, glanced up at Sea View House, then sighed.

"Is it such a hard decision?" he asked quietly.

"This is a small town. I can't afford to screw up."

Again. Unspoken, but understood as clearly as if she had shouted it.

"It's a good town, Rachel. I can feel it. And it's your home."

She looked at him then, her smile as sweet and hopeful as that of a child opening a birthday present. But then she shook her head. "You're only a tourist, Jack. Here for a while and then gone."

A sharp pain pulsed in his gut, and he almost reeled with surprise. "The year's just starting," he replied, his voice husky. "Don't rush it away."

She cocked her head. "All right. See you in thirty minutes. I'll provide a salad."

Yes! He wanted to punch the air in victory. Instead, he nodded.

RACHEL HEADED DOWN the corridor to the school cafeteria on Monday, wishing that Jack would stop nesting in the back of her mind. Their impromptu meal had been filled with conversation, both informative and interesting. She'd learned that he needed Lou's expertise in researching existing young-adult material in areas relating to marine biology, the lobster industry and conservation issues. He simply had no time to visit the library himself.

She was delighted that he cared so much, that he wanted to go beyond the standard textbooks. Maybe he needed assistance in organizing materials so he could come up with weekly plans. She could help him with that. And then he'd be sure to cover the entire curriculum.

Her thoughts drifted from Jack's teaching methods to her habit of checking out the cafeteria during various lunch hours, making sure enough teachers were on duty and the students were following the rules and behaving themselves. Not that she alone had responsibility for the general conduct of the student body, but she was part of the team. Bob Franklin rotated in and so did Dr. Bennett. Actually, Dr. Bennett had told her he liked being there for a part of each period. He wanted all the students to know who he was.

As she entered the large room, the din of hundreds of conversations accosted her ears. The tables were crowded with youngsters. All girls at some tables. All boys at others. A few were mixed. Some kids were walking around, looking for a spot, looking for friends.

Rachel empathized. She watched a young girl, lunch tray in hand, hesitantly approach an almost-full table and sit down. No one spoke to her. But neither did they tell her the spot was taken. Could have been worse, as Rachel knew from personal experience. Too much experience.

Rachel did a visual inventory of faculty. Each of the three sections required one teacher. She spotted Mr. Maggio at the far end of the room, walking up and down the aisle. Good. He was a solid teacher with common sense as well.

Her eyes roved toward the center of the room and she spotted Julie Jacobson, one of the new teachers, looking a little overwhelmed. She'd help her out as soon as the section Rachel was standing in had a teacher of its own. In the meantime, she began to walk up the aisle, stopping occasionally to chat with a group. One table of girls was deep in conversation. Rachel was about to pass by when she heard Jack's name. She paused to listen.

"Dr. Levine's so cool. The coolest teacher in the school."

"He's a real *man.* Not like the clueless *boys* in our classes."

"I'd love to be stranded on an island with him."

The last girl's eyes were almost closed as she spoke, her words having a dreamlike quality. Rachel wanted to groan. Crushes. And if this table was typical, how many more fifteen-year-old girls had come under his spell? And would in the future?

She continued her stroll when she saw the man in question approach. His eyes lit up when he saw her.

"Sorry I'm late. How're you doing?"

"No problem, Jack, but…we need to talk." She glanced over her shoulder. Three pairs of eyes were focused on Jack. She turned to face him again. "Uh, don't look now, but you've got a fan club over there. Can you come by my office later and we'll talk?"

"I'll only have five minutes," he replied.

"Taking the boat out again?"

"I need the daylight."

She nodded. "Five minutes is all we need. See you then." She made her way to the center section and chatted with Julie Jacobson, who seemed glad to see her.

"If they start throwing food at one another, I won't know what to do."

Rachel sympathized. The young woman was on her first teaching assignment. Of course she felt intimidated. "If there's any disruption, you tell a student to get another teacher, so you're not alone." Rachel pointed to Mr. Maggio and Jack. "You know there are at least three adults here at all times. If you'd like, I'll help you out for the first couple of Mondays."

The new teacher seemed relieved. "Thanks. Thanks a lot. I know Jack could probably handle anything that came up, but he's far away."

She'd have to nurse this one through to confidence, thought Rachel. Hopefully, the newbie had more to offer in the classroom. Her plan book was excellent.

"Ms. Goodman, how about if Jack and I patrol together? I'd be a lot more comfortable." Julie Jacobson gazed across the lunchroom at Jack with the same dreamlike expression the girl at the table had worn minutes before.

Rachel couldn't remember ever being that young. "Sorry, Ms. Jacobson. Each section needs to be monitored at the same time."

"I figured. But it doesn't hurt to ask." She turned to Jack's section, spotted him and waved.

He nodded.

Rachel was glad she'd arranged to talk to him. She might need ten minutes of his time. But, in the end, she got no minutes at all. He sent her a note rescheduling for the next afternoon.

Heavy rains predicted offshore. Have to get away and get back fast. Tomorrow instead? Jack

She looked out the window of her office. The day was clear, the sun still shone. But she knew the fickle New England weather could turn in an instant. She crumpled the note and threw it away. And searched the skies again.

At Sea View House that evening, she was restless. Couldn't concentrate and couldn't stop herself from thinking about Jack. She finally put on a sweat suit and set off along the beach. A good run would get rid of her excess energy and make time go by faster. The sky was overcast when she left, the sea choppy. But it wasn't raining. She left the porch light on and headed north.

Thirty minutes later, fat raindrops started to fall, slowly at first, then faster. She was a distance from Sea View House and would be soaked by the time she got there. She berated herself as she headed toward home, thinking about a hot shower and cup of hot tea. When lightning started to flash over the water, she knew the rain was the least of her problems.

She jogged to the first cross street and left the beach, then made her way one short block to Beach Street. She turned left toward Sea View House. Now she wouldn't be the prime target for a bolt of lightning. The houses were a lot taller than she was.

A horn blasted next to her. She looked up, saw Jack's black truck and felt herself sag with relief.

"Get in," he ordered.

"I'm soaked." She gestured to her clothes.

"This isn't a Maserati. Come on."

She climbed up and slammed the door behind her.

"What the hell are you doing out in this storm?" Jack shifted into Drive and pulled away from the curb.

"I can ask you the same thing…and you were in a boat!" said Rachel, arms folded across her chest.

"I wasn't out in the storm. Look closely. I'm dry."

She glared at him. "Well, good for you. Then what took you so long? I don't have a crystal ball to know you're not drowned." She turned away and stared straight ahead.

He pulled into their driveway and switched off the

engine. “Rachel?” His voice was soft, intimate in the enclosed cab.

“Hmm?”

His fingers cupped her chin, gently turned it toward him. “Were you worrying about me?”

“Of course not! You’re Dr. Jack Poseidon-Neptune Levine. The sea is your home. Why would I worry about a little lightning?”

Suddenly, she couldn’t talk. Her mouth was very busy doing something else. A whole lot of something else. His kiss aroused her instantly. His arms tightened around her, and she melted against him, feeling his heart thumping on top of her own. She raised her head to better taste his kisses—urgent, demanding. He was a man, not a boy—the teenager girl was so right about that—and Rachel felt herself respond as a woman. An interested woman. Which wasn’t in her current plan.

When she could breathe again, she stared at Jack. He looked as dazed as she felt.

“What the hell just happened here?” he whispered.

“I have no idea,” replied Rachel, her words trembling. “And I can’t afford to find out.” She opened the passenger door and darted inside the house.

CHAPTER EIGHT

JACK WATCHED HER RUN to the back of the house. What a kiss! Rachel had actually broken her no-mixing rule. She'd cared about him, cared enough to be angry and worried. A couple of powerful emotions. But he certainly was *not* ready for the kind of kiss that made him want to get involved with the woman behind it. Involved...as with emotions. Feelings. No, siree. Not even for Rachel, whom he admired. She was becoming a good friend. A very good friend. He'd assign her to the "women friends" box in his mind.

For a moment, he was content. He leaned back in his seat and breathed. His stomach settled, and his breathing slowed. A minute later, he got out of the truck and opened the side door to Sea View House. When he mounted the stairs to his apartment, however, his thoughts bounced back to that...that...lip action. To the mistake. Surely, he'd forget about it in no time. In fact, they both would. Too bad it had been such a terrific kiss.

Rachel would probably bury herself in her work, in those plan books of hers. Or stay in her office. He paused for a second. No. No, she wouldn't hide out.

She'd actually been quite visible around the school—in the cafeteria every day, in the halls during class changes. She wanted to get to know the students. No hiding away for Rachel Goodman.

He'd bet good money she'd handle her personal life with the same attitude she handled her job. "I can't afford to screw up." Her words echoed in his ears, and he shook his head. He couldn't even imagine her screwing up. She was so dedicated. So serious about everything. She needed to take a lesson from him. Work hard, play hard. And keep personal feelings out of the equation.

He took a hot shower and plopped onto his bed, yawning, eyes closing. He'd been out on the ocean almost every day without a break.

He felt himself drift, drift away…and suddenly was sitting straight up, eyes wide, heart pounding and sweat dripping from his forehead. His arm trembled as he lifted it to wipe away the moisture. He breathed deeply.

He'd been dreaming…about Rachel. The vivid scene rolled through his mind again. Rachel drowning in a thunderstorm. Wearing a white bathing suit. He'd seen her from the deck of a ship and tossed her a life preserver. But she'd missed it. He'd grabbed a rope, tied himself to it, and peered through the teeming rain. Poseidon had already claimed Kevin during a storm like this one. He was not getting Rachel, too! He scanned the ocean's surface, and when lightning flashed, he spotted the white suit and leaped into the roaring waves.

He gripped the rumpled sheet. Slowly, his breathing

returned to normal, and he glanced at the clock radio. The luminescent hands stood at two-fifteen. "What the hell was that all about?" he murmured. "Rachel can swim like a fish! Crazy, dumb dream."

He heard the frustration in his own voice and methodically adjusted the blanket and fell back against the pillow. Jack Levine did not lose sleep over a stupid dream! But his eyes burned as he stared into the darkness. *Kevin.* It always came back to Kevin. The best friend he'd ever had. His blood brother. Born on the same day in the same hospital. And inseparable—until the ocean, which Kevin and his dad depended on to sustain their lives—claimed them instead.

Fresh grief caused him to blink rapidly to suppress his tears. He'd never forget the McCarthy men. Never! And he would not lose another special friend to Poseidon's whims! Not even in a dream.

THE KNOCK AT RACHEL'S office door diverted her attention from the spreadsheet she was studying. Jack Levine stood on the threshold, filling the entire room with his energy.

"Come on in." Rachel waved him over, glad her voice sounded professional. "Sit down."

He lowered himself to the chair across from her, pushed back and stretched his legs in front of him. "Hi."

Nothing special in his inflection, and Rachel was glad.

"This will only take five minutes, but an important five minutes, I'm afraid."

He raised his brow.

"The girls in the cafeteria yesterday, Jack..."

"Oh, yeah. They get crushes. You mentioned it." He shrugged. "Normal for teenage girls, isn't it? To get crushes on teachers?"

"Definitely. But I don't want you or any staff member caught in an awkward situation." She tapped a sheaf of papers on her desk. "I actually have this topic on the agenda for the next faculty meeting. But since yesterday in the lunchroom, I just wanted to remind you about teenage girls."

He raised a brow. "What about them exactly? They were human the last time I looked."

She chuckled without glee. "Very human, with out-of-whack hormones. Sensitive about a lot of things. Sensitive about everything! Laughing one minute. Crying the next. Boy, do I remember."

"And your point is?" asked Jack.

"Be aware of their feelings, be sensitive yourself—but maintain your distance."

He rose from the chair and leaned over her desk, his scowl as dark as night. "Just what the heck do you think I'm going to do? What are you accusing me of?"

She sighed. "Relax, Jack. I've given this speech a dozen times in the last two years—especially to teachers who become a target of admiration. Which you have."

"For God's sake!" He sat down again. "I like working with the kids...this is the age where their curiosity about the natural world can be channeled into something significant. Like your nephew, for instance."

Rachel's ears perked up. "What about David?"

"He's gone out with me on *The Wanderer* several times. During the summer," he added.

"I thought he worked for the marina."

"We rearranged his schedule as needed. He handled the boat while I dove. He helped me label samples and pack them, and asked a load of questions, most of which started with the word *why.* He knows a lot about the ocean—the normal chemical composition and what's not healthy. He's got a curious mind."

And his dad hasn't noticed. "So what are you trying to tell me, Jack? That I should discount the classroom? Discount student grades?"

"I'm trying to tell you that not everything is learned from a textbook. And both girls and boys need to be exposed to the natural world."

A headache started to emerge, and she rubbed her right temple. "I agree, but at the same time you are responsible for planning lessons and covering the syllabus so that the kids pass the state tests." She turned away from him. "I'm so sick of repeating myself."

"Then why don't you relax and let the teachers teach?"

She eyed him. "Because for the past three years that didn't work. I'm supposed to improve the picture."

He said nothing.

"I'll be visiting classrooms regularly. Every classroom. Not just the new faculty, but the old-timers as well."

He nodded, no expression on his face.

"Oh, for crying out loud, Jack! You've taught college students and graduate students—but our kids are teenagers. Don't be so resistant to a little help."

"I don't teach parroting skills, Rachel, at any age. And that's what you want for these tests. That's also what turns off a lot of kids. I teach critical-thinking skills. The kind that last a lifetime." He stood up and extended his hand. "Let the games begin!"

Her headache exploded as she rose from her chair. Her hands remained opened flat on her desk. "It's not a game, Jack. It's their futures. College admissions…"

"Exactly," he said softly. He reached out and pressed his fingertips against her temple, making slow circles. "Take care of yourself." She remained silent. He turned and walked to the door, then looked over his shoulder. "Thanks for the warning about adolescent girls." He left the room.

Slowly, Rachel reseated herself and reached for her bottle of buffered painkillers. She couldn't fault his intentions, but he wasn't going to make her job any easier.

BY THURSDAY AFTERNOON, Rachel had visited ten classrooms, monitored the cafeteria twice more and had broken up a group of jock types when they'd overrun the corridors that morning, forcing other students against the walls. She'd recognized some of the glaring faces: a couple were on the football team.

"This isn't a football field. It's a hallway. Set an example. Save your energy for tomorrow night's game. Now, *walk* to your next class, and pay attention."

She'd felt their resentment; they didn't enjoy being reprimanded in front of other students. But they'd brought it on themselves. Rachel shrugged. The corridors belonged to everyone. Intimidation had no place in school.

She thought no more about the incident until the next morning when Bob Franklin walked into her office.

"It's just high spirits!" he began without preamble. "And that builds school spirit. I don't need my players getting distracted the day before a game." His glare was more hostile than the boys' expressions had been.

"Have a seat, Bob." Rachel had been around athletes for years. She'd seen the best caught up in the tension of the moment. But she was disappointed that a man entrusted with an athletic director's responsibilities would resort to intimidation himself.

"Seat? I don't have time to sit and debate. I have a game to manage."

"There is no debate," Rachel said. "There's only one bottom line. And I'm sure you'll agree."

"Is that right?" He stood with his hands on his hips, his chin thrust out.

She nodded. "We do not tolerate bullying in this school." She leaned forward. "Do we?"

"They have a game tonight! Yesterday was anticipation. Excitement and high spirits. Not bullying. I'm sick of every damn problem in this school being blamed on athletics. My teams put this school on the map around here. My kids win scholarships for college. Just butt out, Rachel."

Rachel shook her head. "Can't do that, Bob," she replied softly. "If the team members, or any student for that matter, resort to bullying, I'll bounce them so fast, all you'll see is the blur."

"On whose authority? You just deal with academics."

"Aren't we all responsible for the safety of every student? That's the bigger picture, Bob."

The walls shook and her door bounced back open when he slammed it. "Idiot," she murmured. She stretched her arms overhead and took a deep breath. Odd, she had no headache from this encounter.

A knock sounded on her open door, and Dr. Bennett stood there, a question on his face. "His exit was quite a punctuation mark. Is there anything I need to know?"

Rachel filled him in. "The real kicker is that I love sports. And he knows it. I'm looking forward to the game tonight myself."

"Bob takes his job seriously. And he's not the root cause of why we needed you here." The principal held out two computer printouts. "These are the latest statistics on the region's unemployment rate broken down into all kinds of demographics, including single-parent households. And here are Helen's statistics on the number of our students holding part-time jobs and living in single-parent households. The correlation is high."

"So, a lot of our kids might be working to supplement

their families," said Rachel. She looked at her boss. "Now we need to track down actual youngsters and their actual grades from last year. I'd expect to see that the working students' performances dropped after they got jobs. But let's check it out."

He nodded. "Helen's gathering that data now. However, the question is, what are we going to do about it this year? And the answer to that, my dear, falls to you."

IT WAS A PERFECT EVENING for a football game. A little nip in the air, clear skies filled with twinkling stars, leaves crunching underfoot. Autumn in New England. Rachel felt content as she inhaled the familiar scents of the season. And after many years' absence, she also felt happy to once again attend a Pilgrim Cove Regional High School football game.

The team looked good. Rachel stood on the sidelines in an area designated for school officials, binoculars in her hand, trying to identify each player beneath all the equipment. In her own mind, there were three players who she thought were above the rest. She drew an asterisk next to their names on a printout she had gotten from school. She idly wondered if Bob Franklin would agree with her.

"Don't tell me you're working instead of just enjoying the game on this gorgeous night."

She turned toward the familiar voice and waved her sheet at Jack. "Have you been here long enough to have an opinion about what you see out there?"

He shook his head. "Afraid not. I just got back from

delivering some cases to the lab at MIT. You know, the Massachusetts Institute of Technology. But I thought I'd drop over for a little while and show some school spirit." He yawned big and loud.

Rachel giggled. "With support like that, who needs you?"

His eyes shone as he looked at her. "Watch it, boss. You're taking a big risk." He yawned again.

Rachel shook her head. "Somehow, I don't think so."

"Had I known the game would draw a crowd of this size, I might not have bothered," Jack admitted. "I've been out every day this week. Today was my short day."

Rachel scanned the bleachers behind her and across the field. They were filled to capacity. "The whole town must have shown up."

"Five towns, isn't it?" asked Jack.

"Right. Not to mention the opposing team's supporters."

"I thought I saw Bart Quinn from a distance, but I can't figure out why he'd bother to be here."

"Are you kidding?" said Rachel. "First of all, the coach is his son-in-law. You know, Tom Sullivan. Second, he has a grandson in the school. But third, do you really think the ROMEOs miss anything that goes on in town? The whole gang's here. They even changed their Friday-night card game to Thursday."

Jack started to laugh. His fatigue seemed to melt away in front of her eyes, and Rachel felt herself smile.

"That's better," she said softly.

He studied her quietly. "You're very sweet."

She felt heat rise to her face, glad the lighting cast some shadow where they stood. "That is certainly a minority opinion around here," she replied, indicating the high school building and the team. "But that's okay. I'm not in a popularity contest."

"No," he said. "Not with your job. And besides, it's not your style."

"So right."

Noise from the crowd grew, and she pointed to the field. "We're tied, and watch, watch... The running back's going for a field goal. And he-e-e makes it!" She shoved her paper under Jack's nose. "He was one of my picks. Look. The quarterback, the running back and the linebacker. They are good. Tom Sullivan really knows what he's doing."

"Uh—Rachel?"

"Yes?"

"I hate to break this to you, but the players in those three positions...?"

"Yeah?"

"...are supposed to be good. Any coach would have put those three out there."

"But not all schools have a coach who can develop the talent. We're lucky we do." She glanced at the paper again. "The kids are Jimmy Williams, Steve Yelton and Donnie Schroeder."

"It's halftime," said Jack. "I've got a Schroeder in one of my classes."

Rachel watched the youngsters make their way to the locker room, helmets under their arms. She watched each face as the boys trotted by. "Damn it," she whispered.

"What's the matter?" asked Jack.

"Two of them were part of the hallway ruckus yesterday. They needed a real attitude adjustment."

"Schroeder seems like a nice kid. Don't borrow trouble. Maybe it was just an incident. A small incident."

"I hope so." But she wouldn't count on it. Winning gave players a high, and friends put them on pedestals. Football gladiators sparked the admiration of everyone, especially when they triumphed in their hundred-yard arena. It was a lot for a kid to handle and still keep his feet on the ground.

Music sounded, and Rachel turned toward the field again. "I forgot about the halftime show."

"So you weren't a cheerleader?"

She eyed him. "Give me a break. I was too tall, too gawky and way too unpopular to bother even if I had been interested."

"So I've heard," he said.

Rachel froze. For a moment. Then pasted a grin on her face. "Then for once, the gossip is true. Whatever stories you hear about me from Mrs. Drummond and others are absolutely true."

She turned away, needle-like daggers piercing her heart. The pain was so unexpected, she lost her breath for a moment. Jack hadn't seemed the type to linger for gossipy tidbits.

"I believe the stories now only because *you* say they're true."

She blinked quickly, the pain dissolving. "You're very sweet," she said softly, echoing his earlier words. Pivoting toward him again, she met his gaze, and they both began to laugh.

"What a lovely sound you two make," said another voice. "Laughter is like music. Soothes the soul."

Rachel glanced at her mom, who was walking toward them.

"Hi, Pearl," greeted Jack. "I absolutely agree with you about that."

"Good. I hope you'll also agree to have dinner with us next Sunday," said Pearl. "It's Rosh Hashanah, and unless you're going home to be with your family, we'd love for you to join us." She looked at Rachel. "Isn't that right, honey?"

Rachel's eyes narrowed. Rosh Hashanah was the Jewish New Year, definitely a family time and the beginning of the holiest days of the calendar. But she didn't trust her mother. Her matchmaking mother.

"Mom, you're putting Jack on the spot here. He may have other plans—"

"But I don't. I just spoke with my mom yesterday. My folks were invited to visit their close friends in Rhode Island for the holiday, but tney wouldn't go until they knew my plans. I told them to have a good time, that I was all set. And now I am." He shook Pearl's hand. "Thanks very much. I appreciate the invitation."

Pearl beamed at Rachel. "See, Rachel. He's new to town, and it's the High Holidays. He shouldn't be alone when he can be with us and have a nice home-cooked meal."

Jack actually looked pretty happy about it, thought Rachel. Must be the food. "I hate to burst your bubble, my starving friend, but if you're thinking it's a quiet intimate family dinner, forget it." Rachel glanced at her mom. "How many this year?"

"Oh, all the usual suspects, but I guarantee plenty of food. Look, there's Dad. I've got to run. Frankly," she added in a low voice, "I like basketball better."

"Of course you do," said Rachel. "Your grandson's on the team!"

Pearl chuckled and left with a wave. Rachel just shook her head. "She's very obvious, isn't she?"

"She's *obviously* a very nice lady who knows when a single guy could use a home-cooked meal."

"If that's supposed to be a hint, you can forget it," replied Rachel. "I've been living on peanut butter and jelly sandwiches myself. No time for culinary efforts."

"I know what we can do about our dilemma," said Jack. "That is, if you're game."

Uh-oh. If he was going to invite her out for dinner, she'd have to turn him down. This time around, she was not going to provide any fodder for gossip at all. Of course, Jack would think she was a coward. But...she mentally shrugged her shoulders. So be it.

"So what do you say?"

Huh? Jack seemed to be waiting for an answer. "Would you…ah…mind repeating the question?"

He raised a brow, and the corner of his mouth lifted. "Does that mean nose-in-the-book, nose-to-the-grindstone Rachel Goodman was actually daydreaming? You sounded like one of the kids."

She felt like one at the moment.

"How about coming out with me tomorrow on *The Wanderer*? We'll catch our dinner, I'll get some work done, and we'll have fun."

She was tempted. Very tempted. A day on the ocean sounded wonderful. Fishing, swimming, relaxing. There would be very little probability of them being seen and becoming an item for speculation. On the other hand, there was always a chance—a big chance—of making another mistake. Another kiss that she'd think about for days. "At what wee hour of a *Saturday* morning had you intended to start out?"

He eyed her carefully. "For you, boss, we'll go late. How about…hmm…six?"

She appreciated his humorous tone, but six? "How about seven?" she countered.

He grinned. "Sold."

Suddenly suspicious, she put her hands on her hips, her foot tapping the ground. "You set me up again, didn't you?"

His eyes sparkled. "Now, you know a gentleman never tells." She refused to feed him the next natural line. Was he a gentleman? She had her own ideas about that. Was she immune? No. Was she going to spend the day with him, anyway? Yes.

"And a lady doesn't keep a gentleman waiting," said Rachel. "I'll be ready at seven."

"Good."

THEY DIDN'T REACH THE marina until almost seven-thirty, after stopping at the Diner on the Dunes to pick up sandwiches and drinks. Rachel had shown Jack the fruit and bottled water she'd taken to share with him. *Woman food,* he'd thought, glad he'd placed the to-go lunch order with the diner.

The docking area of the marina looked like a floating outdoor parking lot. All sizes and types of boats gently rocked in the water. Some boats were outfitted for serious fishing with captain and mate chairs elevated; some craft existed purely for pleasure, both motor and sailboats.

"I guess we're not the only ones wanting to spend a day on the water," said Rachel, following Jack along the pier.

Jack scanned left and right. "It's September in New England. How many more days of good weather do you think we'll have? No one's going to miss taking advantage of a sunny sky. Especially not those two." He waved at the couple in a nearby boat. "Morning, Chief. Morning, Dee. A great day to be out."

Next to him, he heard Rachel mutter under her breath. "Darn it! Just my bad luck."

"Well, look who's here!" said Chief O'Brien, standing up to greet them. “Jack’s got a different Goodman with him this time. Traded David in for Rachel. Good choice, my man.”

“Hush up, Rick,” said Dee, standing at his side. “You’ll embarrass her.”

Jack glanced at Rachel’s flushed face, then saw her square her shoulders and look the chief in the eye. “No phone calls, Chief. You hear? I don’t need every ROMEO at the diner making us a topic of breakfast conversation. I’m just helping Jack with his work, and that’s all. This is a business trip—sort of.”

The chief’s brows rose to his hairline. He turned to his wife. “Who are these people, honey?”

“Never saw them before in my life,” she replied on cue, before winking at Rachel. “Come on, Rick. We’ve got things to do.”

As the older couple refocused on their chores, Jack heard the chief say, “Seems to me I’ve been in this situation before—with Sam’s boy, Matt. He had a dozen red roses for Laura, and when he saw me—poor boy—his face turned as red as the flowers. I promised not to say a word.”

“And look how well that turned out….”

Their voices faded as Jack and Rachel continued along the pier. Rachel looked straight ahead.

“Small towns can have their disadvantages,” remarked Jack offhandedly.

“I keep reminding myself about the lack of privacy,” said Rachel, “but it’s a losing battle. It really is, especially for someone who was born here. Everyone knows everything or will know it in five minutes or less. Grrr…"

"I like the personal space here, the location. The beach. I touch down in cities when I have to, but give me a coastal town any day."

"Do you go out there all year round, Jack?" Rachel asked, nodding at Pilgrim Bay, which led to the ocean. "Even in winter?"

"If I want to be paid, I do!"

Was that a frown on her face?

"It's dangerous work," she said softly, confirming his impression. "Even for a pirate."

He knew that only too well.

"I'm careful," he began. Then shut up as her words registered. "What? What did you call me? A pirate?"

Blushes became her. The pink glow on her cheeks, the shine in her eyes. He saw them both before she turned away and lifted her face to the morning breeze. She was as lovely to him as the morning itself. His body stirred in agreement. Maybe this outing wasn't such a good idea, after all.

IT WAS EASY TO SEE that Jack loved his boat and wanted to show it off. "She's a beauty, isn't she?" he asked, extending his hand to Rachel as she climbed on. "Welcome aboard *The Wanderer*."

She searched his face for a moment. "*The Wanderer*," she repeated quietly. "Very appropriate, I think."

Then she put her hand in his and felt his strength in

the fingers that held hers, his strength and his warmth. She glanced up at him towering about six inches above her. For the first time in her life, she actually felt petite. A strange experience for her, uncomfortable in some ways, but nice in others.

"Thanks," she said, letting go of his hand once she was on board and on her own two feet again. "How about a tour of this lady?"

In Pilgrim Cove, everyone put out to sea sooner or later. Rachel's folks always had a skiff; nowadays her dad and brother co-owned a comfortable fishing boat. She was familiar with most kinds of pleasure craft, and recognized Jack's as being a sports cruiser, built more for comfort and accommodation than for speed.

"I'll guess she's thirty feet long with a nine-foot beam," said Rachel as she scanned the craft.

"On the nose," replied Jack with an admiring grin. "Originally made to sleep six, it offers the comforts of home."

Rachel didn't doubt the truth of his statement as she placed her beach bag on the rear bench seat, realizing she'd have plenty of room to stretch out and doze if she wanted to.

"That bench seat flips up and over so you can face aft and fish. I've got rods on board. And this forward bench seat slides to create a sun pad if you want to catch some rays. Not that I advise it. Too much sun is harmful."

Next, she followed him to the lower deck. "Wow,"

she said, slowly studying the galley. It was nothing less than a full-service kitchen, with a half-size refrigerator built in, a large sink, microwave and two burner cook-top. The cabinetry had dark wood accents, and recessed lighting glowed from above.

A microscope was bolted on the countertop near the sink, and cabinets and drawers lined the walls beneath.

"I enlarged the galley to get more counter space and a storage area for my work, so I had to give up room in the cabin," explained Jack. "That's why she doesn't sleep six anymore. But don't worry, I didn't give up the head—it's fully enclosed."

"And I appreciate that!" A real bathroom on a boat. True luxury.

Next, Rachel peeked into the cabin where cushioned benches lined the walls and provided plenty of storage underneath. She turned to Jack, who seemed to be waiting for her reaction. He didn't have to worry about that. "I am speechless. She's not just beautiful, she's gorgeous! Now I understand why you're always away."

The Wanderer *was his real home.* Not his home-away-from-home. He must he have invested a small fortune in the boat, and he obviously loved her. His voice warmed when he spoke about her, and Rachel had seen him stroke her railings as though stroking a lover's skin.

She kept her thoughts private, but the implication of what she saw was plain. Jack Levine was the proverbial rolling stone. Or, in his case, perhaps a rolling wave, never remaining on shore for more than a visit. Always looking for the next tide out to adventure. A wanderer.

"What's wrong, Rach?" asked Jack, concern lacing his voice. "You look so sad all of a sudden."

She pasted a smile back on. "Not sad. Just feeling the good vibrations on this rowboat."

He laughed at her joke and stepped into the galley with their lunch, chatting about his work. Rachel leaned against the counter, relieved that he had accepted her glib answer.

"It's certainly not a real lab, but it serves the purpose," said Jack, stowing their sandwiches in the fridge. He winked at her. "Normally, I put fish specimens in here for safekeeping until I can transport them to the lab."

"Where would that be?" she asked.

"MIT for this project," he replied. "But it depends on who's contracted me. I go to Woods Hole, the Boston Aquarium and a variety of research and academic institutions from Canada in the north to Florida in the south."

His words confirmed her impression. He never stayed in one place too long. "What else do you sample besides fish?" asked Rachel, starting to become interested.

"Oh, sediment and mud samples from the bottom of the ocean. I've taken sediment from the Charles River in Boston to see if it matches the Pilgrim Cove samples. Don't know yet, but if its positive, it would mean chemical pollution such as lead, chromium and mercury has made its way over."

She wrinkled her nose. “Doesn’t sound very appetizing.”

“But knowledge is power,” he replied. “With the information we gather, we can figure out how to go about restoring a healthy marine environment. And that’s the whole point, isn’t it? Polluted oceans affect everyone.”

“Is that what you’re teaching in class?” Rachel asked. If Jack could infuse his students with his own enthusiasm, he’d make a lasting impact on them.

“That’s the single most important idea I want them to walk away with.”

She had no quarrel with his statement, and as she followed him back up top, she made a mental note to visit Jack’s class during the week. Plan books couldn’t tell the whole story by a long shot. Hopefully, Jack would make science come alive for the students.

He untied the ropes that held *The Wanderer* to the dock, and slid into the seat at the control console. His actions were precise and confident. With his hand on the ignition, he turned to her. “Ready to go?”

“Let ’er rip.” She took the seat across the aisle from him, stretched her legs in front of her, her arms along the back, feeling totally safe and comfortable. As though she’d been there a hundred times before.

The engine came to life, and Jack steered the boat slowly out of her slip, away from the marina, and followed the shoreline of the peninsula from the bay side to the Atlantic side.

Rachel stood and walked to the forward rail, her eyes

on the open sea. Sunlight glinted on the small breakers, making a million patterns of dazzling light. The horizon stretched forever. She felt a smile cross her face, a bubble of excitement fill her.

"It's positively awesome!" she said, twirling toward Jack, her enthusiasm matching her words. "I'd almost forgotten how beautiful it is out here."

He was silent for a moment. "Beautiful?" he finally said. "Go look in a mirror! I've never seen you so relaxed. So full of joy. Look in the mirror and see what I see."

Her legs felt weak, and she sat down again quickly. Unless he'd taken acting lessons, the man was sincere. "Why are you saying such things, Jack? You don't have to give me compliments. I'm an average, everyday woman. And that's okay with me."

Jack glanced at her, then studied his charts and slowed the engine. He steered the boat as if looking for a particular spot. "There's nothing ordinary about you, Rachel," he finally said. He turned the key and silence filled the air.

"Don't you think it's time to let it all go?" he asked softly, twisting in his seat to look at her. "Adolescence is over. That was then. And this is now. You're not the same awkward kid you were. In fact, you're one of the most coordinated, graceful people I know, smart, ambitious and one hell of a beautiful woman besides. You've got the whole package."

Her mouth opened, but no words came forth. Never a game player, never a bar-hopper, and definitely not a

Sex and the City type, she was hopeless at repartee. Was there even a clever retort to such a comment?

She didn't need to say anything, however, because Jack wasn't finished.

"I'd kiss you right now and never stop, but I have the advantage." He looked at their surroundings. "Where could you run if you wanted to?"

Running away was the last thing on her mind. Running her fingers through his thick, wavy hair—now, there was a thought.

CHAPTER NINE

JACK FLIPPED A SWITCH on the console. "I'm lowering the anchor here to take some water samples, and then we can swim."

She didn't reply, and he wondered if she'd heard him. No matter. He had to keep busy, had to keep his mind off Rachel Goodman. The day suddenly loomed long and difficult.

He opened the bench seat to get the equipment he'd need. In less than two minutes he'd slipped test tubes into their holders along a twenty-foot pole he'd assembled earlier.

He hoisted the apparatus and carefully slipped it down into the water, trying not to create any disturbance so that his samples would accurately reflect true conditions at each level.

Jeez! He was making a big production about a procedure he could do blindfolded. Which proved he was desperate for distraction. He hadn't looked at Rachel for at least...thirty seconds. Turning to remedy that situation, he was in time to watch as she removed her blouse, then her shorts, and stood silhouetted against the morning sun in a white bathing suit that clung to every tempting curve. He couldn't move. He forgot to breathe. Like an angel, she was illuminated in a halo of light.

He stared at her wide-eyed and barely blinked. But then his stomach tightened, and he shivered as a kaleidoscope of images rolled through his memory bringing a nightmare to life. A white bathing suit. A turbulent ocean. Rachel. Bolts of lightning. Rolls of thunder. Rachel. *Rachel under water.* Rachel drowning.

He gasped for air, his imagination so vivid that he reached for her…and felt his pole slip from his hands. Heard it plop as the top portion hit the water. "Damn!" he shouted, now fully alert. He'd lost the entire setup.

Rachel turned toward him. "What happened?"

He shrugged his shoulders. "Nothing important." And it was true. He could replace the pole and test tubes. He glanced at Rachel and watched her apply sunblock to her long, shapely legs.

No one and nothing could replace her.

HE WAS DRIVING HER CRAZY. And not with lust. Why was he acting so weird? He'd been glancing at the sky all morning and then he'd stood at the rail like a lifeguard watching her swim. She didn't need a lifeguard. She'd wanted him to swim with her. His conversation had deteriorated into grunts whenever she'd questioned him. They would have eaten lunch in total silence had it not been for the CD system in the cockpit. As far as she was concerned, they'd wasted a beautiful day. Or at least half of it.

"Don't you think it's time to go back?" she asked when they'd cleaned up after their midday meal. They were sitting across from each other on the upper deck in the shade of a canvas canopy. She was still drinking her diet soda.

Jack glanced at his watch. "It's only one o'clock."

"I know...but let's face it," she said. "Something went wrong today. Neither of us is having a good time. I don't know what I've done, but..."

He stood up quickly and walked to the railing. "It's not you. It's me." He tilted his head and searched the sky.

"See!" said Rachel, joining him. "You're doing it again. There's barely a cloud unless...you've gotten a weather report I don't know about?"

He shook his head, and she turned away from him. A mix of embarrassment and anger unsettled her. She should never have agreed to accompany him. She knew better than to mix business with pleasure.

Suddenly, she felt Jack's warm hands on her shoulders. "I'm sorry, Rachel." His whisper caressed her ear. "I'm sorry for ruining our day."

His sincerity confused her further. And when she felt him massage the back of her neck, she knew she'd have to dig deeper. The man was worried about something. As much as she hated to give up the massage, she stepped away.

"Then tell me what's going on. Why are you so...so uneasy?"

For a moment, she thought he wasn't going to answer. In fact, he was the one who seemed embarrassed.

"I dreamed about you," he began. "In a white bathing suit. There was a storm, and you were in danger. All I knew was that I had to keep you safe."

The guy looked big enough to be a one-man army, and he was worried about a dream? She would have laughed out loud except he looked so troubled. "Sounds more like a nightmare," she replied, keeping her voice light. "So, what happened in the end? Did you keep me safe?"

A glorious smile answered her. "Oh, yeah," he said, his voice husky as he stepped closer. "I'd never let you drown." But she was drowning right now. Drowning in his tender expression, drowning in the warmth of his eyes and in the gentleness of his touch on her cheek. She wanted to cuddle into his palm. Instead, she tilted her head back and whispered, "Thank you."

And then she drowned in his kiss.

RACHEL STRODE THROUGH the corridors of the high school on Tuesday morning, still thinking about that kiss and the ones that had followed, and how quickly the afternoon had slipped by once Jack had talked about his nightmare. She was still somewhat surprised. She knew that dreams could be powerful, could sometimes be extremely vivid, but for Jack to be unnerved? The man was a scientist! And then she'd come up with the only logical explanation—superstition.

Sailors were a superstitious breed, and Jack was definitely a sailor. When she'd teased him, he'd denied the charge vigorously, but she noted the twinkle in his eye.

"If I were superstitious," he'd said, "you'd have to be buck-naked on my little ship. Every sailor knows that a woman on board makes the sea angry. But a *naked* woman calms the sea down." He'd wiggled his eyebrows. "Ever wonder why so many ships have figureheads of bare-breasted women?"

She smiled as the memory teased her. In the end, they'd had a fun afternoon chatting and going farther out where they'd caught a mess of bluefish. They'd grilled their dinner at Sea View House, and then walked along the beach, relaxed in each other's company. And when they'd said good-night on the back porch, she'd seen desire heat his eyes. He'd wanted her, but he'd resisted. Had he been waiting for her cue?

She found herself mulling over the question because she was determined to be cautious herself. Sure, she was attracted to him, but taking big risks in a small town was not a wise move. Especially for her. She had too much to lose regarding both her career and her reputation. Caution on both their parts could only be a good move.

At the end of the corridor, she entered a stairwell and climbed one flight to the science wing. She'd set aside time this morning for classroom visits and looked forward to seeing the "cool" science teacher in action. Her nephew had clued her in on Jack's growing popularity. His actual description had been that Jack was "way cool."

Rachel exited the stairs and peeked into the first room along the hall. Mr. Brooker, a chemistry teacher, was pacing and lecturing. Rachel entered the room in time to hear Mr. Brooker ask about the differences between an atom and a molecule. Most students seemed to be paying attention, but some looked puzzled, some looked bored and at least two yawned. She quietly took a seat in the back and settled in to observe.

During the next period, she visited a basic biology class before finally approaching Jack's class in marine biology. The door was closed, and through its glass panes, Rachel could see that the room was dark. She opened the door slowly and realized that the class was watching a video about the ocean. Jack came to the door, a smile on his face.

"Want to join us? Plenty of popcorn's still available."

She sniffed. He wasn't kidding. "I won't come in today," said Rachel, "since you're showing a film. I can easily come back at another time."

"No problem. See you later."

She waved and returned to her office, her mind now focused on the memo she was planning to send to all families with a child on a school sports team. The memo would reinforce the "No pass, no play," policy that the students had been told about in school.

She stopped to knock on Bob Franklin's open door. "Have a minute?"

He nodded, a frown almost cutting his forehead in half.

"Just wanted to let you know about the memo. I'll have it ready by the end of the day, and we can give copies to the kids tomorrow."

"Not a good idea. It'll just add more stress. The boys

are already under a lot of pressure to perform." He turned back to the work on his desk.

"We really are on the same side, Bob," she said softly. "I want those kids to succeed at everything."

The man spun in his chair. "There are only twenty-four hours to the day, Rachel. And they have to sleep!"

She took a breath, determined not to lose her temper. "We're not asking for A's. Only that they pass everything. Surely you want that, too."

He met her glance without flinching. "A winning season is more important. They can study after the season is over."

"Which is after Thanksgiving! If they screw up for three full months, how will they ever catch up with the rest of their classmates? Final grades will be out in December and those count toward college admissions. We've got a number of juniors and seniors playing school sports. It *will* matter to them."

"They'll get in because they play great ball, not because they're scholars. What's wrong with your memory? Being a jock didn't hurt your college admissions any. And my boys can do the same." He rose from his seat, steel-gray eyes burning into her brown ones.

Rachel stood taller, glad she was wearing two-inch heels, glad she could meet his gaze without flinching. "I am getting pretty tired of listening to my past being misrepresented. If you'd taken the trouble to ask *how* I got into college, you would have learned that in addition to my rank as a swimmer, I earned a combined fourteen hundred on my SAT scores." She leaned back against the door frame, her hands gripping the wood, her blood heated. But she controlled her voice, and it remained low and calm. "Can we count on all your boys doing the same?"

Gotcha.

He didn't answer, but his eyes narrowed as he processed her words. Time to make an exit.

"I'll get copies of the memo to you by this afternoon," she called over her shoulder, as she walked through the door.

She went to her own office, closed the door and collapsed into her chair. In truth, she was shaking a bit. She'd trained herself not to back down, but she hated confrontations. Much preferred open, honest discussion. However, Bob Franklin had managed to make himself scarce whenever she'd wanted to talk about the teams. She shrugged and faced her computer screen. It was time to write the memo.

In the end, she wrote two. One to the students and families. And one to the teachers and coaches reminding them about the after-school tutoring service. She encouraged them to communicate with one another especially if they had concerns about specific students.

Satisfied that she'd covered all the issues involving sports, she turned her mind to other concerns. The kids with learning problems, the kids with after-school jobs, the kids with attendance problems whose parents didn't give a damn. She'd concentrate on kids who weren't being challenged and on the teachers who didn't care.

The rest of the week flew by. She didn't see Jack again, never had a chance to return to his classroom, and didn't see him at Sea View House, either. She heard him, however, returning home after ten o'clock each night and climbing the stairs to the Eagle's Nest. It was not possible for him to be taking samples that late, so he was probably out with friends in Boston. Dinner. Perhaps dancing. Very possible. He was definitely a social animal. And the Pilgrim Cove-to-Boston ferry service ran every half hour until ten at night.

The day she'd spent with him on his boat seemed a long time ago. She'd even succeeded in putting him out of her mind. At least until Friday—when she found him leaning against her car, obviously waiting for her.

JACK WATCHED AS SHE approached, her expression more curious than pleased.

"What's up?" She juggled her purse, got her keys and inserted them into her car door.

"How about dinner this evening? I haven't seen you all week, and I'm taking the night off."

She placed her tote bag in the car, then turned to study him. "Turning in early? Good idea."

He rubbed his hand across his face. Definitely time for a shave. "I must look worse than I feel."

She eyed him. "Late nights can do that."

"It can't be helped. But I'm feeling great, and we

need to talk. So, how about it? Either the Lobster Pot or Sea View House."

She didn't answer for a long moment. And then she turned him down. Nicely. "I wouldn't mind the company, but going out with you is a bad idea. For both of us."

She wouldn't mind his company? Leave it to Rachel never to inflate his ego!

He put his hands on her shoulders. "Let me set you straight, Rachel. I don't give a flying fig about what anyone says about me, and I don't intend to live like a hermit in Pilgrim Cove."

"But..."

"Listen, you may have problems you don't even know about, problems that have nothing to do with me. Dinner *is* a good idea."

Her eyes widened. And he was sorry he'd frightened her. "But you can handle them. It's early days yet."

Under his palms, he felt her whole body rise and fall as she breathed. Then she shrugged his hands away.

"Going out in public will only compound any problems I've already got. So, the answer's still no."

He sighed. "Stubborn woman! I'll call Polini's for a pizza."

"Not pizza. You wanted a hearty meal tonight."

"Don't tell me you're offering to cook?" He already knew the answer to that. Her culinary skills extended to using the outdoor grill and tossing a salad.

Sure enough, she said, "Don't be silly. My hot dogs

aren't the answer, but I'll treat you to a compromise. How about Chinese takeout?"

"Sold."

Her expression sobered. "I can't say I'm exactly looking forward to our conversation."

"You'll handle it."

But three hours later, as they sat across from each other in Rachel's dining room, he wasn't sure. She was smart, energetic and caring. She wanted Pilgrim Cove High to be the best. But she was either blind or truly stubborn. For every warning he gave her, she had an answer.

"The teachers are beginning to resent you. They think you don't respect them, don't trust them. They complain that you're always breathing down their necks."

"You bet I am! They're grumbling because they know I won't put up with laziness," said Rachel. "They're grumbling because I visit their classrooms. Some of them haven't changed a lesson plan in twenty years! What's worse, in some classes, the kids are afraid to ask questions. Heck, I was almost afraid to ask questions. So, if I'm rocking boats, I'm glad."

"You can't fight everyone, Rachel. There's talk about you in the staff lunchroom. Every day." He tried to speak gently, reasonably.

"There's always talk when someone comes on board and makes changes. They'll adjust. I know they want our students to perform better on the state tests. So they need to do things differently."

"And you're holding the carrot and the stick."

"I guess I am."

"There's more."

She looked him squarely in the eye. "Don't tell me the staff is going on strike!"

He chuckled. "No, no. It's not that bad yet. And the point is, Rachel, not to let it get that bad. Parents are starting to get involved because their kids' teachers aren't happy. One talks to the other. You should know how that goes in a small community."

She looked past his shoulder. "Thanks for your concern, Jack. I'll do what I think is right."

"The students are rumbling, too. Not only the football team, but all the athletes and their friends who don't play, not to mention the coaches and gym staff."

Now he watched her pace the room, her top teeth biting her bottom lip. "It's called standards, Jack. We have standards. For the life of me, I can't figure out why everyone is so surprised. Wasn't the 'no pass, no play' policy ever enforced before?"

A good question. He shook his head. "I'm new here, newer than you. I don't know."

"I guess time will answer that question, too."

Her voice was soft, her eyes warm and resigned. She began clearing the table, and he stood to help her. "How about a walk along the beach?"

She perked up instantly as he'd anticipated. He knew her well enough to know she needed physical activity to keep her sane and happy. And he liked seeing this woman happy, even if he didn't fully understand why.

All he knew was that he respected Rachel, respected her efforts. Maybe that was why he'd decided to reveal what he knew. Rachel's happiness was becoming very important to him.

ON THE FIRST NIGHT of the Jewish New Year, Rachel stood in the middle of her parents' living room, in the center of the large group of Lou and Pearl's friends, and wondered for the thousandth time in her life how her mom managed to make entertaining look so easy. She asked Pearl, who was standing next to her.

"It *is* easy! Everybody brings something. You and dad set up the extra tables, and you'll head the cleanup committee, so what's so hard?" Pearl gave Rachel a quick hug and went over to speak to Bart Quinn. Probably to thank him for his contribution. Homemade gefilte fish.

Rachel waved at Bart and covered a grin. Her mom was no dope. Thea and Maggie had the freshest fish in town at the restaurant, so over the years Pearl bought her whitefish and pike from them, and eventually taught Bart's daughters how to make the traditional dish. Now Bart brought it every year and her mom cooked one less item on her menu. This year, Bart also brought his granddaughter and great-granddaughter, Lila and Katie Sullivan.

The house was crowded. Doc and Marsha Rosen—who'd made perfect stuffed cabbage, not too sweet, not too tart—were chatting with Rick and Dee O'Brien.

Rachel still felt more comfortable calling the former police chief "Chief," the way she had when she'd been a kid.

Kate and Mike Lyons were talking with Jack. No surprise there, given their mutual interest in the coastal environment. Her eyes kept returning to Jack, however, as she mingled with the rest of the ROMEOs—Sam Parker, Joe Cavelli and the Bigelows. There was something different about her upstairs neighbor today. She couldn't quite figure it out yet. Maybe his clothes? Sport shirt, slacks and a jacket that now hung over the back of a chair. It was the first time she'd seen him in anything dressier than a jersey. His face…clean-shaven, no trace of a shadow. She continued to study him. Haircut! That was it. The carefree pirate was totally gone. And in his place stood a gorgeous, grown-up, responsible adult.

Her heart thumped so hard, she pressed her hand over it. Suddenly, his eyes caught hers. He cocked his head in inquiry.

"Haircut?" She mouthed the question, feeling heat travel from her chest to her neck and face. She tugged a few of her own strands to illustrate.

He nodded, eyes crinkling as he smiled, and she felt herself blush harder. Time to help out in the kitchen. She power-walked herself to safety.

Susan and Jennifer greeted her. "The chicken soup's piping hot. Ask your mom when she wants to serve."

"Serve? With all the appetizers out there, no one will be hungry for the meal."

Holding the ladle, Susan put her hands on her hips. "Rachel, Rachel. Don't you know by now that everyone always devours your mom's soup? Doesn't matter how many hors d'oeuvres there are."

"I guess I forgot."

"You've been away too long," said Susan. "I'm glad you're back."

Footsteps sounded at the kitchen door. Her dad and brother stood there. "Three-minute warning," said Alex. "That's the message from Mom." He turned toward Susan. "Don't get too used to having Rachel around, Susie. At the rate my sister's going, she'll be gone by the end of the year."

"What do you mean?" asked Susan, stepping toward her husband.

"She's going to mess up again, except now it's not her classes, it's her career. Just ask her. Or ask David."

Rachel could barely breathe past the lump in her throat. Criticism from Alex was one thing, but David? Her nephew had waved from across the room when she'd arrived, but hadn't walked over to greet her. She'd thought nothing of it since he'd been engrossed in conversation. But was there another reason?

Suddenly, a warm arm rested across her shoulder. It was Lou who answered his son. "She's improving the school, Alex. And it's a big job. What you've been hearing is the sound of growing pains."

Time stretched with the silence. Rachel would remember the moment forever. She exhaled and leaned against her dad, enjoying his support and approval more than she could ever have imagined. It was worth everything. Even if her brother was proved right in the end. Suddenly Cornelia Stebbins's words popped into Rachel's mind. She turned in her father's arms. "Dad? Remember Cornelia Stebbins?"

"That old battle-ax? She didn't retire soon enough," replied Lou. "Why?"

And suddenly Mrs. Stebbins didn't matter. Rachel started to giggle, but then her eyes filled. "I'm fine. Don't worry. Just so relieved."

Lou looked confused. "Rachel, why do you ask? What did she do to you? Or say to you?" Now he was getting upset.

Good Lord. Alex and Susan were standing there. She'd forgotten all about them. But, what the hell? She might as well clean the wound once and for all.

"Mrs. Stebbins told me that you'd have been better off if I'd never been born. She said that you were embarrassed to have me as a daughter. She felt sorry for you. 'Alex is so bright and handsome, and you, Rachel, are such a disappointment. He's given up on you.'" She remembered every word verbatim.

"That witch!" said Lou, hugging her. "That liar! Not a syllable is true. Not one." He took a tiny step back so he could stroke her cheek. "Rachel, Rachel. Do you know how hard your mom and I tried to have another child after we had your brother? Do you know how happy we were when you were born?" He blinked fast and shook his head. "It took us ten years! We were overjoyed. We felt blessed having you."

She believed him, of course she did. But the echoes of old memories were hard to erase in a few seconds. "But…but what she said seemed to make sense! After all, you never expected anything from me. As if you didn't care, or as if you thought I wasn't smart enough or as capable as Alex."

"No, no. Nothing like that," said Lou. "I just didn't want to push you…all the psychologists said that every child develops at her own pace. And I read all the books. You were unhappy enough with life, and I certainly didn't want you to compete with your brother. The books said every child is different, so I didn't push for high grades. Sometimes—maybe more often than we want to admit—grades aren't everything."

Rachel heard the hubbub around her. A low cacophony of voices. Family. Friends. Celebration. *Rosh Hashanah.* A new year was starting. Another new beginning. She would have smiled, but something dropped onto the corner of her mouth. Something salty. She raised her fingers to her cheek. Her face was wet. So was her dad's.

She grabbed him, hugged him and felt his arms around her, squeezing with the strength of a boa constrictor. And it felt wonderful. After so many wasted years. All those years…

"Soup's ready." Pearl's voice came from the near distance.

Her dad relaxed his grip, and Rachel glanced around. Alex looked shocked, and Susan gestured for him to help Pearl.

"What else don't I know about?" asked Lou.

Rachel patted her dad's hand. "It's okay now. The truth is what's important. But, Dad—here's another important thing. I don't want another Cornelia Stebbins on the staff ever again. I won't have it."

He nodded. "I'm almost afraid to ask—how's Edith Drummond?"

Rachel grinned. "Her methods are a bit old-fashioned, and she has too much ego. But her heart's in the right place. I can handle her."

"'Atta girl."

THE LONG TABLE STRETCHED from the dining room to the living room and was really a series of add-ons covered with white cloths. The twenty-one people sitting around it seemed to be having a good time. At any rate, Rachel observed, they talked nonstop. Amazing since most of them saw each other several times a week!

Rachel sat on a chair nearest to the kitchen. Jack was diagonally across from her, with David on his left and pretty Lila Sullivan on his right. To the right of Lila was her eight-year-old daughter, who had attached herself to Jennifer and then insisted the teen sit next to her for the meal. Jennifer complied more than graciously, perhaps enjoying the admiration of the younger girl.

The blessings over the wine and challah were over.

Rachel had heard Jennifer describe the specially braided egg bread to Katie and had heard Katie's reply. "I know all about challah. We eat it at home, and I eat it at your grandma's house all the time, too!"

The soup had been served, bowls refilled, emptied again and stacked in the dishwasher. Rachel relaxed in her chair, knowing everyone would slow down now and sit around the table for a while.

Lila and Jack seemed to be chatting like old friends, although they hardly knew each other. Nobody could resist Jack's charm. Lila glanced up.

"Rachel, did you know that Jack's never taught high school before? I'm surprised you hired him without experience."

"Don't blame me," she replied with a smile. "The board did the dirty work. But he's taught before at the undergraduate level."

"Hey, ladies. I'm sitting right here," said Jack. He turned back to Lila. "Rachel knows I took this job at the last minute when I learned that the funding for the Pilgrim Cove water project was cut in half. Contracts come and go depending on grants available. I don't stick around too long in any one place."

"Sounds like a precarious way to live," said Lila.

"How so?" Jack replied. "You depend on commissions, don't you? Nothing's guaranteed."

"True, except..." Lila glanced at Rachel, her expression a mixture of pleading and pride.

"What she's trying to say without sounding like a

braggart, is that Quinn Real Estate is known far and wide. If anyone can be certain of earning a living, it's Lila and Bart."

But Rachel's mind was whirling. While she was aware of the special circumstances of Jack's assignment in Pilgrim Cove, she hadn't thought about how long he might stay in town.

"Your granddad's a lucky guy," said Jack.

Lila's pink blush only made her prettier. Rachel sighed. Whenever she blushed, she felt as if she was having one of her mom's hot flashes. Oops. She'd been corrected already. Pearl insisted they were power surges.

"I'm the one who's lucky," said Lila quietly, glancing down the table to where Bart sat talking with the Bigelows. "My granddad understands me. Always has. That's why we live together and work together."

"Since Katie was born, right?" asked Rachel.

Lila winked. "Yup. How many people do you think could have stood up to my mother, a woman who thinks she knows what's best for everybody? Granddad simply said, 'Lila and the baby will live with me, Maggie. You and Thea have a business to run.'" At the table, Lila grinned at Rachel, then looked up at Jack. "Of course, *he* had a business to run, too, but that subject never arose!" Lila paused for a moment before asking, "So, how's Sea View House?"

Rachel and Jack spoke in unison. "Love it." "It's great."

"When you have a minute, explore upstairs," said

Lila. "There's a widow's walk on the roof. You two would really appreciate the view."

Rachel made a mental note to do that.

"And you know what else about me and Mommy and Papa Bart?" came a high-pitched voice.

Rachel, Lila and Jack looked at Katie, who seemed to be doing some heavy thinking.

"I'm afraid to hear," said Lila.

"What?" asked Jack.

"Mommy went on a date!" The little girl's head nodded up and down like a vertical pendulum. "With Sara's daddy. She's in my class at school. And Sara slept over with me and Papa Bart."

"And me," inserted Lila quickly and clearly. "After all, who made pancakes early in the morning?"

"But you didn't play games with us like Papa Bart did and let us stay up way, way late! It was fun."

Rachel watched the child peep at her mother from under her lashes. Something else was coming. Poor Lila!

"Maybe you and Sara's daddy can have another date," said Katie. "Sara says Dr. Fielding must like you a lot 'cause he asked her if *she* liked you, too. And he never asked before."

Lila's blushes now looked painful. "This subject is closed, young lady. Understand?"

"But you never learn anything if..."

"Put a lid on it, Kathleen."

Jack started to laugh, a deep chuckle. Rachel joined in, then reached for Lila's hand and squeezed. "She's a terrific kid, Lila. And you're a terrific mom. But you and I both know, there are absolutely no secrets around this town." She paused and met the other woman's gaze. "I wish you the best."

"If I only knew what that was...." whispered Lila, her voice anxious.

Rachel stared at the younger woman. Lila and Jason Parker had been so much in love. Would someone else always be second best for Lila? Rachel's heart went out to her. But it was time to lighten the mood. "Right now," she said, "the best thing to do is clear this table for dessert. No one can resist my mom's homemade apple pie."

A groan traveled around the table as everyone patted their too-full stomachs. Rachel noticed, however, that dishes began to be stacked in a hurry.

Her dad approached Jack and tapped him on the shoulder. "Would you like to attend services with us tomorrow morning? I should have asked you earlier."

Jack at services? Jack? The man worshiped the sea! Poseidon. Neptune. He placated the gods with naked ladies on his boat. And besides that, he was a scientist. A man of rational thought—superstitions not withstanding. He was also a carefree wanderer. Not traditional or spiritual. Probably hadn't been to a synagogue in years. What was her father thinking?

Jack stood up and shook her father's hand. "I'd be happy to. Thanks for asking. I was planning to find my own way there, but it's nicer to go with friends." He turned toward Rachel and tsked. "You'd best close your mouth now. I'm not a heathen. Just ask my mother. She'll vouch for me."

"A very objective opinion, I'm sure," Rachel teased.

"You'd be surprised."

CHAPTER TEN

PARTICIPATING FULLY in the New Year services, Jack proved not to have been a heathen, but at work he certainly was a rebel. Rachel paced her office several days later, more agitated than she'd been since starting her job. It would take every bit of her willpower not to tear into Jack the moment he showed up. How could he have taken his class to the beach! No permission slips filed. No communication to her or Dr. Bennett. No hint to anyone of his intentions. He'd simply gathered his students and disappeared.

Footsteps sounded outside her office. She stood in front of her desk and took a deep breath, then another. *Keep your cool.*

"Hi, Rachel. What's up?"

His casual manner, casual words, casual attitude—all struck an exposed nerve inside her.

She grasped the edge of her desk behind her. "I'll tell you what's up," she replied, her eyes glued to his face. "Safety. Liability. Ever hear of those two little words?"

She watched a frown slowly form on his face as her meaning sank in.

"You mean the little field trip?"

She threw her hands in the air. "Give the man a gold star!" His frown intensified, and she was glad.

"Sarcasm doesn't become you," he said. "Not your style."

"*My* behavior is not in question here," she said. "*Yours* is." She motioned to a chair. "Have a seat."

"We didn't go swimming, Rachel," Jack replied. He waited until she walked behind her desk before sitting down. "There was no danger to anyone. I've taken lots of groups to examine the beach habitat during my career."

"*Those* students were over eighteen years old. *Our* students are minors and need parental permission to leave these premises. How could you have just walked out like a papa duck with his little ducklings in tow? Where was your head?" She practically threw herself against her chair in frustration.

"Every single student is back safe and sound," said Jack. "And they had a terrific time. Learned a few things, too."

"I'm not questioning the benefits! But *you* were lucky. *We* were lucky. God, when I think what could have happened." Her hands fisted on the armrests, and she shivered.

"Would you lighten up?" asked Jack. "Nothing happened. Next time, I'll get permission slips." He stood and leaned over her desk, his face close to hers. "We get along a lot better at Sea View House. Or on my boat. Or at your family's house. Everywhere but at work."

She paused at his words. He'd made a point. The only common ground they had at school was that they both cared about the students. But their approaches were as different as sand and water.

"How did your classes do on their first unit test?" she asked. The same departmental exam was administered to all students studying the same discipline. Jack's students took uniform biology and earth-science tests. She had to trust Jack with the marine biology class because it was unique.

He met her gaze calmly. "Not well."

She winced. "How can I help?"

Another frown settled on his face, and he stepped away from her desk. "I don't want your help," he said. "You want me to teach a test-prep class. You want the kids to perform like parrots, regurgitating information for the sake of a test. I want to open their minds, to help them appreciate their role in the universe."

Glad she was already seated, Rachel felt her stomach tighten at his attack. In a perfect world, he'd be right. "Those are wonderful goals, Jack. But in real life, the kids and the school are measured by statewide exams."

"They'll do better by midterm," he replied. "They need more time to learn to process information differently." He leaned over her again, his expression now gentle. "Trust me."

She shook her head slowly, however, and sighed. "Famous last words as we both drown." She raised her chin and leaned back in her chair. "I'm sorry, Jack, but *you* are going to have to trust *me.* It's my job to steer this ship into port, and I have to insist on some structure and planning. You need to cover the material in the books!"

His eyes ignited. His gentleness disappeared. "Why don't you check the attendance stats? Who has the most students show up? Me! Why don't you ask the kids how they feel? You think you're steering the ship? Baby, you're missing the entire boat!" He left the room without another word and seemed to take all the oxygen with him.

Tears burned Rachel's eyes, and she blinked quickly, then wiped the corners where drops had escaped. Emotions would not interfere with her logic! She'd handled Bob Franklin. She'd handled her old English teacher. And she'd assisted the new teachers in adjusting to the school during their first weeks. But Jack's derision cut her to the bone. She hadn't counted on having to "handle" him, too.

Suddenly, a kaleidoscope of childhood images blended with her present life, and tears threatened once more. Why did she always seem to lack support from the people she loved the most?

Hold on! Love? What was she thinking? She didn't love Jack! In fact, he drove her crazy. She inhaled and exhaled until her breathing returned to normal. Sure, there was a spark between them, and their kisses were…well, more than good. Definitely "above average." Maybe "excellent." But thankfully, she and Jack had snuffed out the spark before it could develop into a blaze. She almost laughed with relief.

NEVER HAD A WOMAN BROUGHT him to such a flashpoint before. Never! He held a Ph.D. in marine biology, was a guest lecturer at Harvard, MIT and Boston University whenever asked, had worked on behalf of both the United States and Canadian governments' environmental efforts—and all Rachel could do was belittle his work!

He crashed into someone entering the administrative suite. "Excuse me," he muttered, turning aside.

"Well, who ticked off the popular science teacher?"

Jack spun around and glanced at Bob Franklin, whose expression held genuine curiosity. "Women!" Jack replied.

Franklin laughed, but his eyes narrowed. He jerked his head toward Rachel's office. "That particular woman?"

Something in the director's tone made Jack pause rather than seek commiseration. He didn't respond.

"Don't worry about it," said Franklin, slapping him on the shoulder like a pal. "You're not the only one. It hasn't taken our Ms. Goodman long to get herself into hot water. Mark my words, sooner or later that water's going to bubble at a full boil." He turned and walked toward his office. "Can't come soon enough for me," he said.

Jack stared after the man, his own anger at Rachel forgotten. Rachel had laughed at his concerns about her effect on some of the staff; she'd poo-pooed the undercurrents he'd picked up in the lunchroom. Five minutes ago, he, himself, had wanted to strangle her, and he was a friend! If every instructor eventually felt the same way, she'd pay a high price for her so-called standards. She'd be the "rightest" woman in her professional graveyard. She didn't deserve that fate. If he could save her from Poseidon, maybe he could save her from herself.

Jack continued walking until he was behind the school at the football field. At the end of the day, the field was full of boys doing drills, learning plays. Tom Sullivan had produced a top-notch team. They'd won two of their first three games this season. Jack knew that Rachel had attended all of them.

He scanned the team, recognizing a few youngsters from his own classes. They performed better on the athletic field than in the classroom, but at least were interested enough to ask questions.

Tom glanced up, and Jack waved. The coach motioned to the kids to continue their workout and came over to the sidelines.

"They look great, Tom. You're doing a good job with them."

"Thanks," replied the coach. "I'm real happy with them so far. The older boys, especially, have come a long way in the last couple of years. It's satisfying to watch."

"I know what you mean," said Jack. "You're making a difference."

The coach shrugged. "I try. Seems I'll need a few

extra prayers this year. When report cards are issued, we'll probably be up the creek. Some of the best players are the worst students, but hopefully, Bob will work something out."

"You mean with Rachel?"

Tom eyed him. "I guess that's who carries the clout now."

"You have a problem with her?" Jack heard the accusation in his voice, or was it defensiveness?

But the coach shook his head. "Personally? Nah. In fact, I like her. She's working damn hard from everything I hear, but some of these kids will need a miracle to pass everything."

"I guess maybe that's why I'm here," said Jack. "Have you talked to the players about after-school tutoring on the days you don't practice?"

"Sure I have. We sent the memo home. The parents know. The guys know. But it doesn't mean anything during the season. In the fall, it's about football! That's the way it is."

And no different from any other high school in the country. "Tell you what," said Jack. "I'll hang around after practice today and personally invite them to stay late this week. I'll tutor any subject. There's still some time before report cards come out." He'd do it not only for the boys' sakes, but for Rachel's. If everyone passed, confrontations would be avoided and Rachel's life would be much easier.

But Tom laughed. "A great offer, Jack. I appreciate

it. But have you ever seen the boys after practice? All they want to do is shower, eat and sleep."

"Then how about six-thirty in the morning?" asked Jack. "Early works for me, too."

The coach gave him a thoughtful look, but then nodded. "Okay. We've got nothing to lose. Maybe one or two might take you up on it. Hang around."

Jack watched Tom jog to the field, again wondering at his own behavior. At his feelings for Rachel. He'd always made a point to keep things light, to never get involved, and here he was, drowning! Drowning. He pressed his lips together hard as the "d" word passed through his mind. The ugliest, most painful word in the language. At least, for him. The urge to work on his book—Kevin's book—made his fingers tingle. He'd learned that however painful he found facing his past and what had happened to Kevin, he could count on the writing to bring him relief.

A WEEK LATER, ON FRIDAY afternoon, Rachel met with the staff of the Guidance Department in Judy Kramer's office. Judy, who chaired the department, had given Rachel full support from the beginning.

"Are you Wonder Woman incognito?" asked Judy. "Where did you ever find the extra funds for psychiatric services? I can't tell you how many kids fall through the cracks of medical insurance."

Rachel leaned back on her chair and chuckled. Judy was totally committed to helping every student succeed, and she handled a lot of tough cases. "Money always brings smiles," said Rachel. "I'm glad I was able to get it."

She enjoyed the praise. In fact, she needed to hear it. She gazed at the others in the room, grateful to have some positive feedback after six weeks on the job.

"How's the peer-tutoring program working out?" Rachel asked.

"Attendance is increasing every week. And they're staying until four o'clock," replied Judy.

"It's a win-win for the kids who are tutoring and for the learners," said one of the other counselors. "Even the teachers are impressed."

Now Rachel wanted to cheer. Many on the staff had been skeptical when she introduced the program. Thought the sessions would be a waste of time without a real teacher. Rachel suspected their uneasiness might stem from fear of being upstaged by some of the better student tutors. But the staff had come around at least on this issue, and Rachel felt satisfied.

"There's going to be some fallout on Tuesday when report cards are distributed in homeroom," said Rachel. She handed a printout of student grades arranged by caseload to the appropriate counselor.

"There's always some fallout with grades," said Judy. "On the top end as well as the bottom."

"Well, this time, expect the worst," said Rachel, staring at the papers in her hand. "For starters, the football team is going to be shaken up big time. Jimmy Williams, the quarterback, is out. And so is Steve Yelton, the running back."

Suddenly, an uneasy silence filled the room. Rachel could hear the rhythmic clicking of a distant photocopy machine as it ran off a long job. She heard a car backfire in the street outside. Looking into the faces of her supporters, she felt her stomach plunge to the floor. "You, too?" Her voice almost cracked.

"We understand where you're coming from," said Judy quietly, "but we don't agree in this particular situation. Sports competition brings the school together. In fact, a football game brings the whole community together. It also brings in money. These boys have been on the squad since their freshman year, and their parents are all for them playing—despite their grades. Grades that have never been more than passing. They're not scholars, Rachel."

Rachel took a steadying breath. Then another before answering. "And since when do we allow parents to dictate the terms of their children's attendance here?"

"Your theory's got merit," said one of the guidance counselors, "but in practice…it won't wash in Pilgrim Cove. New Englanders love their football. Good football."

"At the expense of these boys' futures?" She leaned closer to the counseling staff. "Come on, now. Do you really think they'll turn professional and have big careers? Every one of them? Not likely. But I can guarantee they'll all need a high school diploma to get anywhere in life."

Another silence followed her speech, and disappointment flooded Rachel.

"Kids have big dreams," Judy said quietly.

"Dreams are fine," said Rachel, "but our job is to provide the safety nets."

No further comment came from the staff, and Rachel stood, her hand gripping the back of her chair. In the end, she was alone after all.

Gesturing to the printouts, she said, "Please keep these locked in your desks. Grades don't come out until Tuesday." She turned to leave, then looked back. "Whatever happened to the 'no pass, no play' policy? Has no one paid attention to it until now?"

Judy looked startled for a moment, then studied her list of grades. "We've abided by it. These boys usually managed to pass all their courses." She looked at Rachel. "But not this time."

Rachel's mind raced. She opened the printout again and searched for the boys' names and their teachers. Mrs. Drummond. Mr. Maggio. Other old-timers. Emotion filled her. Redemption.

"My God!" she said. "I think I get it. Teachers finally feel confident enough to tell the truth. Confident enough to fail a star athlete."

Confused faces stared at her.

"*Finally* confident?" asked Judy. "Mrs. Drummond thinks she owns the place!"

"I'll check on what I'm saying, but I believe Mrs. Drummond has been pressured on this issue," said

Rachel. "Made to feel she had to go along. Probably for years." Full of conviction again, Rachel went to the door with a sure step. "And suddenly she doesn't."

"Rachel—"

"Yes?"

"Be careful," said Judy. "The impact from this particular fallout might have the force of an atomic bomb."

"Then I'll have to try to defuse it." She headed for Dr. Bennett's office, and then…she'd treat herself to a long swim in the high school pool.

HE LOVED THE SPARKLE in her eye. He did not love the fact that she'd lost weight. He blamed it on her job. In the lane next to Rachel, Jack paced himself to her perfect freestyle, admiring her form in more ways than one. He hadn't expected to go swimming that afternoon, but when he'd stopped at Rachel's office to invite her to the football game with him that evening, she'd invited him to join her in the pool. She didn't have to ask twice! He'd grabbed a suit from his truck and met her poolside. Towels came courtesy of Pilgrim Cove High.

They'd now completed three steady laps, and Rachel grasped the pool's ledge and turned toward him with a teasing grin. "Warmed up enough for a little race?"

"You might not win," he said with a chuckle, also pausing.

"But I might," she replied, echoing his thoughts. "At any rate, I need some competition to keep my edge!"

"Then how about making it *real* interesting?" asked

Jack. "If I win, you'll have dinner with me tomorrow night at the Lobster Pot."

Her eyes widened, and he thought she'd turn him down as usual. But then she met his warm gaze and slowly nodded. "All right," she said.

He wanted to cheer. He wanted to kiss her. He wanted to take her in his arms and feel her body next to his, her long legs wrapped around him. In the cool water, his body heated up. His imagination had never been as vivid, as wild. And all he could do at the moment was look at her and grin.

"Have I really made you so happy," asked Rachel, "merely by saying that I'll race with you?"

"Yes!" he replied without hesitation. Why wasn't he afraid to show how he felt? Why did he want this woman to know? A confusing first for thirty-five-year-old Dr. Jack Levine.

THEY'D NEVER ACTUALLY gotten around to racing each other in the pool, so how had she wound up here at the Lobster Pot with Jack? She could barely believe she'd agreed to join him. That she'd broken one of her own rules. But when she'd seen the desire, the heat, and more importantly, the hope in his eyes, her own heart began to beat a hot Latin rhythm. And she wanted to dance. Needed to dance. It had been a long time between dances.

Rachel glanced at the man behind the wheel of his truck as he pulled into the restaurant's parking lot.

Funny, he'd hardly spoken since he knocked on her door fifteen minutes ago, taken one look and muttered, "I'll never get through this night."

She knew she looked good. Her short burgundy suede skirt was topped by its matching belted jacket, while her legs looked sensational in knee-high boots of the same color. A pink shell provided contrast. It wasn't an outfit to wear on a job interview!

She'd been about to make a flip comment when she found she couldn't talk at all. He looked civilized, but the pirate was back in a short-sleeved gray silk shirt open at the neck, darker gray slacks and a black leather jacket, unzipped. It was more his attitude than his clothes, however. He stood tall in the doorway, arms resting overhead against the frame. His dark hair fell over his forehead, and as he'd looked at her, his eyes sizzled. And she couldn't speak. Instead, she reached for her handbag and followed him back outside to his pickup.

Now he pulled into a parking spot far from the main entrance. "I know the lot's crowded, but I think there's a couple of spaces closer to the entrance," Rachel said, pointing toward the big double doors.

Jack shut the engine and removed the key from the ignition. "Walking in the cool fresh air," he said deliberately, "is good for our health." He opened his door and got out. By the time she jiggled her door handle, he was at her side helping her down. And holding her in his arms for an extra second...or two.

"Hell," he murmured. "I knew I wouldn't need this when I'm with you." He threw his jacket onto the seat, slammed the door and reached for her, his arm encircling her back as they walked to the entrance of the Lobster Pot.

She leaned into him slightly, comfortable and intrigued. Definitely enjoying the pressure of his body against hers, enjoying the spicy fragrance of his cologne.

"My goodness!" she said, lifting her face toward him. "Are we actually on a date?"

Deep, genuine laughter was the immediate answer. As well as a hard, fast hug. "Sounds good to me," Jack finally replied.

Sounded good to her, too.

Wide wooden terraces surrounded three sides of the building, but no diners were outside on the chilly night. They walked up two steps and opened the door.

The restaurant was busy. "It's Saturday night, and it's the best place in town," said Rachel as Jack gave his name to the hostess. "We should have come earlier."

"No problem," replied Jack. "We'll have more time on our date this way."

She felt herself blush and looked around for distractions.

"Well, as I live and breathe," said Bart Quinn, walking toward them. He pumped Jack's hand and accepted Rachel's kiss. "If it isn't the whole of Sea View House coming to get a decent meal." The agent studied Rachel, then looked at Jack, frowning. "And it's about time.

She's becoming skin and bone. What took you so long? You know the lass is not her mother's daughter in the kitchen."

A flush crossed Jack's face and Rachel was astounded. The man almost looked guilty.

"My fault entirely," she said. "He's asked a number of times."

"And you turned the good man down?"

Rescue came in the form of fast-moving Maggie Sullivan. "There you are, Dad. Lila and Katie are waiting for you. And here's Rachel Goodman. How are you, dear?" Maggie gave her a hug. "Good to see you."

"You know Jack Levine," said Bart. "Don't you?"

"Sure do," said Maggie, smiling up at the big man. "Welcome back." She turned to her father. "He's sampled our fish chowder a time or two in the past."

Maggie glanced at the hostess's list. "You're next and a table's ready. Come on. I'll seat you myself."

Rachel and Jack followed Maggie into the main dining room. "I'm salivating," said Rachel. "And my stomach's rumbling!"

Maggie laughed heartily as she led them to their table. "Just what I like to hear. I'll send your server over right away. Can't have any of my customers fainting from hunger in my restaurant!" And she was gone.

"Whew!" said Rachel, smiling up at Jack. "She's still a whirlwind, always was, always will be. Same as her sister, Thea. Knowing Bart's daughters, I'm sure Thea will be by to say hello before the night's over."

Rachel slowly studied the room and started to chuckle. "Take a look," she invited Jack. "I was wondering if any new items had been added to the walls lately."

"That's a good one," said Jack, pointing to a poster of Pilgrim Cove whose caption read "A hull of a place to live."

"Cute," said Rachel, nodding her head. "But I think the best one is their slogan smack in the middle of the wall. "The Lobster Pot: Where no lobster is a shrimp!"

"It *is* good," agreed Jack with a smile as he accepted the menus from their server. "Thanks. We'll be just a minute."

He handed a menu to Rachel. "Whatever you want, and leave room for dessert."

Feeling totally at ease, Rachel could have chosen anything on the menu and have been happy. "Everything looks good."

Jack glanced at the waitress. "Any recommendations?"

"The salmon is wonderful today—fresh delivery this afternoon."

"Salmon for me," said Rachel.

"Make that two," said Jack. He reached for Rachel's hand. "And next week, we'll try something different." He paused. "Heck. Let's come back tomorrow night."

Next week? Tomorrow? Her heart rate elevated, and when she looked into his eyes, their normal light green color was streaked with golden hues. She pressed her fingers against his. "Let's enjoy tonight."

"I'll drink to that. Wine?" he asked Rachel, and she nodded.

The meal was delicious. And people stopped by to say hello. Mike and Kate Lyons. Chief O'Brien and Dee. People she'd known all her life.

"In a small town, it never ends, does it?" asked Jack. "It's so like my own hometown in Maine. Too small. Too insular. I loved it as a kid, but later…later, I had to get out."

She heard a strained note in his voice and wondered about it. It wasn't unusual for small town kids to want something bigger.

"Pilgrim Cove has easy access to Boston, so most people don't really feel hemmed in like in other places."

"How'd you make out in Kansas?" asked Jack. "No coastline, no ocean, no big city where you lived."

Suddenly, Rachel sat very still. Kansas. She'd hardly thought about Round Rock recently. "I liked it very much," she finally replied. "I guess I'm a small-town girl at heart. At least, when I'm in the right town."

Jack's hand clasped hers. "Pilgrim Cove can be the right town for you, too."

She shrugged. "Maybe, maybe not. Remains to be seen."

"Sometimes, Rachel, what we think we want the most isn't necessarily what we need," he offered in a soft tone.

She pushed back in her seat. "Whoa! Mr. Philosopher," she said, unlacing her fingers from his. "You worry about Jack Levine, and I'll worry about Rachel

Goodman." But now her hand was gently trapped under his larger one, and she glared at him.

"That wasn't a criticism. Just concern."

She blinked and relaxed again. He wasn't lying. The concern was etched on his face and reflected in his voice. Her fingers resumed their dance with his.

"I'll manage," she said.

"Starting now, you will. Look who's here." Jack rose and extended his hand to the newcomer. "Hi, Tom. Maggie has you working day and night, eh?"

Tom Sullivan shook Jack's hand, then smiled and greeted Rachel. "Glad to see you out and about. Enjoying your meal?"

She motioned to the table. "Clean-plate club. We all know Maggie and Thea are the best cooks in town."

The coach patted his middle. "Too much so, sometimes."

Rachel laughed. "The kids burn it off you, I'm sure. And by the way, that was a good game last night. You're heading into a winning season, Coach. Congratulations."

"You were there?"

"She's been at every game so far," inserted Jack. "Which is more than I can say for myself. I'm busy with two jobs. Working conflicts with working sometimes, if you know what I mean."

"Don't apologize," replied Tom. "I hold two jobs, also. Sometimes I think it's three—the classroom, the coaching and the restaurant. But that's the way it is, and I have no complaints." He waved and was gone.

"There goes a happy man," said Jack.

"For now," she added, then wished she'd held her tongue.

She felt Jack's eyes studying her. Saw him shake his head slowly. "No, Rachel. He's a happy man. Period."

"But..."

"Doesn't matter what happens on Tuesday with report cards. He'll deal with it." He motioned to the back of the restaurant. "There's his happiness. His wife and family. For Tom Sullivan, that's what it's really all about."

Rachel stared down the length of the room, then back at Jack. Her thoughts rearranged themselves. Tom had seemed genuinely friendly toward her. Of course, he'd known her her whole life. And was almost old enough to be her father, but still...he knew she could really make his job difficult.

She looked at Jack. Maybe he was right. "How did you suddenly get so smart? Maybe you're a philosopher after all!"

"I don't know about that, but I'm definitely not philosophically opposed to dessert. Pick the richest one on the menu."

She sighed. "Every one of them looks good, but I'm really too full."

"Easy fix," replied Jack with a grin. "We'll order two to go, and I'll make the coffee back at our house."

"*Our* house? Sounds funny, doesn't it?"

"No," he replied. "I don't think it sounds funny at all."

CHAPTER ELEVEN

EITHER THE PIRATE HAD changed or her impression of him had changed. Rachel glanced at their entwined hands as she and Jack moseyed along Pilgrim Beach, their desserts stored in her fridge. A slight breeze chilled the air, but the glowing harvest moon illuminated the sand and offered a sense of warmth. The twinkling stars and the steady rhythm of the ocean kept them company as they strolled.

She couldn't remember the last time she'd opted for such a slow gait. She'd certainly never seen Jack move at less than warp speed, either. Something had definitely changed.

"This has been…a perfect evening," said Jack, his voice deep and warm. Sincere.

Rachel glanced up. No smart-ass grin lurked, no punch line followed. The man wasn't joking. Her fingers began to tingle as they rested in Jack's hand. Was there more behind his words? And did she want to hear it?

"What a nice compliment," she replied. Her own voice sounded low and raspy, and impetuously, she squeezed his hand.

He paused in his step and turned to face her. When he looked down, his green eyes glowed…searching, and his fingers gently traced the line of her cheek, then her bottom lip. Back and forth. "So full, so enticing…"

She couldn't move—he stroked her top lip next—and the exquisite sensation on her mouth made her hunger for more.

"So pouty…" he whispered, leaning in for a taste.

"They are?" she murmured, raising her chin to better feel his touch.

And suddenly, she was wrapped in his arms, secure in his embrace, his kisses raining on her mouth, her neck and that sensitive place behind her ear. Her eyes closed and she shivered, tilting her head and reaching blindly up to return his kisses with her own.

Then she didn't have to try. He was there. His mouth captured hers, and she gave back the same sweetness that she received. Tender. Eager. Then burning. He excited her like no other man she'd known. Like a tempest ripping through her. She'd known this would happen, had known for weeks—maybe since the pirate had stood in the classroom doorway—that she'd lose herself with Jack if she'd ever give herself permission.

Her knees weakened. She clung to him. And for the first time in her memory, Rachel Goodman allowed herself to trust someone. With her life. With her happiness. Maybe with her soul.

When she opened her lids, she saw her answer. Warmth radiated from Jack's eyes, from his soft smile. She felt his tenderness when his hand gently cupped her cheek. And when his smile became a grin, she saw complete joy infuse him. Jack Levine loved her!

But that couldn't be right. Jack Levine was a sailor with a woman in every port. When he docked in Boston, he always returned late. A big social life would explain it. When he showed up anywhere with his come-hither grin, women surrounded him. Jack Levine couldn't love only one woman if she were the last woman in the world. Of that, Rachel had no doubt. So, she must have imagined the expression on his face.

She blinked hard and glanced at him again. There! His pirate smile was back in place, and she breathed a sigh of relief. She couldn't handle more complications now.

"Ready for that dessert?" asked Jack, taking her hand and leading her back toward Sea View House, his thumb stroking her palm.

She shivered. Then felt hot. Despite her reservations, the dessert she wanted was walking alongside her.

THEY'D SHARED THE BOSTON cream pie, then he'd kissed her hard on the mouth and said good-night. They'd followed the same routine on Sunday evening after their second visit to the Lobster Pot. And on Monday morning, Rachel's memories of the entire weekend revolved around Jack, food, kissing and walking on a moonlit beach. Not a bad way to spend a weekend.

Somehow, between working and daydreaming, the

morning slipped away. But by three o'clock, Rachel was entirely focused once again on her job.

She made her way to the athletic director's office. Out of courtesy, she'd give him a heads-up on the next day's events. Two key players would be removed from the football team. His office was empty, however, and Rachel walked to Dr. Bennett's office instead.

The principal looked up from his desk and smiled. "Leaving for the day?"

"Not yet," she replied, standing near the door. "Just wanted to touch base with you in case a couple of angry young men storm your office tomorrow afternoon or Wednesday."

"Our star football players?" he asked. "It won't be the first time nor the last that I've dealt with upset students. Parents, too, I might add."

She nodded.

Dr. Bennett sighed and shook his head. "Can you find out why these kids let their grades drop after passing all their subjects during the last two years. I thought football was so important to them, but maybe it's not. Maybe they're afraid to say they've had enough."

Rachel's breath caught as she stared as her old mentor. Did Dr. Bennett have no idea that the faculty might have been intimidated by the athletic director?

"I thought they loved the sport, too," she replied, as she left his office and headed for her own. She needed time to think!

She closed her door and began pacing. How could Dr. Bennett be so unaware?

A knock at the door interrupted her thoughts. She pulled it open and there stood Jack, all six foot three of him, granite solid and smiling at her. Then frowning.

"What's wrong?"

She pulled him inside and closed the door again. "It's going to be worse than I thought," she began as she resumed her pacing. "I don't even know if I should share this with you, but I've got to tell someone! It's because Dr. Bennett's got a heart of gold that he never suspected anything. He sees the best in everyone, and that's why he was so good at helping me. But this…this is different."

She looked at Jack expectantly. He was leaning against the door frame, shaking his head. "Rach, I don't know what you're talking about."

As she explained, his face clouded until she could almost hear the roll of thunder. "Rachel, are you afraid?" He stepped toward her, his arms opening.

She held up her hand to stop him. "Afraid? Of the kids? No. Of course not. It's just…I hadn't expected to uncover…uncover…*slime*…among the staff. And that's making me a little sick." It was the truth, and she pressed hard on her roiling stomach.

"Bob Franklin seems to have insinuated himself between Dr. Bennett and the staff. He must be telling the teachers that Dr. Bennett said to pass the kids in enough subjects so they can play. Bennett never knows how the kids are really doing in class. The teachers think they're following Dr. Bennett's directive. Franklin looks like he's running a great sports program. The Guidance Department is in the dark, too. That's how Franklin's gotten away with it. Those boys didn't suddenly lose interest in academics this year. They never had the grades in the first place."

When Jack approached her this time, she didn't stop him. And when he embraced her, she leaned against his broad chest, wishing she could just disappear into him. Wishing she could hide and be protected forever. Reality pierced her immediately, however, and she stepped back.

"It is pretty ugly," Jack said. "I'm sorry the boys didn't show up for tutoring. I guess they wanted to sleep in."

"Thanks for trying," replied Rachel.

He brushed away her thanks with a flick of his wrist. "What can I do to help you?"

She shook her head.

"How about if I sit here as an auditor when you tell the boys they're off the team," suggested Jack. "So you won't be alone."

Reaching for him, she squeezed his arm. "Thank you, but no. I can handle the boys." She peered up at him. "I think I just needed a friend."

His arms tightened around her. "Rachel. Honey. Anytime—day or night. Whatever you need, I am here for you." He kissed her. "Don't you know that yet?"

"I—I—I think I'm a slow learner sometimes."

His laughter was exactly the medicine she needed.

Amazingly, she heard her own voice join his, and felt her tension dissipate.

"Then aren't you lucky that I'm a patient man?" His eyes gleamed with warmth and humor before he looked at his watch.

"I've got a date with your dad at the library. Do you want me to postpone?"

"Not at all," she replied. "I'm leaving here in a few minutes myself."

"Pack up now and I'll walk you to your car."

"I need a little time. Go ahead. Your book project is waiting. Or is it the pollution project? Or the lobster project?" She shook her head. "I can't keep up with you and your research."

"Want to walk on the beach later?"

"Sure." She waved him off, then mumbled to herself. "I just wish he'd finish at least one of those projects…."

As she left the administrative suite, Bob Franklin walked in and she paused in her stride. "Do you have a second?" she asked.

"For you? I *live* for my chats with you." His dislike was evident in his tone and expression.

"I do not appreciate the sarcasm, Bob." She would not be intimidated by a bully. She held his gaze without blinking.

He stared at her in silence.

"Just an advance warning," she said, leading him back toward the privacy of her office before continuing. They stood in her doorway. "Jimmy Williams and Steve

Yelton are going to be cut tomorrow. You might want to talk with Tom Sullivan this evening about substitutions so when the team practices again you'll be ready with an alternative plan."

His cold blue eyes would have made her shiver if she'd allowed herself to. "You're really going through with this?"

"*I'm* not doing anything. The boys each flunked two of four major subjects. You should know the state's rules better than I do. They're spelled out in the MIAA Handbook," she said, referring to the Massachusetts Interscholastic Athletic Association rules. "The two boys are out for the next marking period. And they did it to themselves."

The man's coloring turned florid. "You just don't get it, do you? Well, you won't get away with it. Those rules are broken all the time, and we've got a reputation to uphold, championships to win and money to bring in. The boys did just fine until you showed up. No one on the school board or in this town will back you. And believe me, sister, I'm not keeping quiet."

She shrugged. The rules were clear in her mind. "Do what you want," she replied. "But not tonight. Report cards haven't been distributed yet. Good evening." She reached for her tote bag and left the building.

It wasn't until she sat behind the wheel of her car that she began to shake.

SHE WOULD HAVE BEEN ABLE to deal with the boys by themselves, but she hadn't counted on four angry parents and a group of students—members of the football team—waiting for her when she pulled into the school parking lot early the next morning. Seemed that Bob Franklin couldn't keep his mouth shut. Report cards were still in the office, but these parents had already received the news of their sons' change of status.

She got out of the car, and was surrounded. Harsh voices pelted her. Youths' and adults'. Dozens of questions and accusations swarmed in the air.

"We need Jimmy and Steve on the team. You don't understand!" That was Donnie Shroeder, the loyal linebacker.

She'd have to take charge or be devoured. She held one hand up like a cop, happy that her cell phone was in her purse if she needed to call for help.

"Stand back! Everybody. Now!"

The shouting stopped, and the group shuffled a step backward.

"Donnie Shroeder, Lincoln Smith, Mike Perrini," she said, pointing at each player as she spoke, "since school is not officially opened yet, you will remain outside until it is. Then you'll report to my office. Understood?"

The boys glanced at one another, then nodded.

"I didn't hear you," said Rachel pointedly.

"Yes, ma'am."

"Thank you." Positive reinforcement for manners, as meager as they were.

She turned toward the two families. "You're welcome to come inside, but I will meet with only one family at a time. If that's not acceptable, you can return later and explain to my boss why you refused my offer of privacy to discuss your concerns."

She waited a moment, and when neither family left, she said, "Okay, folks. Let's go in."

But the discussions were fruitless. The anger and disappointment of both parents and students created a wall that Rachel couldn't break through.

"Everybody knows teachers don't fail the players," said Mr. Yelton. "They give 'em a D, but not an F. Our kids never claimed to be Einsteins."

Nods of agreement by his wife and son.

"That behavior is totally against the code of ethics we live by in the world of interscholastic sports," said Rachel.

"Since when?" the man replied, his voice rising. "Since you changed the rules? Why don't you go somewhere else and make boys miserable? Playing means everything to my son." Steve's father rose, leaned across Rachel's desk and glared at her. "And you haven't heard the end of this yet, lady, not by a long shot. Steve'll be back on the team by the end of the week."

"I'm afraid not," said Rachel softly.

The man gestured to his wife and son, and all three stalked out of the room. Rachel leaned back in her chair and closed her eyes.

Just as she raised her lids, two men appeared in her doorway. Bob Franklin and Jack Levine. She ached for Jack's gentle touch, but made her expression blank as she looked at Bob.

"Having second thoughts?" he asked with an innocent smile.

"Not a one."

"It's not too late to change their grades, you know. We can avoid all the nastiness that's going to happen next." He turned toward Jack. "She's been complaining about you, too, pal. Your students aren't passing, either. But the truth is that this woman doesn't know how to do her job at all. Ever since she got here, the school's been a mess."

Rachel saw Jack's eyes blaze. Saw his arm flex as he turned toward the athletic director. Good God! Just what she didn't need. "Jack!" He looked at her, and she shook her head, hoping he'd get the message.

She focused her gaze on Bob Franklin. "I've got four words for you…no, no, better make it seven." She enunciated clearly: "Massachusetts Interscholastic Athletic Association—Code of Ethics." She stood and walked in front of her desk. "How many rules have you broken over the years, Bob?"

His jaw tightened. His expression turned ugly. "Don't think you can threaten me. I built these teams!" He turned and left.

"Close the …" She didn't have to complete the sentence. Jack had pulled her door shut and was wrapping his arms around her before she could organize her thoughts. So she didn't think. She just rested against him.

"I'm going to beat the sh…stuffing out of him," he said, continuing to hold her.

Her head snapped backward. "No, no," she said, with

rising panic. "Please. You can't do that. Don't even think about it."

"Okay, honey. Okay. Then he'll just have to walk the plank!"

JACK'S HUMOR KEPT RACHEL going for the rest of the day, especially during the time when doubts crept into her mind. Maybe she was causing too much trouble. If she hadn't taken this job, the Pilgrim Cove football team would be intact and perhaps go on to victory. Morale in the school would be high. The community would be happy with the strong football team. Now maybe her entire hometown would be sorry she'd returned. She had certainly not anticipated uncovering such a mess.

She purposely chatted with Mrs. Drummond during the teachers' lunch period to confirm the grades she'd given the two boys.

"No homework turned in, no tests passed. No passing grade," Mrs. Drummond said. "I thought sports were supposed to improve the boys' ambition to do well. That's what they tell us, anyway."

"Normally it does, Mrs. Drummond. I've had wonderful success in my other two high schools. But here—" she shook her head "—it's not the same." She wasn't going to go into any detail yet. No names. No accusations.

"You mean, 'Something's rotten in the state of Denmark?' Or should I say, Pilgrim Cove?"

Rachel didn't respond.

Mrs. Drummond patted her on the arm. "You're doing a good job, Rachel. An honest job. I'm proud of you."

Rachel couldn't speak. Just stared at her old nemesis.

"Don't look so surprised! You're Lou Goodman's daughter, aren't you? I've got eyes! You care about the students, just like he does. Or did." She sighed. "I miss him. I miss our book talks. Always enjoyed keeping up with Lou. A very smart man."

Rachel listened hard. So interesting to see her dad from the perspective of his peers. "Go visit him at the public library. He volunteers there a lot."

"I know. And I have. But it's not the same. Oh, well. Life goes on."

"Thanks, Mrs. Drummond," said Rachel. "Enjoy the rest of your lunch."

She returned to her office to find Tom Sullivan waiting for her. She liked the coach but didn't quite know what to expect from him.

"How can the boys get back on the team?" he asked without preamble.

"They can qualify for next year's team," she replied, "if we're only talking football. They can qualify for winter sports if they get their grades up next marking period, which ends at Thanksgiving—also the end of the football season. So, I'm afraid that football is over for them this year."

"Are there any ways around this? Anything we can do? A special exam, maybe?"

He was a problem solver. Not a blamer. "I like the

way you think, Tom," she said, arms behind her as she leaned casually against her desk.

A knock sounded at her open door. Her nephew, David, stood there for the very first time since she'd started her job. She glanced at Tom. "Word sure travels fast around here." Then she motioned David inside.

"Nobody's home," he said, "and I feel sick. Can you give me a ride?"

"Of course," she replied, walking to him and touching his forehead.

He pulled away. "I'm not a baby."

"Oh, right. Sorry." She returned her attention to Tom. "About our discussion—I'll review the MIAA handbook carefully over the next day or two—in fact, you should, too—and we'll talk again by the end of the week. In the meantime, they're benched."

"Fair enough," said the coach, walking to the door. "And thanks, Rachel."

"You're welcome."

Then she signed David out and drove him home. As he unbuckled his seat belt, he turned to her.

"Aunt Rachel, can't you let them play? Give 'em another test or something. They'll study this time and pass."

The boy was flushed, and Rachel wondered if his illness was a reaction to the situation with the boys.

"I wish it were that easy, David, but it's not. If they pass the next marking period, they can play winter sports, like basketball or ice hockey. I'm doing a little research on other options, but don't count on anything."

"Maybe Jack can think of something," replied David. "He always comes up with great ideas."

Rachel chuckled. "He's smart, but he doesn't have the power to change the MIAA rules. Sometimes, David, the best lessons are the hard lessons. Jimmy and Steve will buckle down to their schoolwork from now on. In the meantime, go inside and get some rest. I'll call you later."

She never got the chance. Her phone at Sea View House rang that evening, and when Rachel picked it up, she heard her brother's voice.

"What the hell is going on in that school, Rachel?"

She plopped into a kitchen chair, happy to take advantage of its support. Her brother's tone promised another confrontation. "What's going on is called standards, Alex, or following the rules. And how's David feeling?"

"Not well, thanks to you."

"What do you mean, thanks to me?"

"The kids are on his back because you're his aunt. They think he can make you reinstate those boys. And they're leaning on him."

Now Rachel sat up straight. "Define 'leaning.' Has he been threatened?" she asked, her muscles tensing in every limb. "Alex, I'll file charges with the Pilgrim Cove police if this is true. No student will get away with threats."

"No. No. Not threats exactly, but they're making him uncomfortable. Harassing him in the halls. In the lunchroom. In class. Why are you being so hard-nosed?"

And why did nothing ever change between her

brother and her? "I didn't write the rules, Alex. Those boys each failed two out of four major courses. Therefore they cannot play."

"So, bench them for a week or something. Lousy academics is more reason for them to play and make their mark for an athletic scholarship. You used athletics to go to college. Why shouldn't they?"

Why did Alex continually harp on her history? "These boys don't just have lousy grades, they're failing! My grades may have been poor, but I did manage to pass my courses. And you always seem to forget that I scored high on my boards."

"Well, good for you," he replied sarcastically. "David won't."

Her heart sank. Her brother's call was really about his own son. He was a worried parent. "Alex, I promise you that David will find his way. He has a good mind. A creative mind. Give him the space to develop his abilities without breathing down his neck."

"After you become a parent, you can give me advice. Not before. Damn it, Rachel! I was hoping things would be different this time, but you're still a spoiled brat. Always wanting your own way and still getting it. Like when we were kids. I was the one who had to work after school when I wasn't baby-sitting you. I was the one who had to get straight A's. I had to buy my own glove and cleats and pay my own admission to a movie. And I was only fourteen. So don't ever, ever say that I was their favorite child. That's crap."

The phone clicked in her ear. She couldn't move. Didn't have the strength. The receiver fell from her hand, bounced on the table and landed on the floor. The house was silent except for the sound of her own breathing. Her dreams for a better relationship with her brother were gone.

So why was she reaching for the receiver and dialing his number? She heard it ring. Heard Susan say hello.

"Your husband's an idiot, Sue. But would you please put him on the phone?"

"Gladly. I'm happy that these leftover resentments are finally being aired. I like peace in my family."

Silence.

Then her brother's voice. "What?" he barked.

"Take your sky-high IQ and use it, Alex. There are ten years between us. Our parents were ten years longer into their marriage when I came along. When Mom went back to work and you baby-sat, there was finally a second income. More money in the family.

"What do you want from me, Alex? I was eight years old when you went to college. Tell me, how did I ruin your life?"

Silence again.

"It seems to me," said Rachel in a quiet tone, "that you have it all. You're happily married, have two great kids, a job you love...so I ask again, how did I ruin your life?"

This time he replied. "My brain says you're right...I guess it's my emotions that are fouled up. I can't believe how hard it is to get rid of those memories. They must be embedded or something."

"You've got two great kids, but they're different from each other, just like we were. If you don't let them flower in their own way, Alex, they'll end up like us! Is that what you really want?"

"No, no. I don't. I'd like them to be friends."

"And what do you think our parents want of us?" she asked softly. "What do you think I want, Alex? That was part of the reason I took this job."

"Truly?"

"Believe it."

"Okay, Rachel. I do believe it. We may have our faults, but the Goodmans don't lie."

"That's right. We do other things that come back to bite us!" She tried to lighten the mood to match her heart. Her brother believed her, and that was a step in the right direction.

"I do love you, Rachel. But I need time to get to know you as an equal. I need to get over the past so I can embrace the present."

"Oh, Alex. Thank you. I can't ask for more."

She replaced the receiver, and went in search of a tissue. The Goodman family was going to be fine. Her relationship with her dad was strong; the one with her brother would be the same.

She glanced at her ceiling, toward the Crow's Nest. Jack was away that evening, dredging up more water samples and taking them into Boston. She was on her own.

Outside, darkness had fallen, and Rachel noted the days getting shorter as autumn headed toward winter.

The air inside wasn't cold, but she shivered. For the first time since renting Sea View House, she felt isolated. Vulnerable. She made a point of locking the windows and setting the alarm system.

She changed into a sweat suit, donned thick socks and meandered into the comfortable living room, her reading material in hand. The MIAA manual. All the rules governing interscholastic sports. She stretched out on the chintz covered couch and opened the book, but her mind wandered back to the school and to the personalities of those involved. Too bad people were so much more complicated than rule books. And then she thought about herself. Was she not also guilty of seeing the world through her own filter? Trying to foist her ideas on others? But wasn't that why she'd been hired in the first place?

She'd probably fail here. In her own hometown. She ached at bringing such disappointment to her parents when they'd had such high hopes at the start. She sighed deeply. But the playing field hadn't been level, and she'd stumbled into something that was bigger than she was.

Had any athlete ever failed a course in the years since Bob Franklin had taken over as director? Or was he too clever for that? Maybe he gave the okay for the less important contributors to flunk to avoid suspicion.

And maybe she was simply writing a script for a bad movie! Maybe she was blowing everything out of proportion. How would she ever find out? She knew that grades were saved in the computer system, but the task of assessing each athlete's value to a school team for the last several years would be almost impossible, especially since she didn't know the youngsters herself.

Her dad had always preached that knowledge was power. She looked at the book in her hand. If she were going to go down, she'd do it fighting. She began to read.

CHAPTER TWELVE

"WHAT SHALL I TELL the BOYS today?" Tom Sullivan hovered in Rachel's doorway the next afternoon.

Rachel managed to dredge up a tiny smile. "I need more time to evaluate what I read last night. I need to figure out if it's worth turning the school upside down."

The coach's eyes narrowed. "I reread the handbook, cover to cover, too. Maybe we can come up with something. Two heads are better than one."

Her smile became easier. "I know." She checked her calendar. "Tomorrow, lunchtime. Let's talk here in my office. In the meantime, the boys don't play."

"Okay." He waved and left. Rachel rested her head in her hands.

What a day! Nonstop phone calls, visitors. Jack had stopped by every five minutes—at least, it seemed that way. If he were an M.D. instead of a Ph.D., he'd have checked her heart rate every time. She knew she looked awful because the mirror didn't lie. She could probably pack the bags under her eyes. She was running on little sleep, a lot of caffeine, a whole lot of nervous energy.

And now Dr. Bennett stood in her doorway, a deep crease in his forehead, yellow legal pad in his hand.

"Got a minute?"

She nodded. "Of course."

He closed the door and held out the pad. "I've been on the phone with practically every member of the school board. They've been getting calls from parents who want to know what's going on regarding the football team. And I mean lots of calls."

Her heart sank. He was going to fire her right now, after less than two months. How unique was that? "I guess I'm not surprised. At least, not too surprised."

Dr. Bennett sat down before he replied, before he held her undivided attention with only his glance. "Rachel, you're going to have to fill me in on every detail. On your conversations with everyone involved. Teachers, parents, staff and students. I need to know how to respond to these calls."

Had she heard him correctly? "You mean, I still have a job?"

He chuckled, but not happily. "My dear, there's always the possibility that *I'm* the one who won't. In the end, the operations of the entire school fall on me. Including any scandal. I'd hate to retire early under a cloud."

"What?" Rachel jumped from her seat. "Dr. Bennett, you're the best thing that ever happened to our students. You've got the biggest heart, you understand adolescents better than anyone in this building...the kids line up to talk to you. They stop you in the halls. I've never seen a principal like you. The board can't fire you!"

She shouldn't have drunk so much coffee. Too restless to sit down again, she walked behind her chair. "I'll think of something. Don't worry. You're worth too much to this school. Who cares about Bob Franklin, anyway?"

But he was shaking his head and smiling. A genuine smile. "My goodness, Rachel. Thank you. Your loyalty makes me proud. I knew I was right to hire you."

"Thank *you,* sir," she replied, sounding like a ten-year-old.

His laughter made her feel a little better, and an hour later she felt a whole lot better after their discussion. Not that the facts had changed, but sharing them relieved some of her stress. He agreed to join her and Tom at lunch the next day. Together, they would try to determine if there was a way of legally reinstating the two boys on the team. Rachel wanted to be prepared with a plan or two before the meeting. When Dr. Bennett left her office, she turned to the pages she'd marked in the handbook the night before and began writing.

She noted when the building emptied out. Somehow the quiet pervaded even the inner sanctum of the administrative wing.

Jack came by and tried to talk her into working at home. He left calling her a "stubborn woman" to her face and who knows what under his breath. She'd promised him a walk on the beach at whatever time she got to Sea View House.

"Go, go home," she'd said, shooing him away.

He just stared, his eyes dark with frustration. "Damn it, Rachel! You'd make a saint angry! Why do I even care?" That's when he left, mumbling too low for her to hear the rest.

But his words nagged at the back of her mind. She'd try to explain later that she had to see her projects through to the end. She couldn't relax until her commitments were met.

It was eight o'clock by the time she was satisfied with her preparations for the next day's meeting. She glanced out her window. Darkness had descended. No moonlight brightened the night sky that evening. Rachel locked her office, set the alarm and left the building by the side entrance. She pushed the door hard until it locked behind her. Then she walked to the front parking area where her vehicle rested in its assigned spot.

And her world spun out of control again.

Flat tires. The two facing her were flat and the car was level. So all four had been slashed. A paper was on the windshield. With bold black letters. But she couldn't read it from where she stood. Her heart began to pound.

Someone had sent an ugly message. Were the boys behind it?

The parents? Their friends? She backed up against the building, trying to hide herself in deep shadow. Should she try to return inside the building? Would she be safe running to the car?

She opened her purse and reached for her cell with

sweaty hands. The phone slipped and crashed to the concrete. She groaned and fell to her knees, her eyes still scanning the parking area. She stretched her arm blindly in front of her. "Got it!" she whispered.

Without any delay, she raced for her car, grabbed the note, used her remote opener and…froze. Couldn't move. The back window of the Explorer was shattered. Fragments everywhere inside and out. It took a moment to breathe. With shaking hands, she pushed the phone's on button. The face lit up. She felt tears run down her cheeks as she punched Jack's number and climbed into the front seat.

HE COULDN'T MAKE OUT HER words at first. All he recognized was her voice. In the end, he got to the school in under two minutes.

As soon as he pulled up next to her, she jumped from her vehicle. He went to her, held her tightly and guided her to his truck, then kept her on his lap in the front passenger seat. He felt her shivering, all the way down to her feet. He had no blankets, so he wrapped her more snugly in his arms.

"It's all right now, sweetheart. Shh… Shh…" He made soft noises, but his muscles tensed, ready for action. Problem was, he didn't know who to blame. And his first concern was Rachel.

Finally, she just lay against his chest, her breathing back to normal. He kissed her hair, her temple. She didn't seem to want to budge. And that was fine with him. "You're safe, Rachel. We'll get to the bottom of this."

"Look, Jack," she said, handing him the crumpled note. "It says, 'Let Them Play.'"

"Looks like we have motive," he replied. "We can start by calling the police."

Incredibly, she shook her head. "No. No police. Call Charlie Cavelli at the garage. But don't talk to his dad. Joe would call my dad right away, and we don't want that."

He'd go along with her request for the moment, let her ramble as he reached for his wallet where he'd placed the special ROMEOs' business card. Printed clearly was the number to Cavelli's auto-body shop as well as the numbers of every other ROMEO family business or home.

Jack punched in the number and reached Charlie just as the businessman was closing for the day. "Just wait till my brother-in-law hears about this. He'll want those kids off his team now for sure."

Jack remembered that Charlie Cavelli and Tom Sullivan had both married Bart's daughters. So now the families were related.

"Rachel says not to tell your dad about this—it's the ROMEO thing."

"Nothing stays a secret around here," replied Charlie. The phone went dead.

"He'll be by in five minutes," said Jack, kissing Rachel's temple again. He loved having her in his arms. He loved feeling her weight against him. "Maybe six."

"Good," she said, snuggling into him again.

"Now, I'm calling the police," said Jack.

"No!" Rachel sat up so quickly, she knocked the rearview mirror askew with the back of her head. "Give me the phone."

He held it out of her grasp. "First, tell me why."

"Because if the police get involved," she said without hesitation, "the kids could wind up with a juvenile record. I don't want that to happen."

"Why not? They deserve it. Look how frightened you were. Look at the damage to your vehicle."

"I know. I know. But they're young and angry," she replied, calmer now—in fact, she was trying to soothe him. "They didn't understand the effects. They didn't think in terms of consequences."

"And I can't think of a better way to learn! It's a lesson they'll never forget."

But Rachel was still shaking her head. "No. We'll solve this in-house. Having a record is too high a price to pay for a prank."

"A prank? Woman! They destroyed your property! Your heart's too soft underneath your business suit. You were shaking like a leaf when I got here. Hiding in your car. This action is beyond a prank. Rachel...Rachel..." He kissed her on the lips, those luscious lips that had quivered with fear earlier. "If anything worse had happened..." He couldn't finish the thought, so he tightened his embrace and felt her body lean into him. God, he loved her so much.

He what? He stopped breathing. His thoughts spun like a rowboat twirling in the rapids.

"Tell you what…" said Rachel, her voice trailing off.

He barely heard her.

"Tomorrow, I'll call Rick O'Brien. He'll nose around and keep his eyes open. We'll find out what happened. He's the only ROMEO who knows how to hold his tongue."

It took a moment for her words to register. Then he nodded. "That's great." What he didn't say was that they might still have to go to the active police force. One thing was for sure. He wasn't going to sit still while Rachel might possibly be in danger.

AT THREE-THIRTY THE NEXT afternoon, Rachel felt light enough to dance on the ceiling. She and her cohorts had devised a plan at lunchtime, and the plan had worked better than she could have imagined.

Now she sat at a round conference table in the principal's office with Dr. Bennett, Tom Sullivan and Bob Franklin.

"Thank you, gentlemen." She nodded at her boss and the coach. Then she held Franklin's gaze. "They had a choice, and they made it. As far as I'm concerned, the question of Steve Yelton and Jimmy Williams on this year's football team has been resolved. They're off the team until next year. And their participation then will depend on them getting their grades up."

"That was hardly a choice you gave them," said the

athletic director, his foot tapping the floor. "What kid would agree to have the whole school retested so he could get back on a team? Every student in the school would hate him. So now we've got a team with a lousy quarterback."

"But those are the rules, Bob," said Dr. Bennett. "And you know that as well as we do. 'No special privileges—are to be granted to athletes.'"

Rachel reclined against the back of her chair. Her hands rested on the arms.

"You don't get it, do you, Bob? Don't you see what happened here? Sure, they had a difficult choice, but maybe you've got a former quarterback who grew up today. What you forget is that these boys are high school students who happen to play football. They're not football players who happen to go to high school!"

"Yeah, yeah, yeah. Maybe you're more concerned that they have time for an after-school job to pay for your tires."

She heard a gasp from Tom, but she kept her gaze on Franklin. "Do you actually condone what they did?" she asked quietly. But then she quickly raised her hand in a stop motion. "On second thought, don't answer that. I'm not pressing charges—they and their parents should be grateful."

Tom stood up. "I'm very satisfied with this outcome, and very happy that the situation didn't drag on. Rick O'Brien is still the police chief to a lot of people in town. His involvement made an impression. If we're done here, I'm on my way." He turned to his immediate supervisor. "We still have a team, Bob, and they'll do their best. That's all any coach can ask for." He waved and left.

Rachel rose, stepped to Dr. Bennett and shook his hand. "As far as I'm concerned, this situation is resolved."

Her mentor nodded. "A very satisfactory ending. I'm more than sorry about your car and your experience last night. Go home and have a good weekend."

"Thanks." She walked toward the door and heard Dr. Bennett say, "But it's not over for you, Bob. Or for me."

She slipped out of the room. Her part was finished, and the relief was exhilarating. Then she spotted David and grinned. If the kid hadn't burst into her office searching for the boys who'd scared his aunt, she might never have found out who the culprits were.

"How's my hero?" she asked, opening her arms and giving her nephew a quick hug. "What timing! How'd you find out about what happened last night?"

"Are you kidding? The whole school knows!"

"Not from me," said a deep voice in response to David's comment. "Can I be your hero, too?"

She looked up into Jack's laughing face, and then didn't want to laugh. A layer of truth shaded his question. She saw the need in his eyes.

He seemed to recall where he was, turned to David and winked. "What's your secret, mate? Did you vanquish her enemies? Tie them to the mast?"

"No," Rachel replied for him. "Just came into my office determined to deal with the criminals who'd vandalized his aunt's vehicle and scared her to death. He came in roaring, threatening to beat their lights out." She paused for effect as they reached the front door of the school. "Of course, Yelton and Williams were with Dr. Bennett next door, so no actual bloodshed occurred."

"Just pure luck. Right, David?" said Jack. "One more question that has me wondering. How did the news about the flat tires spread all over the school?"

"Simple," David replied. "Those idiots told a few of their friends. And that's all it took." The boy's expression reflected such disgust that Rachel and Jack burst out laughing.

"How about dinner tonight at the Lobster Pot for my two best guys? My treat," said Rachel.

"Great! But can we go early?" asked David. "Not just because I'm starving already, but I'm meeting the guys at eight."

"Works for me," said Jack. "I've got a date with some books tonight. Some your grandpa pulled for me."

"And I'm doing nothing tonight!" said Rachel. "So going early is fine with me! Sometimes doing nothing is the best activity of all."

RACHEL LEANED OVER HER bedroom mirror and placed a pair of silver hoop earrings in her ears. Her dark eyes shone, and a definite smile reflected back at her. She felt good! She looked pretty good, too.

A loud knocking on the back door interrupted her

musing. She strode to the kitchen. "It's open," she called.

Jack filled the doorway, his whistle of admiration making her blush. Rachel stood still, but he sauntered toward her, his intention obvious. "So beautiful," he whispered before he bent his head and tasted her lips.

She ignited like paper to a flame. She felt his touch from her head to her feet.

"Mmm," she murmured when her mouth was free again. "Nice."

"We can skip dinner…." His voice trailed off as he studied her. "No. Forget I said that."

For a second, her feelings were hurt. Did he not want to explore their relationship? Take it to the next step? But when she studied his expression, she understood. Playtime was over. No flirting. No teasing.

He was waiting for her signal.

She looked away. "My nephew called," she said, switching the subject. "A slight change in plans. My brother's whole family is joining us."

"Your plastic will be getting a real workout," he replied lightly, as though their prior conversation had never happened.

She shook her head and reached for her purse. "That's the funny thing. Alex is picking up the tab."

"Seems like a peace offering to me."

Fifteen minutes later, Rachel hugged her niece and greeted her brother and sister-in-law in the entrance of the Lobster Pot.

"We need a table for eight," said Alex to the hostess.

"No problem." The woman made a mark on her chart. "Follow me."

Alex turned to Rachel as they walked. "The folks are coming, too."

"Figures." Rachel chuckled and looked up at Jack. "They always want to be in on the action. Which reminds me..."

But the hostess seated them at a large round table just then, and Rachel had to wait a moment. Now she glanced at David, who sat on one side of her. "Do they know about..."

"Sure do," replied Alex before David could answer. He glanced at both David and Jack. "I'm glad neither of you wound up using your fists."

"I woulda," said David. "In a second. They went too far. Aunt Rachel's working hard at the school. Not that I really understand what she's doing. But if she hired Jack, then she did a great thing."

"Well, thanks, David," said Jack. "It's good to hear."

"I can't take credit or blame," said Rachel, wondering if she'd have to repeat that fact forever. "I inherited him."

Her nephew patted her arm and grinned. "Then you should keep him. He's great. Give him a raise!" The boy pointed down the aisle. "Here's Grandma and Gramps. I bet they think the same thing."

Alex and Susan were both beaming at Jack, whose face was getting ruddy.

"Oh, my," said Pearl, taking her seat. "What are we all talking about?"

"Doesn't matter," said Jack. "David is going to change the topic right now. Isn't he?" His expressive eyes reinforced the message.

"Okay," said David, looking around the table as though a topic was floating in the air. But he was smiling.

It occurred to Rachel that for once, her nephew was enjoying the attention from the family rather than hating it. She was curious to hear what he'd say.

"Let's talk about the Earth."

Next to her, Rachel heard Jack moan under his breath, saw his eyes close. She paid closer attention to David.

"See this lemon?" the boy said, reaching toward a bowl of citrus fruit in the center of the table. "That's the core. In the real planet Earth, the core has two parts. The inner part is very hot and heavy, probably composed of solid iron and nickel. The outer core is molten metal." He turned to his younger sister. "That means melted."

"I know what *molten* means. Birds moult when they lose their feathers."

"That's not the same thing at all! Birds don't melt." He reached for an orange and cut it in half, then scooped out the fruit. A messy process. He covered the lemon with the orange shell. "That's the middle layer, the mantle. Volcanoes start out near the upper part of the mantle. They *spew* their magma through fissures left by earthquakes. The magma is called lava when it hits the surface."

Rachel watched, listened and was fascinated as David took a grapefruit, representing the earth's crust, cut it in half, carefully nudged the fruit away from the skin, and covered the lemon and orange shells with the grapefruit rind.

"This is just a kitchen model," said David, pointing at his creation. "It's like a starter kit." He went on to discuss how the shock waves of earthquakes can be simulated in a laboratory with a model. "They don't use fruit rinds," he said with a grin. "They use aluminum and other materials. But the Earth is a pretty cool subject."

Rachel studied her family. Her brother looked shocked, actually had tears in his eyes; Susan's mouth was agape. Jennifer appeared confused. Rachel's parents were beaming. Jack's face revealed nothing, but his eyes scanned the table faster than hers did, then scanned the room. He looked like a man trying to make an escape.

"Jack!" Alex's voice called from across the table. Next to her, Jack shifted in his seat as he looked at the man. "Thank you."

Jack dismissed the gratitude with a wave of his hand. "It's my job."

"Dad," said David. "Jack's is the best class I ever had. And we never get any tests!"

"Thanks, Dave," said Jack with a crooked smile. "Looks like your aunt is ready to faint."

She didn't faint, but the chowder stuck in her throat when she heard David's words. If Jack didn't give the kids class tests, they'd never pass the larger department tests, and certainly not the statewide tests at the end of the year.

She glanced up at him, but his focus was on David again. He was smiling and teasing the boy. David sat taller, eyes sparkling, and Rachel hesitated to spoil the mood. But, as if he could sense her attention, Jack leaned toward her, then said under his breath, "Okay, Rachel. I'll throw in some tests. If you think the kids need it, I'll do it."

Relief filled her. She reached for his hand and squeezed it. "Thank you."

CHAPTER THIRTEEN

LATER THAT EVENING, Rachel wandered through the Captain's Quarters, too restless to read or watch television. Jack had gone upstairs to work on his book. He was quite mysterious about it. Even after all these weeks, she didn't know any details. She pushed it out of her mind. If he didn't want to talk about what he was writing, so be it. She had more than enough on her mind.

She looked out the kitchen window and considered a walk on the beach, but the sky was clouded and moonlight was scarce. Not that she was afraid. After strolling on a moonlit beach with Jack, however, the solid darkness was just not inviting. Then she thought of the widow's walk on the roof. She felt herself grin. It was the perfect time to explore!

She unlocked her front door and used her key to open the entrance next to hers. She found the light switch easily enough, and saw she was in a narrow hall with an open staircase. She began to climb. On the second floor, she realized that Jack's apartment, while also on this level, was not accessible from the hallway. Twenty-five years ago, before remodeling, this level of the house had contained bedrooms and a bath. Now it was simply a way station to the third floor. She took the last flight two steps at a time.

A shuttered window almost covered the entire back wall—the side of the house facing the ocean. After manipulating the hooks, she opened the shutters to reveal huge picture windows. Had the sun been shining, she knew she'd enjoy the pleasure of a spectacular seascape—the same vista as she'd get from the roof. Now, however, the dark night blended the sky and ocean, making the horizon invisible.

Sitting on a two-foot-high platform in front of the window was a strange-looking light fixture. It looked like a beehive chandelier with tiers of glass prisms. A curved mirror lined the back of the apparatus.

Interesting, but she was clueless. Her real goal was the short flight to the roof. Just as she approached it, she heard a knocking at the wall. "Rachel? Is that you?" Jack's muffled voice floated to her.

"Yes," she called. "I'm exploring. Come up through the front."

He joined her a minute later. "What are you do— Oh, wow! Just look at this!" He fixated on the beehive, and his eyes glowed. He walked around it, examining it from every angle. Rachel was content to watch him discover whatever it was that made him so excited.

"This may be an original Fresnel," he said, circling once again. "The Smithsonian's got one, and so does the National Museum, but there were plenty of others along

America's coastline." He looked at Rachel as though she had the answer. "Do you think it is too small to be an original?"

Rachel leaned against the wall, forcing herself not to laugh out loud. "I have no clue what it is or what you're talking about. But it's good to see you so happy."

Then he kissed her. Quick and hard. "This, my dear, is a Fresnel lens. Or a copy of one. This baby is what prevented shipwrecks all along the American coastline, at least after Congress decided to cough up the money to install them in our lighthouses."

Rachel studied the lens. "But where's the light source? You can't light a fire indoors to reflect in the prisms."

"Not fires, Rach. A lamp inside the lens. Or a floodlight." He searched the walls. "Aha! Look." He pointed to a large switch. He moved toward it and flipped it. "Bingo!" he exclaimed, just before the light inside the lens dimmed away to nothing.

His disappointed expression was so comical, Rachel couldn't contain her chuckles this time. "You look like a kid with no birthday presents."

"Oh?" His eyes darkened as he stepped toward her. "I'm not worried about birthday presents," he whispered as he cradled her. "I've got a perfect package right here."

She leaned into him and simply rested her head against his shoulder. No arguments. No complaints.

"Rachel," he said, loosening his hold. "I really want

to test another bulb in the lens. Be right back." He headed down the stairs.

Rachel eyed the short flight to the roof. She climbed and pushed the safety bar up and over, then used her key to unlock this door, too.

She stepped outside and felt she was on top of the world. An elaborate wrought-iron railing surrounded the square platform on which she stood. The wind chilled her, but it also encouraged the clouds to play hide-and-seek with the moon. Some light filtered through and was reflected on the water.

Footsteps vibrated beneath her, then on the steps as Jack reappeared. She held out her hand and he took it, wrapped her in his arms. "It must have been awful for the women who stood here waiting for their men to come home from the sea," she said, leaning against him.

She felt his arms tighten. "Storms at sea are terrifying." He spoke with certainty, as if he'd experienced it firsthand.

"In those days there was no sonar, no navigational systems," she said. "It was really dangerous." She twisted around to look at him. "But you have all the latest gear on your boat, don't you, Jack?"

He kissed her. "I sure do. Not to worry."

"Good."

"A standard bulb works in the lens," he said, "so the electricity's flowing, but I'm going to replace the old floodlight." He led her back inside. "I'll check with Bart, but it seems to me that this lamp was here for a reason. I can't imagine any other house having one."

"I'm sure they don't," said Rachel. "And it's no mystery now that I know what that lamp is. It's the basis of the Sea View House story, or I should say the William Adams family story. The great-great-grandchild of the original William Adams, who founded this town, was caught offshore in a small fishing boat during a thunderstorm."

"When was this?" asked Jack.

"About 1790, I believe. Anyway, the sky was dark and neither he nor his companions could see the direction of land. Lightning flashed high up but didn't illuminate the ground. Finally, a lightning bolt struck a huge oak, which burned steadily, leading young William and his friends to shore. Right here."

"A nice story," said Jack.

"Young William decided to build a house on the same spot and to keep a lamp burning in the topmost window—a beacon to any sailor who might need it. He called his home Sea View House. Said it was a lucky house. And that's how its been known ever since."

"Of course," said Jack, closing the door to the roof, "he didn't have a Fresnel lamp to reflect light. Not back then."

"He probably used oil lamps. A lot of oil lamps to create enough light. Obviously, his progeny improved the system."

"It sounds like the Adamses liked to plant themselves in one place," said Jack.

"I guess they did," agreed Rachel, closing the shutters over the large window. "In fact, until about twenty-five years ago, the latest William Adams lived in this house. Then he decided to remodel the house and set up a trust. Bart Quinn and a board of directors have been seeing to it ever since."

"Nice story," said Jack again as they descended the steps. "Bart never gave me the details."

Once on the street level, they locked the door behind them and stood on the front porch. "Cup of tea?" she asked, indicating her apartment.

He covered a yawn. "Sorry. I'd like nothing better, but I'm off early in the morning."

She paused by her front door before going inside. "Jack?"

"Hmm…?"

"You're working more than full-time. You're tired."

A sleepy smile crossed his face. "Is that concern I hear? No need to worry. I'll catch some Z's tonight and I'll be fine," he replied. "I work hard and I play hard. It's the way I am."

"Well, don't fall asleep at the wheel."

"Hasn't happened yet!"

He started walking down the porch steps, his movements still graceful despite his fatigue. "Good night."

"Wait a minute." He turned and looked at her again. "I want to thank you for what you've done for David. It wasn't just your job, like you said. It was—is—a big deal to us. To my family. But most of all, to David. So, thanks. Many thanks."

He didn't reply. Just retraced his steps until he was

abreast of her. "I'd work with him a million times over to see that starry look in your eyes."

"Wha..."

"The one that's there right now." His words were softer than summer clouds, his lips just as gentle when they brushed against hers. "So sweet, so sweet," he murmured.

Lulled by his soft voice, she swayed against him. His arms wrapped around her, holding her tight. She sighed, pressed closer, and had no desire to move away. Being in Jack's embrace felt right. Absolutely right.

HE WOULD DO ANYTHING for her, anything except force-feed information to his students. On the Friday before Thanksgiving, Jack sat at his desk in the science lab staring at the results of the midterm exams his classes had taken the week before. Not a pretty picture. But worse was the image of Rachel's disappointment when he told her. He closed his eyes and a laughing Rachel appeared behind his lids. Sparkling. Eager. Determined. She wouldn't be laughing today.

Well, it couldn't be helped. He opened his eyes again and glanced around the room. Rock samples. Fossils. Models. He'd brought them in and used them as jumping-off points for lessons. He could spend a year with his earth-science class just teaching the fossil record of the Grand Canyon!

There was so much for the kids to learn, and he believed they were learning every single day. No, not *believed,* he *knew* they were. So what if they couldn't absorb all the material he presented? That was okay for now. More important, they asked questions. Lots of questions. In general, they were good kids with curious minds. And his attendance rate still held at a record high. He treated these students no differently than he did his college students. He just didn't understand these test scores.

He glanced at his watch, gathered his bad news and went downstairs to Rachel's office. At three o'clock, she'd still be there, then he'd go directly to the marina.

He caught her studying some work on her desk. She didn't glance up at his approach, and he enjoyed the moment simply looking at her. Such a delicate profile, each feature so perfect. She was so pretty, so smart...so, so exciting! They'd had such wonderful evenings together over the last few weeks. He'd been careful, however, not to push too hard no matter that the effort was killing him. He'd never taken so many cold showers before in his life. But Rachel was different from any other woman he'd known. Special. Special to him.

Content to keep looking at her, he didn't say a word. His heart filled now, and his breath caught in his throat. Electric charges seemed to run up and down his body. The longer he stared at Rachel, the stronger the sizzle. They warmed his whole body...these...these feelings. Feelings for Rachel. God, he must love this woman! That's what this craziness must mean.

He raised his head toward her office window. A pale sunlight was fading fast, but it seemed wondrously bright to him. He was in love with Rachel Goodman and could barely believe it.

"Hi, Jack. Have you been waiting there a long time?"

His gaze rested on her. *All my life, sweetheart. All my life.* He didn't say the words aloud.

She tilted her head, her expression curious. "Come on in," she said, stacking her work to the side of the desk and smiling up at him. "What's on your mind?"

He wasn't sure she'd really want to know what he'd been thinking, although her eyes had lit up when she'd seen him in the doorway. But…he couldn't tell her, not in a principal's office, for God's sake. He walked to her desk and held out the test results. "Not what you wanted, I'm afraid." He watched as she absorbed the grades, unhappy because he'd made her unhappy.

"Oh, Jack…" She looked up at him, distress all over her face. "I thought you were giving them practice tests—"

"One," he said, holding up his index finger. "There just never seemed to be enough time for more. So much else to do with them."

But Rachel was shaking her head. "No, Jack, no. You *chose* to use the time the way you wanted to. We've talked about this before. Your classes are not part of an Outward Bound program with exercises on the beach. The goal here is to learn, not to have a good time, or wonder about possibilities yet to come in the world when they don't even understand the world as it is."

She rose from her seat and leaned over her desk toward him. Her brown eyes shone black with emotion. "Your classes are about science! About the basic curriculum that was given to you."

"I'm sorry, Rachel." He took a deep breath. "My ways don't seem to work here for what you want to achieve," he began. "And I don't want to cause problems for the kids, for the school or for you. Definitely not for you." He longed to stroke her forehead, to erase the furrow that lined it. Instead, he continued to speak as calmly as possible. "Maybe you should find someone else for the job."

Her eyes widened, her skin paled, her mouth opened and closed, but no words came out. Jack got nervous. "I'll stay as long as it takes you to find a replacement. Don't worry, Rachel. I won't leave you in the lurch."

Suddenly, she caught fire. She banged the desk with her fists. Her eyes burned, her complexion turned a deep pink, and she whirled from behind the furniture until she stood nose to nose with him.

"You'll quit, Jack? Just walk out? Because it's hard? Because you can't have your own way?"

"Hard?" he replied. "This stuff is kindergarten for me."

"Sell it to someone who'll buy, Jack. What I see is a brilliant scientist without a real career because he jumps from one job to another every year." Her index finger poked him in the chest as her words poured forth. "You've got a doctorate, but you're not tenured at a university. You say you're writing books, but have you finished one? You're a quitter, Jack, even in your private life. No ties to a community, no real home." She whirled away from him and crossed the room.

His ears pounded as her words penetrated. Is that what she really thought of him? Had he misjudged her after all this time together? And she wasn't done.

"At twenty-five," she said, as she faced him once more, "a person has potential. At thirty-five, no one's going to care." She paused a moment, then said, "What happened to you along the way, Jack?" Her voice was husky now, and he saw her swallow hard. And he saw her eyes widen as if she was as surprised by her outburst as he. Maybe she was. But her spontaneous eruption could only mean she spoke the truth hidden in her heart.

Jack hadn't thought hearts could really break—just romantic nonsense in books—but something was piercing his thirty-five-year-old chest on the left side. Something was causing him to blink rapidly. Something was making it hard for him to breathe.

He needed air. Taking a last look at her outrage, he turned and left the room without a word.

WHAT HAD SHE DONE? Why had she said those horrible things? Rachel stood on the far side of her office, unable to move. Her hand slowly came up to her mouth, as if to prevent speech. Too late for that. She had to go after him, had to apologize for taking out her frustration on him. She took a step and stumbled. Her legs wouldn't work, her body was tense and clumsy. Her emotions had drained her strength. She inhaled deeply three times, then managed to rush to the main corridor leading to the front door. "Jack?" she called. No answer. She called his name again.

The hall was empty. In fact, the whole building seemed quiet. She glanced at her watch. Past three-thirty on a Friday afternoon. Of course no one was there. Everyone rushed home to start their weekend. For once, she'd leave on time, too.

She left her paperwork, grabbed her purse and ran to her car. Maybe she'd catch up with him at the marina. She slipped behind the wheel and made her way up Bay Road, but traffic was heavy. By the time she arrived, she wasn't surprised to see his empty slip. He and *The Wanderer* were gone.

She gazed at his docking place, her heart heavy. She'd have to wait until he got home. Waiting alone...with time to think. It was what she deserved! Jack and she—they were great together! He was wonderful. He cared about the world, he cared about people—about the young and the old. He cared about...her. She thought about all the times he'd held her, kissed her. Perhaps he'd loved her. Until today.

Until she'd pushed him away—her usual pattern with men. Before they realized she wasn't as smart or as pretty or as talented as they thought.

But not this time! Not with Jack. She wanted the ending to be different this time because Jack was different. And because she...loved him.

But he'd never forgive her for all the words, all the accusations. And she couldn't blame him.

She bit her lip and started the ignition, forcing herself to pay attention to the road. But a half hour later, as she paced the floor at Sea View House, she couldn't remember the drive home at all. Her mind was filled with memories of Jack—from the time she'd first met him as she swam in the ocean on a warm August night. And then again when she'd bumped into him a couple of weeks later after her interview. She recalled the volleyball game, football games, the day on his boat, the night of her flat tires…. He'd been there for her.

But where was he now? She glanced at the time. Too early for bed. Besides, she had too much energy. She changed into running clothes, donned an extra sweatshirt and let herself out the back door.

The night was cloudy, moonlight undependable. She retrieved a flashlight and amended her plans from a run to an aerobic walk. The waves looked choppy and the rhythm of the ocean was erratic, not the regular pounding of the waves on the sand. She shrugged. At the end of November, winter was almost upon them. Weather patterns changed.

She did a three-mile loop, hoping he'd have returned by the time she got back. She jogged the final distance, but no pickup truck stood in the driveway. Disappointment filled her. She felt tears form. She'd give him the biggest apology ever invented. She'd…she'd even cook dinners. Lots of them.

She entered the kitchen and immediately saw the light blinking on her answering machine. Her fingers trembled as she pushed the button.

"This is Jack." His voice sounded impersonal. "I'm staying in Boston tonight with friends. Just wanted you to know I hadn't drowned." Click.

Now the tears rolled down her face. She didn't try to stop them. She'd hurt him terribly. So terribly, that after doing his work, he'd docked in Boston instead of coming home.

She finally fell asleep in the wee hours, after taking two aspirin, and after tossing and turning until the covers lay haphazardly on the bed. She heard the newspaper hit the house at some point before dawn, then rolled over and slept.

Late the next morning, she awoke with swollen eyes. She glanced out the window at a day that looked as gray and overcast as she felt. She crept out of bed slowly, like an old woman, and sadness filled her. After automatically performing her morning ablutions, she plugged in her coffeepot and went to the front porch to get her newspaper. A small carton sat on top of the flattened paper with her name printed in big letters across the top. She looked up and down the street, but no one was in sight, and she brought the box into the house.

Once in the kitchen, she placed the newspaper aside and opened the flaps of the carton. Bound with a large rubber band was a stack of paper. She pulled it out. A second stack lay beneath. She left that one and focused on the top page of the first.

A True Tale of The Sea
by
Jack Levine

Jack! Was Jack here? Upstairs? She ran outside the back door, shivered in the cold, only to see an empty driveway again. He must have dropped the manuscript off while she slept. Had he even knocked? She shook her head and returned indoors. No, he didn't want to talk. He wanted her to read.

She studied the title page again. Under Jack's name was a note in parenthesis: "Lou—I'm aiming for young adult readers. What do you think?"

So, *this* was the purpose of her dad's research?

She turned the page.

This book is dedicated to the memory of
Kevin McCarthy,
my best friend, my blood brother,
always alive in my heart.
You need to rest now, Kev. Rest in peace.
And I need to live in peace. Finally.

The dedication drew her in. Made her blink. She would find the real Jack in this story. Her hands trembled as she turned the pages.

I always thought my best friend Kevin had everything a guy could want. A great mom and dad. A bunch of little sisters—perfect gofers—and most important of all, generations of seagoing McCarthys behind him. Kevin came from a long line of fishermen. Lobstermen to be exact. His dad ran a lobster boat, and Kevin had learned to pull catches as soon as he could hold a rope. I learned, too. That was the great thing about his dad. He'd take me along with Kevin almost every weekend. Not that I didn't have a great mom and dad of my own. But I hated that my dad worked in a bank while everyone else's father worked the sea. When you live on the coast of Maine, lobstering is the natural way of life.

Rachel barely blinked as she continued to read. Jack was clearly the narrator and his conversational style made the story flow. She began to love these boys! Loved watching them grow up. Their typical adolescent experiences were punctuated with adventures on the ocean. With worries during a bad year and celebrations during a good one. The pages seemed to turn themselves.

I never thought about our lives changing after we graduated from high school. My dad said I always lived "in the moment." And now that I understand what the phrase means, I know he was right. I never planned ahead. Back then, all I knew was that one day followed another with the usual stuff—school, girls, football in the autumn, baseball in the spring and trapping lobster on the weekends with Kev's dad.

But one day, we stood on the stage of our high school auditorium wearing caps and gowns. For the first time, reality began to sink into my brain: childhood was over. But I didn't feel any older or smarter or more mature. I simply felt weird about going off to college when I really wanted to stay on the boat with Kevin and John McCarthy. And Kevin thought I was nuts. He wanted to trade places with me. But that's not what happened.

It wouldn't have happened, thought Rachel. Not in their situations. The parents of these kids had definite ideas and a strong influence on the choices their sons made after high school. She read about Jack's first months in college and how he had kept in touch with Kevin. She read how Kevin managed to spend a weekend on campus with Jack. How they both got blitzed at a fraternity party. How they woke up the next day holding their pounding heads and laughing through the pain, their arms around each other. They'd reconnected in their guy way, assuring themselves that their friendship had remained strong.

And when Kevin left to go back home, we were both in the best of spirits. We'd made plans for my

Christmas break. I'd be home just in time for the last lobster outings of the season. How could I have known that we wouldn't keep that date? That I'd never see Kevin again?

Rachel's fingers tightened around the pages in her hand. She knew what happened next. It was all in the dedication. Somehow Kevin would be lost. She took a breath, feeling Jack's pain, not sure she wanted to read further. But how could she not? He'd given her this story as a gift. A piece of himself he'd wanted to share with her.

I had two flat tires on my drive home, and I got into town late. So late that I overslept the next morning. I couldn't believe I'd messed up so bad. Of course, Kevin and his dad had left without me. A lobsterman starts his day about four in the morning, is on the water by five and doesn't come in until four in the afternoon. But on the day they left without me, the routine was broken. On that day, an unexpected thunderstorm charged in about one, and Kevin's mom expected them to return sooner. The rain came down in torrents, and one by one other boats arrived home. The storm kept getting worse. The men crowded in the harbormaster's office and talked about sudden squalls coming out of nowhere. Then they roamed the docks peering out to sea as if they could wish them home.

Everyone thought Kevin and his dad would pull in any minute, or at least make their way to the closest dock wherever they were. No one had heard from them by radio and they would have made contact if they were in trouble. That's what we all kept telling ourselves. The McCarthy family knew the water and the weather better than anyone!

Kevin's mom waited at the phone. I went back and forth between the house and the dock from the time the rain started. At some point, we called the Coast Guard, but it was almost full dark by then.

The fingers on Rachel's left hand drummed the table while her right hand kept turning pages. She glanced up briefly when the rain started hitting her kitchen window. It was pretty dark outside Sea View House, too. A good day to stay indoors with a book. She glanced down at Jack's manuscript both dreading what happened next, yet wanting to read more.

As I looked out the window into the night, a terrible feeling slammed into my gut and stayed there. I choked on my own saliva, then started to sweat. I could barely breathe.

Fear has no taste. Fear is when your tongue goes dry and everything around you disappears because all you can see is what's in your mind. I knew that ocean. I knew what ten-foot waves could do. How they can toss a boat high or fling it sideways like it was made of paper. And I knew my friends should have been back by now. I left the house and walked down to the dock, my tears mixing with the rain. Kevin and John McCarthy weren't coming home.

In the end, two flat tires had changed my life. Or possibly had cost them theirs. Could I have made a difference had I been with them? Or would the death toll have been three?

The Coast Guard found them. Kevin was tangled in the lines, floating twenty fee down. It took another day to find his dad. He'd been washed up to shore—a heart attack had killed him. The best guess was that Kevin's ankle had been caught in a coil of rope, and he'd been pulled overboard. His dad had jumped in after him, but the strain of trying to free his son combined with the shock of the cold water were more than his system could take.

All our lives hang by tender threads, and theirs had broken. Mine could have broken, too. Each of us lives on borrowed time, and I was going to make the most of mine.

In the kitchen, Rachel brushed her tears away. Everything she knew about Jack made more sense now. He'd spent his life at sea teasing the ocean, tempting the Fates and communing with the soul of his dead friend. And just as he flirted with death, he flirted with relationships.

Not only afraid to lose someone he loved, but perhaps also afraid that someone could love and lose him. Before yesterday's fiasco, Rachel had thought there might be a future for them. But now she had more questions than answers.

One thing she'd learned for sure: Jack had many talents. He couldn't be forced into a mold. He'd reach more youngsters with his book than with her curriculum. Teaching young people to respect and appreciate the environment had always been his goal.

She stood up and stretched, then went to check the driveway again. The rain had continued, and she opened the door to a dark, wet and raw day. The temperature had dropped while she'd been reading. She dashed around the side of the house, but Jack's truck wasn't there yet.

Maybe he wouldn't return that night, either. Her heart sank at the thought, but then she shook her head. No, he'd be back or he wouldn't have left her the manuscripts. She walked back to the kitchen and reached for the second manuscript.

This one was untitled, but it was another story of the ocean, this time focusing on pollution. It wasn't finished, but Jack's research notes were clipped and organized.

A flash of lightning split the air. Startled, Rachel jumped and ran to the window just as a roar of thunder shook the house. The wind whipped the rain against the panes, adding to the loud cacophony. When she looked outside, she could barely see the width of her porch. And where was Jack?

She turned her radio to the Pilgrim Cove weather station. Strange how after all this time, she remembered exactly where on the dial it was. But what she heard did not reassure her. The storm had started at sea and was hitting the coast with a wallop now. Waves were cresting the sea wall, which meant they were over thirteen feet. Craft warnings had been given for the last two hours. Two hours!

Rachel grabbed the phone book, found the number of the marina and dialed. Jack's boat hadn't returned. He'd motored in around nine that morning and docked for a while. Came back, filled his tank and left. Said he was meeting a lobster boat. "In this weather?"

"Wasn't stormin' this mornin'. And you know that lobstermen like fall and early-winter fishing best."

Well, she didn't know and didn't care right now. "So, he's out there floundering in the open water?"

"Not necessarily. No, no. Could be he docked somewhere else to ride out the storm."

"Yes," she replied, her heart lighter. "Maybe he did."

"But he was acting strange, too. No 'good morning' or the like."

She blinked back sudden tears. His mind wasn't on what he was doing. He was thinking about her and their terrible argument. No, not an argument. A monologue. She'd done all the arguing while he just listened and offered to resign. Quietly.

Oh, God! He was a wonderful man. The best. And she loved him so much. If anything happened to Jack, it would be her fault. Definitely her fault. Blinded by her own needs, she'd hurt the person who'd stood by her side from the moment they'd met. And she'd never, ever forgive herself if he met the same fate as his friend Kevin.

CHAPTER FOURTEEN

THUNDER BOOMED. Rain pelted him with the sting of razor blades against his skin. The wind roared, then merely gusted, tossing *The Wanderer* about in the raging sea.

Jack peered through the downpour, cursing under his breath as he fastened his life jacket with numb fingers. Caught in a damn thunderstorm like an untutored landlubber! Lightning crackled, illuminating the grayness around him for a moment, but he could identify nothing. No coastline. No lighthouse. No other boats. No horizon. And certainly no stars to steer by. He stroked the control panel. Hopefully, the lightning wouldn't have affected his instrument readouts.

He cursed as the wind gusted hard again, and he hoped his lobsterman buddy had made it back to his harbor in Maine by now. Common sense told him the guy was fine since he'd been only three miles out from shore. Jack estimated they'd parted company about an hour ago. Plenty of time for the fisherman to moor his boat. Enough time for Jack to be closing in on Pilgrim Cove. On a good day, maybe twenty more minutes.

Rain dripped down his face as he fought the wind to keep his seat at the controls of *The Wanderer.* The electrical system still functioned, and he set the bilge pump and blower to get rid of the water he'd taken on. Something to be thankful for. He tuned his VHF radio to the Coast Guard broadcast channel, but static obscured the broadcast.

Suddenly, the wind blasted against his back. The boat sailed up on a wave as though it were no heavier than a leaf. He clenched his muscles as he waited for the slam back into the sea. The jarring impact came seconds later, and only his own strength saved him from hitting the windshield of the cockpit.

"Damn, damn, damn it!" he rasped. "Of all the lousy luck. I'm in a friggin' downburst." The original storm had spawned a powerful, hard and fast wind, probably gusting to one hundred and thirty miles per hour.

He checked his life jacket for a tight fit, then turned the wheel hard, trying to face the bow into the wind to lessen resistance. "Come on, baby. Turn. Turn." Little by little, *The Wanderer* obeyed, and now the rain sluiced directly against his face. If his compass was correct, *The Wanderer* was now turned toward the open ocean when all Jack wanted to do was head toward land. He had no choice but to ride out the storm. Or die trying.

SHE'D WEAR OUT THE FLOOR with her pacing if she continued any longer. Rachel glared at the darkness outside. It was barely five o'clock in the evening, but it might as well have been midnight. Now she knew what it must have been like for the sailors' wives in the old days, waiting for their husbands to return.

On that thought, she grabbed her keys and ran to the door next to hers and climbed upstairs. She had no idea if Jack had replaced the floodlight for the lantern on the third floor, but she'd find out now.

At the top of the last flight, she turned on the overhead light, then scanned the wall for the switch that controlled the lantern. After spotting it, she raced over, lips moving in prayer to the gods of the sea as well as to the loving God she knew. She pleaded; she made promises.

She held her breath, reached for the switch and flipped it. Bright light filled the lamp. Tears rolled down her cheeks as she opened the shutters over the picture window so the light could be exposed to the world. As she watched, the light rotated and was reflected by the prisms just like a real lighthouse lantern. When she bent down to examine it closer, she saw that the light was stationary, but the mirror turning around it provided the rhythmic pattern.

Rachel stared, mesmerized for a moment, and then felt her mouth curl into a smile. For the first time in many long hours, she felt hope.

Encouraged, she opened the door to the roof. The widow's walk beckoned. She rushed up the stairs and stepped into the fury of the storm. Drenched in seconds, hair plastered against her head, she gazed through the rain toward the Atlantic.

The stygian darkness scared her. She could see nothing in any direction. How could one man, in one small boat, survive in the darkness over an enormous, angry ocean? Her hopes crashed, and her tears blended with the rain running down her face. She stood on the roof of Sea View House and sobbed.

DROWNING WAS NOT AN OPTION. "You've already got Kev. You're not getting me!" Jack gripped the wheel with one hand and the grab bar with the other. He shouted into the night.

The tremendous wind had lessened—the downburst had petered out—but gale-strength air masses still blew. As long as his engine ran, he could maintain some control. He glanced at the fuel gauge. The motor was working hard, using up fuel faster than it would at a normal cruising speed, but he should have enough to get home.

What he wanted to do was turn the craft around and head for land. For a coastline he couldn't see. He'd have to trust the readings on his instrument panel to be accurate despite the storm.

If only he wasn't so cold! If only he could feel his fingers, his feet, his ears. His nose was frozen, too. He wished he were back in Sea View House with Rachel. Had she read his book? The book he hadn't shown anyone else except for her dad, whom he trusted. Did she understand? Did she care?

He began to inch *The Wanderer* around. In the boat's headlights, the waves were high and the rain still pelted the ocean. He rode the rise and fall like the sailor he was, grateful for all the years of experience. Grateful for his sea legs. Grateful for a childhood working lobster boats with Kevin and his dad, John McCarthy. They'd worked hard, and they'd played hard. They'd been a family on that boat just as surely as Kev had been a part of Jack's family on shore. Kevin had hung around the Levine house so much that Jack's dad had called him a "piece of furniture." Jack and Kev—they'd had the best of two worlds.

"Help me out here, bro," whispered Jack as he continued to ease the craft around. "Because something great happened to me. I met this girl. No, not a girl—a woman. I know you'd like her. She's wonderful. Smart. Sassy. And legs! Boy, does she have legs." His throat closed, and he gulped for air. "I want to live, Kev! But I don't want to party all night anymore. I played hard for the both of us, bro. A drink for me. One for you. A girl for me. And a girl for you. But..." He shook his head. "Fifteen years...it's enough."

Lightning spat out of the sky, and in the distance before him, Jack discerned a wide swath of irregular lights. His heart rate sped up; he didn't care about the cold, didn't care about the rain. Those lights had to be the coastline. Had to be land. And somewhere—God only knew where—along that coast was Pilgrim Cove. And Rachel.

"Okay, sweetheart," he whispered, patting the railing of the cruiser. "We're heading for home."

Now, with his bow facing land and the wind at his back, he could make it to shore. Eventually. First, he needed to ride out the storm right where he was until the weather eased. *The Wanderer* didn't have the power to overcome the force of this current and race to shore.

They were lifted and thrown forward by the next wave, then flung sideways. Again, Jack clutched the wheel, angry at himself for rejoicing too soon. The boat was caught in the crosscurrents of the storm, and there were no rules. Just survival.

As he focused on his surroundings, a strange silence enveloped him. He felt no vibration under his hands, under his feet, and the rhythmic sound of the bilge pump had ceased. Jack's insides shriveled as he checked the now-darkened instrument panel with his flashlight. The electrical systems were out. The engine was out. He had no motor, and no control of the boat at all.

He shook his head in disbelief and raised his eyes toward land once more. So close and yet... What was that? He blinked hard and squinted through the rain. Was that a light? To the left. He squinted again and stared at beams of light dancing in the dark, maybe...two miles away.

For the first time since he'd begun to fight the storm, tears filled his eyes. Rachel. His light was Rachel. He closed his eyes and allowed tears to run down his cheeks. "Thank you, God."

RACHEL MIGHT HAVE STOOD on the widow's walk for a minute or five minutes or thirty. She didn't know. Didn't care. Only cared that Jack was somewhere on that enormous ocean, alone, and in the dark.

He'd be wet and cold, colder than she was. With that thought, a shiver ran through her entire body, but whether it was caused by the falling November temperature or by fear, she couldn't tell.

She'd call the marina again when she returned to her apartment. Maybe they'd heard from him. And if not, why not? With all that equipment on board… Her imagination erupted.

Maybe nothing was working. Maybe he'd fallen overboard. Now she hugged herself and started to turn toward the door when, from the corner of her eye, she saw an orange light flash in the sky like a rocket. Staring at the spot, she held her breath and waited. A second flare followed the first, and then a third.

Someone was out there in need of help! Coast Guard regulations called for three orange flares to signal distress. She ran through the door, down the never-ending stairs and back to her own kitchen. In her heart, in her soul, she knew that Jack was signaling for help.

She grabbed the phone and within a minute was speaking to the Boston branch of the United States Coast Guard.

"What color was the flare? How many flares did you see? What's your position? How big's the boat?"

She answered the best she could. "We've got a harbor in Pilgrim Cove," she added. "A good one."

"We've got a cutter out on patrol along the coast, not too far away. They'll start searching. If they find him, we'll send out our biggest motor lifeboat to tow him into your harbor."

"I'll call the harbormaster and tell him to expect you. Please hurry."

She disconnected and made her next call. "I'm going down there," she said to herself after she hung up. But first, she climbed back up to the roof and looked out. Maybe he'd signal again, and she'd get a better fix on his position. The rain had lessened, but no more flares pierced the darkness.

"I love you, Jack," she whispered. "Please hang in there. Please."

Back in her apartment, she changed into dry clothes and stripped the house of blankets. Jack would be cold when they brought him in. She wished she owned a bottle of whiskey. She wished she had the key to his apartment to get him a change of clothes. Heck, who locked doors in Pilgrim Cove? It might be open.

It was. She barged into his bedroom, opened a lot of drawers until she found sweatshirts and pants. Underwear. Socks. Shoes in the bottom of his closet. Everything into a big plastic bag. Time to get into her car. Start the engine. Take a deep breath.

Breathe. In. Out. They'll get him. They'll bring him home. *And I'll love him forever. If she hadn't hurt him forever.* What if he wouldn't look at her? Worse, what if he looked at her with anger? And disappointment? No, no. She wouldn't go down that path. She'd hug and kiss him so hard, he'd know exactly how she felt.

She drove carefully in the rain. She gripped the wheel so tightly, her knuckles shone white. She pulled over at one point and took out her cell phone.

"Dad? Got any of that whiskey you and Bart share? Good." She told him about Jack. "Meet me…meet me…" And she started to cry.

"Pull yourself together, Rachel! If he's hurt or ill, he'll need you to be strong."

Strong. She, who was always in such control! Hadn't everyone called her stubborn? Too strong-minded. And now look at her!

"You're right. You're right. I'm fine, Dad. See you there."

"Five minutes."

She pulled into the parking lot next to the harbor-master's office, lifted the bag of clothes and ran inside.

"Any news?" she called as she stepped over the threshold.

Aaron Cooper looked exhausted. No doubt the night had been a difficult one for the harbormaster and his staff. "The three of us have been listening," he said, waving at his two young assistants also in the office. "And I'm tuned to VHF Channel 16, but nothing yet. That can be good news, too." His obvious attempt to cheer her up wasn't going to work when his brow was creased and his mouth tight.

The door opened and Lou and Pearl joined them, a paper bag in her dad's hand. "Anything yet?" he asked.

Rachel shook her head.

"It's early, Lou. Maybe only twenty minutes since Rachel called it in," said Aaron.

Rachel glanced at her watch. "Thirty-five minutes."

The radio sparked to life at that moment. "Coast Guard *MLB Washington* to Pilgrim Cove Harbor on Channel 16. Switch and answer Channel 68."

Aaron worked the controls. "Pilgrim Cove here," replied the harbormaster.

"Towing a thirty-foot sport cruiser, one passenger. Needs medical attention. Now below deck. Do you read?"

"Ten-four. Slip available." He gave coordinates. "Lights are on and all hands on deck here. Did you get the passenger's name?"

"Jack. Just Jack. We're coming in now."

The room erupted in a quiet cheer. Rachel almost collapsed with relief. She forced her legs to carry her to her father and gave him her cell phone. "Please call Max Rosen. Tell him to bring his medical bag."

Lou nodded.

"I'm going to get the blankets from my car, and then I'm going out there," she said, pointing at the window overlooking the pier. "I'm going out there to get Jack."

HE FELT THE BOAT ROCK HARD. Then hit something. He wouldn't have cared if it had been an iceberg. In fact, he felt like an iceberg himself. He wanted to sleep. He turned his head on the cushion of the berth below deck. Man, did he need to sleep. No more rain. No more cold.

Footsteps above him. And voices.

"Let me through, please. I've got a flashlight, and I'm going to him."

Suddenly, he wasn't sleepy. Rachel? Rachel's voice? He tried to get up and crashed to the floor instead. And then Rachel was there. Her hands on his face.

"Oh, my God! You're freezing cold. But I brought you blankets. Let me help you."

He felt pressure on his face here and there. Was she kissing him? He could only hope. Then she spoke. "Forgive me, Jack. I love you so much. I'm so sorry about what I said. About everything."

"Kiss-s-s me," he said on an exhaled breath of air.

She did.

"Am I in heaven…are you real?"

"Shh. I'm real. But now you're scaring me."

Her lips touched his forehead, traveled across it. "You're frozen," she said.

"No. I'm burning." Frostbite was painful when it started to thaw. She began pushing and pulling him in all directions.

"You're too heavy for me," she said. "I need some help. Don't move."

As if he could. Then he was alone. He listened. Listened hard. And despite the pain in his hands and feet, a chuckle bubbled from deep in his chest. Rachel was in her command mode, giving orders as rapidly as she could think of them. Then more footsteps descended and other people—guys—were helping her get him dressed. Dry clothes. Wonderful dry clothes.

"Here, sweetheart," she said, brushing his lips with hers. "Drink this."

He turned toward her, eager to taste her, then inhaled the aroma of very good whiskey and swallowed it gladly. Heat penetrated his middle and meandered to his limbs. His nose began to tingle. Painfully.

"Rachel," he whispered, "I've got frostbite. Hands, feet, face."

"I'll take a look at you upstairs," said a familiar voice.

"Doc? Doc Rosen?"

"Well, of course," replied Rachel. "Who else would I call?" She kissed his forehead. "We're going to get you upstairs now," she said. "It's still raining, but we've got you totally covered up."

With Rachel's and Doc's coaching, he managed to stand. Then two young fellows half carried him from *The Wanderer* to the harbormaster's office, and he didn't get wet at all. Not even his frozen feet, because of the plastic bags Rachel had put over his woolen socks.

"Just take me home," he said, collapsing onto a chair. "To Sea View House." He glanced up at Rachel and stopped breathing altogether. Tears flowed unabatedly down her cheeks.

"Home?" Her voice cracked on the one syllable, her expression frightened and hopeful at the same time.

He reached for her with a trembling arm. "Wherever you are, sweetheart, sweet Rachel. This sailor is home. For good."

"Well, not quite yet," said Doc. "I'm admitting you to the hospital."

Too much to think about. Jack closed his eyes and knew nothing more.

HE AWOKE TO BRIGHT DAYLIGHT coming through the windows of his room. An unfamiliar room where he lay in an unfamiliar bed. He wrinkled his nose at the scent of alcohol, then paused. His nose! He reached for it, and stilled suddenly. His hand was encased in cotton gloves. Slowly, he moved his fingers. They were stiff, but they moved with barely a tingle. Then he continued the journey to his nose. Stroked it and felt the stroke he made on it. Felt the taps he gave it on the tip. It wasn't cold anymore, or numb, and it—he sniffed—seemed to work just fine.

"Good morning."

He snapped his head around to the voice he loved. "Rachel?" His own voice rasped, and he reached for the cup of water he spotted on the tray next to his bed.

She was there in an instant helping him, but looking pale, tired. He glanced behind her to a lounge chair with a blanket in it, and inclined his head. "All night?"

"Of course, all night." She placed the cup back on the table, leaned over the bed and kissed him gently on the mouth. "I love you, Jack. Why would I be anyplace else?"

A kaleidoscope of mixed-up memories cascaded in his mind. "A light. I saw a light."

Her grin said everything.

"That was you? The lens?"

She nodded. "And I saw the orange flares. All three of them."

"Ahh, sweetheart. See how creatively we can communicate?" He opened his arms. "Come over here."

She lowered the railing and balanced herself lightly across his chest, nuzzling his neck in a way that reawakened other parts of his body.

"I love you, Rachel Goodman. With everything that's in me."

To his horror, she started to cry—again. "Woman! You've shed more tears in twenty-four hours than in twenty-four years! What's going on?"

She just shook her head against his chest. "How can you love me after everything I said? And I'm so sorry about that because I love you so much and would never want to hurt you…." Her words ran on and on.

"Shh. Shh. I've had lots of time to think. Maybe there was a kernel of truth in what you said. But it doesn't matter anymore."

"You know what really doesn't matter? How you shape your career. You do what you want to do, Jack. You're so good at so many things, and some people don't fit into a box. Your book was wonderful. Simply wonderful. I couldn't put it down, and I'm not fourteen!"

She was still running off at the mouth. He kissed her just to shut her up before she embarrassed him with praise. "Hey, no need to go overboard."

"Don't even say that word around here!"

They both started to laugh, then were silent, still sharing a smile while looking into each other's eyes.

"I love you, Rachel Goodman," Jack said once more. "Marry me. Let's make a home."

An eternity seemed to pass before she nodded. "Yes. Yes, of course I'll marry you. I love you with all my heart. And I think it's time for both of us to stop wandering."

Jack nodded. Rachel was exactly right. "Do you have your cell phone with you?"

She retrieved it and started to pass it to him. He held up his gloved hands. "Would you punch in this number?"

He took the phone in time to hear it ring before it was picked up. "Hi, Mom."

Rachel stood like a statue, eyes as big as silver dollars. He winked at her.

"I'm just fine," he answered into the phone, deciding his mother didn't have to know where he was calling from. "In fact, Mom, I'm so fine you need to tell Dad to pick up the extension."

He watched Rachel pace. "Sweetheart, they've waited thirty-five years to hear this announcement from their only child. Let's do it up big."

His dad came on the line. "Some good news? Another award? Another article?"

"Better than awards," Jack replied. He took a deep breath, excitement dancing through his body. "I've met someone. And I'm going to bring her home to meet you. Her name is Rachel."

"Oh, Jack" was all his mother managed to say.

His dad broke in. "You tell Rachel that we love her already. She must be very special if you're bringing her home."

"You're absolutely right."

CHAPTER FIFTEEN

"I WANT TO MAKE LOVE to you more than I want anything else in the world." Jack leaned against the pillow of his hospital bed after returning Rachel's cell phone, and enjoyed watching the blush rise to her cheeks. Enjoyed more, the tilt of her chin, the shine in her eyes. And the sensuous way her tongue brushed against her lower lip.

"Is there a lock on this door?" she whispered, bending over him until their mouths touched.

"Who cares?" he replied. He yanked off the protective gloves and wrapped his arms around her, tugging gently until she rested against him. Warm and trusting. He kissed her hair, her neck, her cheek, and basked in her responses as he felt her shiver against him. He was more than ready to love her.

"Jack," she whispered. "Jack…"

A heavy knock sounded at the door, immediately followed by a voice announcing, "You're being discharged today. Doctor's on his way."

Five minutes later, Doc Rosen and the weekend resident entered the room. "I'm just here to follow up," said the older man. “At my old friend’s—” he looked at Rachel “—your father’s insistence.”

Jack wiggled his fingers and toes. “I feel great,” he said, looking first at Max Rosen then at the medic in charge. “More than ready to leave.” Neither physician would ever know how very ready he was to find privacy at Sea View House. Privacy to make love to the love of his life. He figured a half hour at the most.

Who knew signing papers, receiving instructions and getting the car would take thirty minutes? Who knew that when they were finally settled into the front seat of Rachel’s Explorer, she’d turn to him and say, “Don’t you think we should stop at my folks’ house and tell them our news?”

“We told mine over the phone….” He looked at her suggestively, and she giggled like a blushing schoolgirl.

“Yes, well they live a hundred and fifty miles away. Do you want to take the chance of my folks barging into Sea View House?”

He winced at the thought. “Call them, tell them we’re getting married, and say we’ll be visiting them later today. That should hold them off.”

Rachel’s eyes sparkled. “You’re a genius!” she replied, reaching for her phone.

It didn’t take a genius to see that Rachel wanted to be alone with him…wanted him…as much as he wanted her. Just the thought made him too ready…. “I think I need a cold shower first,” he murmured.

Rachel grinned. “No more cold water for you, sweetheart. But how about a hot shower…for two? And then a blazing fireplace…I've got lots of extra blankets for the floor…and later a glass of wine…."

He felt his jaw drop open as Rachel continued. "I love you, Jack. These feeling inside…they're more than I've ever had…they fill me up…it's scary."

"Yeah," he whispered. "I know exactly what you mean."

LATER THAT AFTERNOON, a beaming Pearl Goodman swung open her back door to welcome Rachel and Jack.

"*Mazel tov, mazel tov.* Congratulations. Come in. Come in. We're so happy for you." She turned to her husband. "Look, Lou. She has the glow."

Rachel gasped. What glow? Could they tell she and Jack had made glorious, delicious, *amazing* love for the last three hours? How mortifying!

"Relax." Jack's voice rumbled in her ear. "She's talking about being in love, not about my delight in finally having the best pair of legs in New England wrapped around me the way I've dreamed about for months."

Now she felt the heat rush to her face. "Hush up!" But he laughed instead, put his arm around her and led her inside.

"We've got a few guests," said Pearl, giving Rachel and Jack each a hug. "Join us."

Before Rachel could ask a question, her parents disappeared toward the front of the house. From the living room, she heard a whirlwind of voices. She squeezed Jack's arm and nodded toward the noise.

"A few guests? She can't count!"

Immediately, comprehension registered in his expression.

"Your mother works fast," said Jack.

"I know," said Rachel, wrinkling her brow. "Smell those aromas? Look at the stove. She's feeding an army."

"Good!" replied Jack, rubbing his stomach at the very moment they both heard it growl.

Rachel took a step back and looked at the man she loved. "I honestly don't know how Mom does it," she said, "but I suppose I could make the attempt to learn…."

She hadn't expected Jack to laugh at her. "I'll be happy if you don't poison me!" he replied.

She jabbed him with her elbow, and had to admit she was slightly relieved. "You do realize, Jack, that the best chefs in the world are men. And with your experience cooking things up in the lab…" Could she have given him a bigger hint?

"You're not scaring me, Rach," he replied, bestowing a quick kiss on her mouth. "Now that I'll be at home more and more, why not?"

They hadn't discussed his work. She twirled around and kissed him hard. "That's for 'being home more and more,'" she finally said, her voice catching, "not for the cooking."

She was rewarded with a hug.

"I have no desire to sail away at the moment. No desire to go anywhere without you. So," he said to her quietly, "how does living in Pilgrim Cove sound to you?"

She stared at him, tongue-tied. Swallowed once, twice. "Not Boston?" she finally asked. "Or Maine, near the lobster coast?"

"No," he said. "Not necessary. Pilgrim Cove is perfect for both of us. Handy for me in the middle of the New England coast. Handy for you in your current position. And perfect for perhaps…raising a family?"

She heard the question in his voice. They hadn't discussed children, hadn't had time for anything but discovering their own love. But her heart soared.

"Yes!" she gulped. "Yes. Definitely. A family." She felt tears form. One dropped to her cheek. He kissed it away.

"Hang tight and follow me," he said, leading her into the living room. She went without a word.

"Bartholomew Quinn," he called.

The agent turned toward him from halfway across the living room. "I hear you, Jack Levine."

"Do you happen to have any nice homes available near the marina?"

Silence echoed in the room after Jack's question. One of those pregnant silences that Rachel had read about but had never experienced until now.

Silence, and then, pandemonium. From Susan and Alex, David and Jennifer, Doc and Marsha Rosen, Sam Parker, Chief O'Brien and Dee. And Kate and Mike

Lyons, who'd been on the same ferry with Rachel the first time she came home.

"Look at those two," said Jack, pointing to Bart and Lou, who were walking toward each other, grinning like two schoolboys with a secret. Without a word, they shook hands, then clapped each other on the back with vigor.

"That's three in a row!" said Bart, crowing with pleasure. "Three in a row. First, Laura and Matt. Then Shelley and Daniel. And now Rachel and Jack. My, oh, my. It's a lucky house, it is."

"Lucky?" asked Pearl. "Maybe. But hot? Definitely. Just like I said last summer, that house is hot!" Pearl's contribution had Rachel groaning. But Jack chuckled and continued to hold her in his arms. "Enjoy the ROMEO and Company show," he said.

Sam Parker walked over to them, hand extended. "Congratulations to you both." He kissed Rachel, then looked at Jack. "Lou tells me you've written a book for teens. And he tells me it's good."

Rachel glanced at her dad. Lou smiled and nodded, but Jack didn't say a word. Just stared at his soon-to-be father-in-law.

"I loved the book," Rachel replied. "But Dad—he *knows* the literature. And if he says it's good...then it is."

"That's what I've been trying to say," said Sam Parker between chuckles. "Talk to my daughter-in-law. Laura has an agent who knows the publishing business inside and out. She, herself, narrates children's books for one of the biggest houses in New York. But it was the agent who got her the audition."

Jack hadn't thought much about the future of his book. Writing it had been the important part. But Sam was right. "A book doesn't do much just sitting in a drawer, does it?" he said. "Thanks, Sam. Tell Laura I'll be calling."

Sam waved and returned to his buddies just as David and Jennifer came over.

"Mom says I should call you Uncle Jack now," said Jennifer.

David looked uncomfortable, however, as though he were sitting on a tack. "Yeah. She said it's either that or Dr. Levine."

"How about sticking with Jack, like you did last summer? Except in school."

"Cool." The kid gave him a high five. "When are you going to tell us the whole story? About what happened yesterday."

"Yeah..." said Jennifer. "Tell us about your adventure in the storm."

Rachel preempted his reply. "Kids, I don't think Jack wants to—"

"We might as well tell it once and be done with it," said Jack, giving Rachel a little squeeze. "I say 'we' because some of it is your story, too."

The older set waved them to the couch. "You're going to have to write the whole tale in the Sea View House Journal, anyway," said Bart. "Just like Laura and Shelley wrote their stories. Think of this as a first draft."

Silence filled the house as everyone settled into their seats. The room filled with a sense of expectation, everyone waiting for a story.

"This is the story of a man, a woman, a boat and a storm. A true tale of the sea." He aimed the narration at David and Jennifer. He started from the time he left the Pilgrim Cove marina under cloudy skies, leaving out the argument or the reason he'd left the manuscript with Rachel. He described the storm, the darkness, the icy rain. The huge waves. The lightning. And then the loss of the motor and all the power.

"But your aunt knew what to do," he finally said. "She turned on the big light at Sea View House. A light so big, I saw it through the rain and the darkness. It gave me hope."

"Wasn't it lucky that you were near us?" whispered Jennifer, leaning against Jack's legs from her seat on the floor.

"Lucky?" repeated Jack. "It was a darn miracle!"

"No," said Rachel. "It was a wonderful miracle." She squeezed his arm so hard, he'd have a bruise.

"And very appropriate," said Pearl.

Now the small audience turned to Pearl. "Hanukkah begins this evening," she said. "The miracle of light. Isn't it nice to know that miracles do still happen?"

THREE O'CLOCK COULDN'T come fast enough for Rachel on this last day before the winter holidays. So much to do at home, but so much to do before she left school for the day.

Footsteps sounded outside her door. Dr. Bennett walked in and extended his hand. "A promising semester, Rachel. It may have had some rocky moments, but the home stretch is looking great."

Rachel stood up, more than pleased with Dr. Bennett's compliment. More than pleased with the final result of the athletic department changes. Bob Franklin had requested an unpaid leave of absence rather than be forced to attend a certified coach-education program. He'd been indignant at the suggestion. Rachel suspected he wouldn't be back.

Tom Sullivan had been promoted to athletic director, a position he was well qualified to handle. The entire faculty had cheered when the change was announced at a recent staff meeting.

"I couldn't be happier myself, Dr. Bennett," said Rachel.

"I think the whole town knows that." The principal winked and waved. "Have a great vacation."

She nodded. "I certainly intend to." It would be a whirlwind week. Jack's parents were driving down the next day and would stay at Sea View House with them. A dinner at the Lobster Pot was scheduled for tomorrow night with the entire family and whoever else showed up. She was pretty sure every ROMEO would just happen to be eating there, probably at surrounding tables! Ah, well. That was life in Pilgrim Cove.

"Hi, sweetie! Ready to go?"

And there was her life. Standing in the doorway, eyes

shining with love for her. She closed her desk drawer, shut down her computer and got her purse. "No homework this week," she said. "No tote bag."

The look in his eyes turned warmer. He took her hand and pulled her to her feet. "I love you, Rach."

She leaned against him for a moment. "I know."

"I've got some good news to share," he whispered in her ear. "I found out about a half hour ago."

She pulled away so she could see his face. Suppressed excitement. "Well, are you going to tell me or do I have to guess?"

Suddenly, all humor disappeared. A serious Jack stood in front of her. "Laura's agent called," he began. "Or should I say, *my* agent called."

"Wow, fast work," said Rachel. "You met him in Boston and signed a contract only about…what? Less than two weeks ago?"

"Yes. That's why I'm so surprised." He grasped her hands and squeezed. "Rach—three publishers are bidding on the manuscript for their young-adult lines. Three publishers want Kevin's story."

Suddenly, Jack blinked hard, and Rachel felt tears well in her own eyes. Her wonderful man didn't even realize what he'd said. To Jack, this story would always be Kevin's. No matter that he had lived it, too. No matter that he had written it.

"And sweetheart," said Jack. "I hope you won't object, but if people actually buy the book, I'd like to give half the royalties to Kevin's mom."

"No one has a more loving heart than you," she whispered.

"I love you, Rachel Goodman, and now I'm going to show you how much."

She expected kisses. Instead, he led her outside to his truck. He wouldn't answer any questions.

Fifteen minutes later, she thought she understood when he pulled into the marina's parking lot. "*The Wanderer* must be back! That's great." And she meant it. Jack had spent untold hours on the phone and in person supervising its repair. "But I hope you're not counting on taking her out now, darling. It's getting dark."

"Shh. Don't say anything yet." He led her onto the dock and toward his slip. She would have walked right past the boat, however, if Jack hadn't stopped walking himself.

"There she is," he said. "What do you think?"

Rachel looked. Everything seemed exactly the same except… "Oh, my goodness. Jack! I don't believe this." The man was incredible. "*Sweet Rachel?* You renamed it for me?" If her voice was pitched any higher, she'd squeak.

Jack grinned, seemingly very pleased with himself and with her reaction. "I sure did. I think it's a perfect name for a beautiful lady."

"PILGRIM COVE AND THE Lobster Pot welcome you to town." Bart Quinn, himself, greeted them at the door of the restaurant the following evening, taking extra time with Jack's parents, Shirley and Arthur Levine. His eyes twinkled, his grin appeared often, and he was obviously having a good time. Rachel poked Jack. "He's letting the leprechaun out."

"And loving every minute," Jack replied.

"But watch his eyes, his expression. Nothing gets past that man."

"We've set up a special table for you tonight," said Bart, leading the way inside the restaurant. "Right in the middle of the main dining room."

"I knew it!" exclaimed Rachel. "A zillion people will be coming by."

"And what's wrong with that?" asked Pearl. "I love sharing happy news."

"Your mother's right, dear," said Shirley. "We're thrilled about you and Jack, and we want everyone to know it. Even if we don't know a soul in Pilgrim Cove."

"Within an hour, you'll know dozens, Mom. Trust me." Jack gently squeezed Rachel around her waist. "It's that kind of town."

Bart joined in again. "Your boy's a quick learner, Shirley. He fit right in from the start. Said the town felt familiar."

"Familiar? Then it must be the New England coast. He's happy wherever there's water."

Jack glanced at Rachel. "Am I standing right here, or what?"

She giggled and pointed to the table. "We've arrived. And look around. Notice the Reserved signs on those three tables."

Just then she glanced down the corridor and saw the Parker crew walking toward them. Sam led the pack. Matt and Laura followed with their sons, Casey and Brian. And Katie Sullivan, too.

"Hi, Papa Bart," said the child, running up to her great-grandpa and hugging him. "I'm sleeping at Uncle Matt's tonight. Mommy's on a date with Sara's daddy again."

"I know that, little one. Don't we all live together?"

Introductions were made all around until the Parker clan sat down at their table. Within the next five minutes, it seemed to Rachel that every person her parents knew found their way into the Lobster Pot. ROMEOs and wives. Mah-jongg players. Card players. Finally, everyone was seated. Rachel purposely sat next to Jack's mom.

"It's not usually *quite* like this," she said.

"But close enough," said Jack, from his seat on her other side. "You get used to it," he added with a grin.

Just then, Maggie Sullivan and Thea Cavelli whirled toward them, arms outstretched, smiles on their faces. "Welcome, welcome. Congratulations to you all." Maggie looked over at Bart. "I see Dad has everything under control."

"Of course I do," said Bart. "In fact, I was just going to give the Levines a tour of the walls."

"The walls?" said Arthur.

"Oh, yes," replied Thea. "We've always got a special art exhibition in the restaurant. Now, some pieces may be better than others, but...we try to have fun."

"And tonight," added Maggie, "we have a new work to add to the collection. In addition, champagne is on the house." She paused. "Who knows? Weddings are in the air. You're all going into Boston next week for Shelley and Daniel's. And maybe, just maybe…there will be another one, closer to home."

Rachel glanced at Bart, but Bart was staring at his daughter, his expression a mixture of pain and resignation. She only hoped that Sam Parker hadn't heard Maggie's remark from where he sat. Maggie Sullivan was banking on her daughter, Lila, finding happiness with the new veterinarian, Adam Fielding. She was banking on Lila forgetting about Jason Parker once and for all.

Who knew what the future held? Rachel pressed her hand to Jack's and felt his answering squeeze. Life was good, and she'd enjoy it.

"Look over there, Shirley." She pointed to a poster of Rodin's *The Thinker,* except there was a huge fish in his lap. Beneath the pictorial was a caption that read, "Fishful thinking."

In the next one over, two kids in a rowboat looked at the viewer and said, "Wouldn't you rudder be fishing?"

"Cute and corny and adorable," said Jack's mom.

"Check out the one about the Chief and Dee." Jack pointed to a caricature of Rick O'Brien wearing his cop's hat and riding on a fish as though he were a cowboy, while Dee sat demurely on the dock. "He wanted to *snapper* up…because she lived inside his *sole.*"

"Now, *that's* a good one," said Shirley with enthusiasm.

Bart spoke up from behind their chairs. "Maggie draws them and Thea comes up with the words. Sometimes with a little help from whoever happens to be around. They've got a new one ready for tonight."

Maggie and Thea approached, each holding one side of a large poster board. They tipped it right side up.

The caricature of Jack wore a sailor's cap and stood on the deck of a white boat with hands on his hips. He had an overlarge chest and overdeveloped muscles. Rachel's facsimile had a crop of dark hair, extra-long legs and a narrow waist. She was on the beach, a fishing rod in her hand, its line thrown into the water. The caption read:

Jack *floundered* around the seven seas,
'Til Rachel said, "He's my *Maine* squeeze."

General applause broke out at the table. "Perfect," said Jack's mother. His father smiled and nodded. "Good job, ladies."

"Hang on a minute," said Rachel, motioning the sisters to come closer. "The boat. It's called *Sweet Rachel!* Now, how did they learn that so fast?"

A chorus of voices replied, "There are no secrets in Pilgrim Cove."

Everyone laughed, and Rachel looked around the table at her family. Was it only last summer that she'd hesitated about coming home? Alex winked at her from across the table while Jennifer leaned against him as she chatted with David. Pearl and Lou's hands were intertwined in full view of everyone. And Jack's parents seemed relaxed and happy mingling with all of them.

Rachel leaned against the love of her life, and sighed a big contented sigh.

"I know what you mean," Jack whispered. "It doesn't get much better than this."

"Amen."